MIRANDA

A NOVEL BY

Jan Hilliard

Other books by Jan Hilliard

A VIEW OF THE TOWN
THE JAMESON GIRLS
DOVE COTTAGE

MIRANDA

 ABELARD-SCHUMAN

London New York Toronto

© Copyright 1960 by Jan Hilliard

Library of Congress Catalogue
Card Number 61-7095

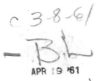
LONDON	NEW YORK	TORONTO
Abelard-Schuman	Abelard-Schuman	Abelard-Schuman
Limited	Limited	Canada Limited
8 King Street	6 West 57th Street	81 John Street

Printed in the United States of America

MIRANDA

Chapter One

Some years ago, before I knew how to be happy, there were
certain dreams that I dreamed over and over. In one of the
most vivid of these, we were all—my mother, my sister Jessica and I—back in that gray seaside town in Nova Scotia
where we lived for two years in the late twenties, in a tall
narrow house of stained brick on a dead-end street called
Lupin Crescent. This street was crowded with identical
deteriorating houses, worn privet hedges, and horse chestnut trees. It was always late afternoon in my dream, when
the rooms of our house were filled with blue dusk; and
there was a lion in the hall.

The lion lay in a shadowy corner under the stairs, on the
strip of flowered carpet beside the radiator. A sleepy sort
of lion, really, it was stretched out with an air of languid
indifference, seemingly half dozing. But, watching without
appearing watchful, its eyes would be fixed on a spot a
little to the right or left of mine, and I knew with terrify-
ing certainty that its indifference was assumed.

I would come in from school, perhaps, from the autumn
streets where the air was thickening with the smoke from
bonfires, and birds like flights of arrows were disappearing
into the leafless trees. When I opened the door of our
house I would note—with no surprise, only a feeling of
dismay, for I had been hoping all the way home that this
day would be different—that the lion was still there. My
mother and Jess went to and fro on everyday errands, seeing the lion but pretending not to, and I knew that I must
keep up the pretense, too. To speak, to admit that I was

3

aware of the sinister presence in the hall would bring ca-
lamity down upon us all, in what shape I had no idea. I
must not show fear, or run.

So, with what I hoped would appear to be a fine show of
unconcern, I would force myself to walk slowly past the
lion, perhaps even humming a tune, on brave days. But
as soon as I reached the living room I would hide in the
farthest corner. Then the lion would move silently and
lazily, still with that air of indifference which I knew to be
assumed, to a place where it could watch me without appearing watchful. Its eyes, half closed and sleepy, fixed on
a spot a little to one side of mine, and then I would have
to pretend that I had not been hiding. Always I was filled
with the despairing certainty that it would, when I least
expected it, stir and look straight at me, and then—I don't
know what then. I would know I was afraid.

Often there were other people in my dream: the schoolteachers and clerks who roomed with us. They were just
out of sight up the stairs, voices and footsteps heard in the
upper rooms. They had seen the lion in the hall below but
had looked the other way, too polite to mention it. It was
not a thing that people spoke about to your face.

I am a great dreamer. I do not attribute this, as some
people suggest, to indigestion, for I never have what could
be classed as real nightmares. There was another dream in
which Jess and I were being chased through a night wood
by wild horses, lean black beautiful horses with flying
manes and red fiery eyes. We ran and ran toward a gate,
and the wood was filled with the drumming of hooves.
Looking back from the gate, which was shut and insur-
mountable, we saw the black horses coming. This was
where I always woke up. I have longed for the talent to
paint this scene—woods and galloping horses and night
clouds, dark trees and wind—but I am not an artist.

I consider this a beautiful dream, though it frightened me. Any student of Freud is welcome to make what he can of it. I do not call it a real nightmare any more than I call the lion in the hall dream a nightmare. It is true I was afraid of the lion, but after waking I remember, more than my fear, the short beaded dresses Miranda, my mother, used to wear, and the heavy musky perfume, like hothouse flowers, and how before she went out she would stand before the kitchen mirror flattening down her spit curls with real spit, her mouth pursed in imitation of Clara Bow's. And for no reason at all I remember as if it were yesterday the hours Jess used to spend every night rubbing her chest with a miraculous cream called Lubriform, guaranteed to induce curves, until her breasts blossomed suddenly and became unfashionably large under the straight dresses of that era, and had to be subdued with a tight bandeau.

We are English. Jess and I were born in Sussex, in a little two-roomed stone farmhouse under the South Downs where our father had been raised by his grim-faced Aunt Eliza. The farm belonged to her. We lived there until I was four years old and Jess was five. We rarely saw our parents in those days, and perhaps that is why we have no fond memories of Sussex. We were too young to remember much, in any case. Our father was fighting in France, and Miranda was too patriotic to idle away her time in the country when everyone else was helping to win the war.

"I must do my bit, too," she used to say, to explain why she could not be with her children. She had a job in London, not rolling bandages for the soldiers—as one might expect from her patriotic attitude—but working as a parlormaid for a Mrs. Fitzhugh, who had a house in Park Lane. Madam—we did not hear her real name often in those days—did a great deal of war work. She entertained officers on leave, and sold Victory bonds, so Miranda could quite rationally explain that by assisting her employer she was doing her bit, too. Jess and I were left in the care of Great-aunt Eliza, who was as old as the hills and not quite all there. Miranda spent a week or so each summer at the farm, but she disliked the country and did not get along well with Great-aunt Eliza. Once in a great while our father came home on leave.

Not being the sort who accepted change readily, Alfie had intended, after the war, to settle down in Sussex and spend the remainder of his life there, on a little farm he had leased next to his aunt's. Miranda soon tired of the country, however, and after about a year of it she persuaded him to leave the farm and move up to London, where he had been offered a job as a bartender by her sister Vi's husband—Uncle Bertie—who ran a little alehouse called The Golden Fleece.

The Golden Fleece was in a working-class section of London, just off the Kennington Road, and we lived nearby, in the upstairs flat of Uncle Bertie's house. It was a small shabby dwelling standing a little back from the street, with a strip of lawn and a paved walk leading up to a latticed porch. We had three rooms on the second floor. I cannot recall all the details of our life there. One thing I do remember is that the place smelled eternally of kippers.

Not long after we moved to London Miranda went back again to her old job with Mrs. Fitzhugh, not "living in" as she had during the war, but returning home each night except when she was needed for some special occasion. Madam's house in Park Lane held a fascination for her. This was not surprising, for she had worked there off and on since she was fifteen. Madam was getting on in years, and she liked seeing familiar faces around her. As soon as she heard that Miranda was living in London, she offered to take her on again.

Miranda was pleased. As she said, "Madam's house is a second home to me, and it will be nice to earn a little extra. There's really nothing for me to do at home." This was true. Jess and I were in school all day, and for a few shillings a week Auntie Vi did the cleaning up and got the meals.

Auntie Vi and Miranda were about as unlike as two sisters could be. Auntie Vi was much older, an overweight dowdy woman who had given up thinking about her appearance; in fact she seemed to feel that there was something not quite decent about anyone's striving to look smart, or above one's station. She disapproved of Miranda's going back to work, and said so. She guessed, correctly, that it was not so much the extra money that tempted her as the opportunity to mingle with the upper classes.

"It's time you learned there's more to life than making cups of tea for Madam's titled friends, and rolling your eyes at the male help," she said.

It is not surprising that my most vivid recollections of London are not of the East End where we lived, but of the fashionable district across the river where Miranda worked. Whenever she had a day off she would dress us—Jess and me—in our best clothes and we would take a tram across the Vauxhall Road bridge to Victoria Station, and from this point go on long excursions through the parks and verdant squares of the West End. We gaped at the houses of the rich and pretended we were persons of importance.

Miranda was like a little girl playing grown-up. Even in those days we called her by her Christian name, never "Mother." She would say, "I'm Princess Mary. Who do you want to be?" When we could not decide, she would say, "Jess, you be the Countess of Asquith, and Rose can be Lady May Cambridge." Another day we might be Sybil Thorndike, Pauline Lord and Marie Tempest, but more often we were royalty or near royalty. We stood outside churches to peer at notable brides and funeral processions. (After standing for hours in a February chill, we caught a very nice glimpse of Princess Mary's bridal veil.)

Sometimes when Mrs. Fitzhugh was away, her housekeeper, an easy-going north-country woman who told bawdy jokes and shook all over laughing at them, would invite us up to the house in Park Lane for tea. Her name was Florrie something-or-other. It seems odd, when I come to think of it, that whereas Miranda admired the upper classes so much, and longed to be one of them, she always picked as her closest friend someone like Florrie: cheerful, a bit vulgar, with no pretense of refinement whatsoever. We would have tea and rock cakes in Florrie's dark little basement sitting room off the pantry, and then Jess and I would be taken on a tour of the rooms abovestairs.

It was a house such as we had never dreamed existed. Even when the furniture was swathed in dust sheets, as it was once when Madam was on a trip to the continent, the place had such an air of elegance and richness that we were awestruck, and spoke in whispers. We could understand why Miranda sometimes showed dissatisfaction with her own home.

Quite often, when we visited Florrie, Madam's chauffeur would drop in for half an hour, and then the party became very gay. His name was Sidney Wilkinson. He was a sandy-haired man with green eyes that drooped at the outer corners and jowls that drooped a little, too. This gave him, on duty, a rather pompous appearance, but when he relaxed in Florrie's sitting room he laid his pomposity aside with his coat, and became heartily jocular. The jokes were funnier than ever when he was there.

He teased Jess and me, whispering, "I'm going to steal your mother. I'm going to put her in my pocket and take her home with me."

Miranda would slap his hand and say, "Now stop it, Sidney. You behave yourself."

Then they would both laugh. It was no laughing matter to me. I thought he meant it, and I had bad dreams. Even after we left London I would sometimes wake up in terror, having dreamed that Sidney was stealing Miranda away from us.

We had five years of London. Then Mrs. Fitzhugh died. In her will she left Miranda a set of three Corot prints and a cloisonné bowl. Miranda stayed at home for a month or so, bored and idle. She began to fret. We were not prospering as she had hoped we would. "We're not getting *on*, Alfie," she complained.

"Well, I was never cut out to work in a pub," my father defended himself. "It's not my line at all. I'd just as soon go back to Sussex."

"We'll never go back there," Miranda said firmly. "What we ought to do is go somewhere entirely new, where we can get a fresh start."

Some story she had read, or someone she had talked to, had given her the idea that there was no future in merely pretending to be a person of importance, when with a little effort she could be one herself. Nothing was impossible. All that was needed was a change of scene. The magazines were full of stories about people who had gone out to the colonies, or to America, and made a fortune overnight.

So Miranda began to plan a new future for us. It would be a great adventure to pull up stakes and go off somewhere to the ends of the earth, get a fresh start. She thought of Australia, Canada, even South Africa. She really wanted to go to the United States, but immigration laws made going there more difficult. "Get a fresh start" was a phrase she used often. Once we had this fresh start everything would be clear sailing. What she really meant was that among strangers who did not know our background we would have a better chance of rising above our present station in life, as it was her ambition to do.

Canada, because it was next door to the United States, and because it was advertised in the English papers as "the land of opportunity," seemed to present the most attractive possibilities. The only trouble was the expense. To get to Canada would take every penny we possessed, and more. Then Alfie, being tired of his job in Uncle Bertie's pub and longing for a change of scene himself, made inquiries at the Empire Settlement Office, which was an organization set up to assist and advise anyone who wished to emigrate to distant parts of the empire. He was told that, since farm hands were so badly needed in Canada, the government of that country was prepared to share the greater part of the expense of transporting agricultural workers from England. They must agree, of course, to work for a certain length of time—I think it was one year—at a preselected location.

"I knew there'd be a catch in it," Miranda grumbled. She had never intended to allow Alfie to go back to farming, but could scarcely ignore this chance to secure passage to Canada for practically nothing. She brooded for a while on the lack of consideration shown by the Empire Settlement Office, then began to look on the bright side.

"It's only a year, after all, Alfie."

"Yes," my father agreed. "They want us to go to the Annapolis Valley in Nova Scotia, where they grow apples—

almost two million barrels a year, the chap at the Settlement Office said. Very pleasant country, nice climate and
all. It says here in this leaflet he gave me: 'One may ride
for fifty miles under apple blossoms.' Think of that!"

"Fifty miles without a town? We don't want to get stuck
in the middle of nowhere."

"Oh, you'll find plenty of towns," my father promised.
The description of the Annapolis Valley had fired his imagination, and now he was the one who was most eager
to get away to the new land. He wanted to get back to
farming, too, for he had always been happy doing that.

"We'll move to some city as soon as your year is up,"
Miranda told him.

"Yes, of course." He was willing to promise anything.

A month later we were on the boat. I should be able to
remember the trip from Liverpool to Halifax better than
I do, for I was just past nine years of age, certainly
old enough to retain impressions. I do have a vivid recollection of the departure—the crowds at the dockside,
laughing, crying, throwing kisses, calling out good-byes.
Nobody came to see us off, for Uncle Bertie and Auntie
Vi could not afford the train fare up from London, but
Miranda stood at the rail waving and throwing kisses, tears
running down her cheeks.

"We don't know anyone there," Alfie said.

This made no difference to Miranda. She loved crowds,
and she was saying good-bye to England. When, as the
ship moved away, the people on the pier sang *Till We Meet
Again* she cried harder than anyone else.

Of the voyage itself, I can recall only that we were all
seasick, that the Atlantic was cold, and gray with fog. We
slept in the crowded, airless third-class quarters below
deck. I was frightened, and longed for the voyage to be
over. We disembarked at Halifax one cold afternoon in

late winter, boarded a train, and were at once whisked across a bleak landscape along a frozen river between hills. Late that night we stopped at a tiny red station where Mr. Saunders, who was to be Alfie's employer, was waiting with a sleigh and a pair of steaming black horses. Jess and I, half asleep, were tucked into the back of the sleigh and covered with buffalo robes. We lay in our warm cocoon hearing, for the first time, the gay jingle of sleigh bells.

It was such a jolly sound that we sat up and poked our heads out into the frosty air. The winter landscape seemed incredibly beautiful. There had been a fall of snow earlier in the day and everything was covered. Every fence post, even, had a little ermine cap, and the bare trees were etched white against a dark blue sky thick with stars. We felt excited, as if we had entered a totally new and wonderful world, just this side of magic. It was a good beginning to our life in Canada.

A week after we arrived at our new home, Miranda sent a notice to the small weekly newspaper which served that part of the country. It read, "Mr. and Mrs. Alfred Arnold, of London, with their daughters Jessica and Rose Ann, have taken up temporary residence in the village of Cheswick."

We stayed in Cheswick for three years. I think Alfie was happier there than he had ever been. I know Jess and I were. (I was happy, but I did not know how to be happy, which is a different thing.) We lived in a small tenant's house across the water meadow from the big farm where Alfie worked, a neat white cottage with a picket fence and old-fashioned flowers, tucked into a fold of a gentle hill, with a pond and a wandering brook and five pine trees against the sky. Looking back later, it seemed to me an enchanted place, a warm and sunny time. A happy family time, too, for we had Miranda to ourselves, really for the first time in our lives. Jess and I knew, when we came in from school, that she would be there waiting for us. It made a difference.

I suppose we did have cold winters in the valley, but I do not recall ever *feeling* cold there, though I do remember skating on the frozen meadow. In early winter the whole meadow flooded, and later froze into a glittering sheet of ice several inches thick. It was a safe place for children to play, for soon the water under the ice drained away into the river which snaked along the length of the meadow, looping and turning. You could always tell where the river was. Along its banks the ice cracked and slanted down into the stream. With our coats held out like sails, we could skim across the meadow as swiftly and effortlessly as birds fly. We coasted down the long hill, too, sometimes on a slick red double runner we had ordered through the mail-order catalogue, more often on a tin tray that had once been lacquered black, with a design of pink roses in the middle.

Miranda entered into the fun. Though she did not like the farm, she was sensible enough to get as much enjoyment as she could out of the time we were forced to spend there—which was only a year, as she kept reminding us. Wearing one of Alfie's mackinaws, a red stocking cap pulled down over her ears, she would go screaming down the hill on the double runner to upset, laughing, in a snowdrift at the bottom. Evenings, when she was in a playful mood, she would sit on Alfie's knee and tease him. He would smile, looking pleased but sheepish, for growing up with Great-aunt Eliza had not taught him how to accept or bestow affection. He did not know how to tell Miranda that she made him happy, but as he hastened home through the fields after his day's work he would wear an expectant expression, and his eyes would light up when she ran to him and called him her grumpy old poop, or met him at the door with a haughty expression, pretending he was a peddler she had no wish to do business with.

In spring I remember best the little streams that ran down the turfy slopes, making a braided pattern in the new grass as they hurried to the pond where rushes grew, and Jess and I lying face downward on a hummock at the pond's edge, watching the minnows and waving algae; and lying in bed at night listening to the spring peepers. Across the meadow we could see the big farm, a green-shuttered white house surrounded by well-kept outbuildings and tall Lombardy poplars, and near by an arched bridge where the river crossed the side road. It looked like an English watercolor painter's dream of summer. There were violets and scented mayflowers in the woods, daffodils along the meadow bank, and blue flags in the swamp.

I remember full summer and the hay being gathered in the meadow, and the smell of sweet fern and wild blueberries, and the orchards hung with red and yellow apples: Bishop Pippin, Ben Davis, Yellow Transparents, Gravensteins. In September, gangs of pickers arrived, whole families of them, and camped on the rise at the far side of the meadow. We were not allowed in the orchards at this time, but watched the excitement from a distance; the tall wheeled picking ladders being moved from tree to tree, the shouts of the workers as they lowered each basketful of fruit to the waiting barrels, the teams of horses—great broad-breasted Clydesdales with polished harness and flashing brass, their manes and tails done up in topknots and laced with red ribbon as if they were on their way to the fair; not at all like the horses in my dream—transporting the filled barrels to the railway siding. When the last tree was stripped the pickers went away, and the orchards were ours again to enjoy until the time of the fall plowing. We gathered the windfalls for our own use.

There is a special memory connected with the five pine trees on the ridge, but it is so hazy, so lost in time, that it is difficult to write of it. On one of those magic days that come in childhood I lay under the pines and suddenly became aware of things I had loved without knowing—in this case warmth and summer, pine needles against the sky as in a Chinese drawing, crows calling far away, the smell of summer, even the roughness of dry cones against my palm pressed into last year's brown needles, flying clouds, and the sea sound of the wind in high branches. I was completely unaware of myself as a separate identity; I was not lost, but achieving a unity with my surroundings as if I had gone beyond the invisible line which separates us from nature. I think only children can do this. They have less of themselves to leave behind. It was one of the happiest times of my life, and whenever nowadays I hear the wind in tall pine trees I shut my eyes and try to recall how I opened that magic door; but the key was lost a long time ago.

In the distance, on either side of the valley, were the hills that we called mountains. They were dark blue, sometimes green, with here and there a ribbon of road looping up, lost for a while, then, narrowing, running on again. In spring the lower slopes were pink with blossoms.

There must have been times when we were not happy in the valley, for there were quarrels and tantrums and scoldings. These did not really upset us much. They were soon over, like summer storms. Miranda never did anything by halves. When she was angry she spoke her mind in no uncertain terms, and when she was gay she was the most light-hearted person imaginable. If she felt like crying she let

go in a flood, and did not hide her face. When the little
dog that Mrs. Saunders had given us died, Miranda cried
for a whole day without stopping.

It was unfortunate that she did not take the trouble to
cultivate the friendship of Mr. and Mrs. Saunders, who
were, after all, her husband's employers. They were, I suppose, as she said many times, nothing but simple country
people. You would never know, to look at either of them,
that their farm was one of the largest and most progressive
in those parts. Mr. Saunders could be mistaken any day
for one of his hired hands. He was a shy man, unused to
city ways, and when Miranda flashed her eyes at him he
thought she was trying to flirt with him. He became horribly embarrassed, and went out of his way to avoid meeting her alone.

I was fond of Mrs. Saunders. The first Christmas we
were in Cheswick she gave me *The Wind in the Willows*,
which I still have. Jess and I used sometimes to go over
to the big farm to play with the Saunders boys, who were
a bit younger than we were. Mrs. Saunders was a plump
woman with a plain country face and a way of looking at
you that made you feel you could tell her anything. It was
lovely to have a mother like Miranda, who was more like
a sister, but once in a while Jess and I wanted one who was
more like a mother. Mrs. Saunders filled this need.

Both Mr. and Mrs. Saunders tried their best to make us
feel at home in Canada, to know and like the country. During our first summer in Cheswick they drove us—since we
had no automobile of our own—on long Sunday tours
about the neighboring villages, stopping now and then to
point out scenes of local or historical significance.

Not far distant—about forty miles away, at the head of
the valley—was the village of Grand Pré, locale of Long-

fellow's *Evangeline*. This was the most famous place in the region. In preparation for a visit to it, Mrs. Saunders had given us a copy of *Evangeline* to read. We drove to Grand Pré one fine Sunday, and stood on the plateau above the village looking across Minas Basin toward Cape Blomidon. The receding tide had exposed the mud flats for miles, and left dozens of little boats stranded there, heeled over, waiting. The flood tide came in as we watched, not creeping, but marching across the flats as if a dyke had broken. Mrs. Saunders, obviously enjoying this chance to show off a famous landmark, began to recite:

> ". . . and away to the northward
> Blomidon rose, and the forests old, and aloft
>   on the mountains
> Sea-fogs pitched their tents. . . ."

Jess and I, having both read *Evangeline,* were thrilled. Here was the very ground on which Evangeline and Gabriel had walked, here were the vast meadows, the orchards and cornfields, the turbulent tides, just as Longfellow had described them. There was Blomidon, too, away to the northward, with tents of sea fog high up against the sky.

Miranda was less impressed, for the simple reason that she had not found time to read *Evangeline*. On the way home, Mrs. Saunders gave a condensed version of the poem for her benefit. Then she had to explain the underlying story, which concerned the expulsion of the French Acadians by the British in 1755. Recounting this bit of her country's history filled her with such enthusiasm and goodwill that she made the mistake of offering to teach Miranda Canadian ways and customs.

"Why should I learn their damned customs?" Miranda demanded as soon as she got my father alone. The story of Evangeline had not gone over too well with her. She suspected Mrs. Saunders of being anti-British. "What's the matter with English customs?"

"She was only trying to help," Alfie said in a placating voice.

"Saying she'd make real Canadians out of us in no time! I never heard of anything so insulting. I didn't come to the colonies to *be* one of them."

"I suppose she thought if we're going to live in this country we'd want to conform to their ways."

"Conform to *their* ways!" Miranda cried, outraged. "Such impertinence! If there's any conforming to be done, they'd better do it themselves."

"It's only that our ways are different, and seem funny to them. And they don't like it when you call Canada a colony. It's a self-governing dominion."

"That's right, stick up for them. They'll be talking like the Irish, next thing you know."

"I only meant that since we're immigrants in a new country—"

"*Immigrants?*" Miranda looked at him as if he had called her a dirty name. "Where would these Canadians be if it weren't for English families like us coming out here, I'd like to know? Immigrants! I never thought I'd hear you talk like that, Alfie."

"Well, if we're going to make a living in this country, we ought to try to get on with the people," Alfie persisted.

"I suppose if we went to the Fiji Islands you'd expect me to go around naked. I don't know how you can talk so foolish, Alfie. As if I'd for one minute consider changing my ways! I call it bloody insolence, that woman suggesting such a thing. I hope I have some patriotism," Miranda added with a pious expression.

Alfie gave up trying to explain his views on this touchy subject. Miranda, like many an English immigrant before and since, honestly believed that if there was any teaching to be done it was up to her to do it, not the other way around.

One Sunday, on our own, we drove over the mountain to the sea. It was Jess's birthday, a Sunday in July. We rose early and by eight o'clock were laboring and steaming up the hill road in a high open touring car we had borrowed or rented for the occasion. The hills were shadowed and smelled of coolness. The road went upward at a steep angle.

We passed a horse and cart, and for a long time were just able to keep ahead of it, though we all rocked in our seats, urging the exhausted automobile onward and upward. When it seemed that the sputtering engine had reached the limit of its power, that we were about to stall and slide backward down the hill onto the horse and cart, we topped a rise and coasted down a short incline, gathering enough speed for the next ascent. We made frequent stops to cool the engine.

When we came to the top of the mountain, there was the sea in the distance far below, fading to the horizon. The remainder of the trip was downhill. We plunged along the narrow road at such a speed that the wind snapped at us, and wayside bushes clutched out to stop us, but the trees rushed by faster and faster and before we knew it we had reached level ground and a sunlit cove ringed with rocks. We parked the car under a tree at the top of the cliff and rested for a while after our dangerous journey.

This cove was on the Bay of Fundy, famed for its high tides, which sometimes reached a height of sixty-two feet,

Alfie said. He had read this in the leaflet supplied him by the Empire Settlement Office. He pointed out the high-water mark on the rocks.

The tide that morning was far out, and nets full of fish were strung on crossed poles stuck in the sands below us. A group of fishermen came in carts, sending the gulls soaring, and began to take fish from the nets. Sunlight glittered on the wet sand and in the sea pools among the rocks as we clambered down to the beach with our picnic baskets and towels. The beach was empty except for the fishermen and the hundreds of flapping gulls.

Miranda tucked up her skirts and ran to the water's edge, singing and calling. Her big-sister attitude toward us was most evident whenever an audience was present. That day her audience was the fishermen, and I feel sure that as she ran on the sands she was aware of the picture they would see: the gay family group comprised of a father and three daughters, the oldest daughter so pretty and full of laughter as she played with her little sisters.

Alfie was only ten years her senior, but he looked older because he was a slow considering man, somber-faced, wearing that expression of patience often seen on the faces of farmers and fishermen or anyone who must depend on the moods of nature. With her skirts tucked up and the wind blowing her dark bobbed hair, Miranda did look young enough to be his daughter. She was short and small-boned, though well rounded. When the fishermen had gone she took off all her clothes down to her pink knickers and cotton chemise, and splashed in the shallow creeping tide. Jess and I went in naked.

"What if someone comes?" Alfie asked, glancing around.

"Oh, Alfie, don't be such a fidget!" Miranda laughed

and kissed him. "Take off your trousers, lovie. Who's to see?"

He rolled up his trouser legs and waded gingerly out, then sat on the sands and watched us, but keeping an eye on the cliff, too, in case somebody came.

We unpacked the picnic basket and shared the sandwiches and hard-boiled eggs. Miranda in her underwear turned a different side to the sun every few minutes to dry herself, while Alfie warned against sunburn, for he had the typical countryman's aversion to exposing his skin to the elements. Miranda pooh-poohed him and lay back like a reclining nude in some old painting. She had a high-colored lusty beauty, a full-lipped changeable gypsy face. The color in her cheeks was not always natural.

After lunch Jess and I went off to gather shells, and when we returned a quarrel was beginning. Alfie had angered Miranda by suggesting that she might like to earn a little extra money helping Mrs. Saunders with her housework. He began to apologize almost immediately.

"I only thought, since you were in service back home—" he began.

Miranda's eyes glittered. "You haven't been telling people I was in service?"

"Well. . . ." He twisted uncomfortably and looked at the sea. "I told them you were with Mrs. Fitzhugh."

"Acting as a companion to Mrs. Fitzhugh is not quite the same thing as scrubbing floors for a great gawky country woman," Miranda reminded in a cutting voice.

Alfie looked up. "I thought you were Mrs. Fitzhugh's parlormaid." There was no hint of sarcasm in his voice. He was too slow and straightforward for that. When Miranda's face went stony he saw that he had made a mistake, and tried to patch things up. "People won't think any less of you. They don't have upper and lower classes

here the way they do at home. Everybody's the same here.
Mrs. Saunders worked in the canning factory once before
she was married."

Miranda was simmering up into a rage. "Do you seriously think for one moment that I would demean myself
emptying slops for your fat Mrs. Saunders, washing her
dirty drawers and her husband's socks, going down on my
knees to scrub her filthy floors? I have some respect for
myself, if you have not. To ask such a thing of me! Of *me!*"
she repeated, throwing back her head and spreading her
palms dramatically over her full breasts. "To suggest that
I lower myself before a crude country woman who worked
in a factory! I think you must be utterly insane!"

"She only wanted you to help around a bit. And she only
worked in the canning factory one summer years ago, to
help with her education. She taught school before she
married Mr. Saunders. He's a rich man. They've got two
bathrooms. All I thought was that you might want to
earn a little extra to buy dresses. . . ."

"You can tell your damned Mrs. Saunders that I would
die rather than lower myself. Two bathrooms! Does that
give her the right to look down on me—a fat country
woman who keeps pigs in her kitchen?"

"It was only a little sick pig she was nursing. You could
eat off her floors."

"The insolence!" Miranda cried, not listening. "And
you, Alfie—I wonder you can look me in the face! If you
can't earn enough money to support your family we had
better all go to the poorhouse and be done with it."

"Well, I only mentioned it," Alfie said in his slow be-
wildered countryman's voice. "I never thought you'd get
so upset."

"Upset? We came to this country to better ourselves,
and now you want me to scrub floors for a woman with

pigs in her kitchen!" Miranda burst into tears. She sobbed wildly, rubbing her eyes with the backs of her hands like a child. She was still in her knickers and chemise.

"Don't carry on, there's a good girl. She never expected you to scrub floors, she's got a hired girl to do that. It was only to help out with the children."

"To pick up after her grubby children and wipe their bottoms, while my own girls shift for themselves."

Alfie looked around despairingly and said, "It was only three days a week."

Miranda sobbed on, rocking back and forth with her hands clutching her hair as if she intended to pull some out by the roots any minute. "I wish we had never come to this bloody country. Common people putting on airs, thinking they're better because they've got two bathrooms!" The discovery that Mrs. Saunders enjoyed the use of two bathrooms enraged her more because the plumbing facilities at our small cottage, though not the most primitive kind, were far from adequate. "Looking down on me, when she can't even speak proper English. Oh, I never heard of anything so insulting! Expecting me to scrub her damned floors!"

When the tears and denunciations had subsided somewhat we looked behind us and saw that the tide was lapping at the picnic basket. The nets which had been far out on the sands that morning were completely covered. A cool wind sprang up and the sea darkened. We dressed and climbed the barnacled rocks to the top of the cliff. Jess remembered the shells we had gathered, but when she went down to fetch them the sea had covered the lower rocks. We finished the sandwiches and went home.

The day was not ruined. Jess and I were not disheartened, for we were accustomed to quarrels of this kind, and took them in our stride. Miranda's anger was not intimidating, in fact we rather admired her delivery of invectives and her theatrical gestures. When she cried, it was none of this half-hearted sniveling into a handkerchief that makes others feel guilty, but an unashamed and noisy demonstration that we could understand. It ironed out tensions and left us as refreshed as if we had had a good cry ourselves. And having spoken her mind and given vent to her emotions, Miranda herself was washed clean of rancor, rejuvenated.

She never forgave Mrs. Saunders, though. From that day at the beach onward, she hated her.

She had come to Canada to *be* someone, had believed that in this new and uncivilized country, as she thought of it, an English family would stand out like a pearl among stones. She had not studied Madam's elegant manners and refined way of speaking for nothing. She knew very well that she was miles above these country people with their vulgar Canadian accents. And yet here was Mrs. Saunders thinking she was just as good as—no, better than—we were. Oh, it was too insulting.

Jess and I were discarding our English accents as fast as we could, were quick to pick up local expressions and styles of pronunciation. Miranda, on the other hand, went out of her way to remind these Canadians that she was English.

She did not make many friends. The village people called around once, and then ignored us. They did not relish condescension. Alfie got along well enough with the men, he was liked because of his unassuming ways, but Jess and I were not too popular at school. The other pupils, having heard their parents talking at home, regarded us as curiosities. We grew accustomed to being not much liked, and the hours we spent with other children became only

intervals between the times we could roam by ourselves
through the woods and meadows at home, or in cold
weather shut ourselves up in a cupboard under the stairs
to read and reread our small store of books.

I can imagine what modern child-guidance experts
would say about this retreat from society, but I don't think
it did us much harm, and it did give us many happy hours
to look back upon. However, it made us unsure of our
impact on others. We never got over the feeling that we had
to earn the good opinion of those with whom we wished
to become friends; and we never made the first overtures
toward friendship, but waited to see how the wind was
likely to blow.

Alfie's year was up, and he could leave the farm if he
wanted to. He did not know how to go about finding another job, and in any case he liked where he was. Miranda
spoke hopefully of going to some city, though it was beginning to dawn on her that there *were* no cities in this
godforsaken country, only bleak towns which seemed dis-
tressingly uncivilized, compared to London. She kept trying to prod Alfie into some sort of action.

"How can you sit there night after night doing nothing,
Alfie?"

"I'm not doing nothing; I'm reading these." He meant
the farm journals. He spent all his spare time studying
them.

"Are you *content* with this sort of life?"

Alfie, who was perfectly content, would try to quiet her
with promises. "We'll get away one of these days, Miranda.
I'll find another job."

"Do you want the girls to grow into gawky things like
that Mrs. Saunders? Wasting our lives in this wilderness,
with people who never heard of culture. . . . And not one
pub in the whole bloody country. I never thought, when

we left London, that we'd end up like this. We're worse off than if we had stayed in Sussex."

Moody, frustrated, she would stare across the valley, drumming her fingers. Out there somewhere beyond the mountains were big bright cities; New York, Boston—still far away. She longed for the stimulation of a city, of people around her, not necessarily people she knew; in fact, strangers were better. All she wanted was that feeling of things happening, of wits being sharpened one against the other, that a city gives. An ant does not need to know every other ant in the hill. Their being there is enough.

The last thing Miranda wanted was to become settled, content with her lot. She feared contentment; it made people dull. And though she could exclaim over a pretty view or a field of wildflowers, she did not want to admire nature to the point where she might forget there were more important things. This, of course, was exactly what Alfie wanted to do—to become settled and enjoy nature in the country. He did not care if other people thought him dull. He did not really care what was going on in the world as long as he was left alone. In the evening, after his day's work, all he wanted was to sit on the porch with his farm journals and speculate on tomorrow's weather. He laid out two tiny gardens for Jess and me, and taught us how to tend them. When, occasionally, he spoke of Sussex—in spring he missed the bluebells—it was not as if he really wanted to go back to his old home, but was satisfied with the memory of it.

One thing that struck both our parents as strange about Canada was the absence of public houses. There were none in the village, none in the town; in fact, it turned out that there was not one in the whole country. "But where do people go?" Miranda asked Mrs. Saunders when we first came to Cheswick. "Go?" Mrs. Saunders had looked at her blankly. "For a drink; to meet their friends," Miranda had explained. Mrs. Saunders told her that Canadians did not drink, and that they met their friends at church socials.

Miranda chalked up the absence of pubs as another shortcoming of this queer country. It was so ridiculous; you could not even buy beer in the shops! Alfie had to make his own, in two big brown earthenware crocks in the cellar. Jess and I helped him.

I hope I am not giving the impression that Miranda was always complaining. Actually, between periods of impatience, she was wonderfully optimistic, refusing to consider any possibility but that one day the tide would turn, opportunity would come knocking, something would happen to give us a flying start toward that goal she had come all the way across the ocean to attain. She intended to be ready for it. We lived as frugally as possible, saving toward the day of liberation.

"Now, Mr. Murphy, don't you come tempting me!" she said to Mr. Dan Murphy who called around once a week in a sort of traveling department store: a truck that was lined all around inside with shelves holding bolts of cloth, cosmetics, needles and thread, patterns, cheap jewelery, shaving soap, candy—almost anything you could think of. "We'll be leaving here soon," Miranda told him. "I'm saving every penny."

"Now, that's a darned shame!" When he smiled at her, he reminded me of Sidney Wilkinson, back in London, though I could see no physical resemblance. "A good-looking woman like you shouldn't have to go without things. Why, you ought to be dolled up in furs and diamonds! See these beads? The minute they came from the wholesaler's I said to myself, 'There's only one woman in the county who'd appreciate the style and value of a necklace like that.' Straight from New York, too."

"You stop flattering me. I can't afford necklaces. I'll take three yards of that green wool and some buttons to match."

"It'll make a dress fit for a queen," Mr. Murphy said, measuring off. "When it comes to style, Mrs. Arnold, you've got the rest of my customers beat a mile. The minute I clapped eyes on you, I said to myself, 'There's a woman with style.' "

We saved on everything but clothes. Here Miranda refused to economize beyond a certain point. She was clever with a needle, and had a flair for style, as Mr. Murphy had noted. All our clothes, run up on the old treadle machine in the kitchen, were in the latest fashion. They were city clothes. Miranda said she would rather freeze than bundle up in heavy coats and country boots such as the native women wore. When we drove into town, using one of the farm trucks, we were the most stylish people there.

The nearest town—that is, a place with shops, a movie, and sidewalks—was ten miles away. Except when the weather prevented it, we drove into this town every Saturday night. Here Miranda was able for a little while to mingle with other people and catch the admiring glances of shopkeepers. She knew she was giving them a treat, after the plain-faced country girls they had to look at every day.

I do not say that Miranda was a perfect wife and mother. I do say that she suited us. She made Alfie happy. When he saw the way other men looked at her he felt puffed up, knowing she preferred him. (She had refused I don't know how many offers of marriage. Half the men in London had pleaded for her hand in vain.) When things went wrong, when Alfie came home looking worried, she would say, "Oh, lovie, what is it? Don't be a gloomy old duck." She would fuss over him and tease him until she made him smile again.

It was not all selfishness that made her want to get away from the farm. She really believed that, deep down, Alfie must want the same things from life as she did. She meant to help him get them.

But the second year went by and we were still there. Mr. Dan Murphy came around every week with his false salesman's smile, staying longer and longer.

"This is no sort of life for you," he was saying one day as Jess and I came in from school. "You ought to be in town, where things are gay, where you'd see some life. What I'd like to do is show you New York. There's a town for you."

"Oh, New York," Miranda said wistfully. "I've seen pictures of it."

"I'd parade you down Fifth Avenue. You'd knock their eyes out." He caught sight of us and said in a changed voice, "Will that be all for today, then, Mrs. Arnold?" and began to pack up his boxes of merchandise, adding something in an undertone to Miranda that made her laugh.

One of the things that Jess and I disliked about him was the way he seemed to be always talking around us, or over our heads. We could never be sure, when he and Miranda both burst into laughter, what they were laughing about. They exchanged glances over our heads.

"He'd never take Miranda away from us, would he?" I asked Jess, remembering my old fears about Sidney.

Jess scowled fiercely. "He'd better not try!"

One day when we had been in Cheswick just under three years, when Jess was going on fourteen and I was a year younger, the opportunity we had been saving for did come knocking. Alfie met a traveling salesman who represented a company dealing in what was loosely described as veterinary supplies. These included liniments, salves, tonics, cures for sundry animal ailments, leather and brass polishes, currycombs and brushes, as well as an assortment of simple household remedies. This salesman called on the general store in each town and visited, besides, a number of the larger farms in each district. He talked with the farmers, and left a few samples of his wares, along with a printed card bearing the inscription, "Samuel Baker, District Representative, The B. F. Whitney Company."

At the Saunders farm Mr. Baker talked to Alfie. They took a liking to one another, and Mr. Baker let it be known that there was an opening for a B. F. Whitney representative in another part of the province. He thought Alfie was just the man for the job. You didn't have to be a slick salesman, he said. B. F. Whitney products practically sold themselves. All you needed was a knowledge of farm animals and their care, a sympathetic ear, and an automobile. The district representative received no salary, of course. He worked on a commission. It was like being in business for yourself.

Left to his own devices, Alfie might have spent weeks considering, weighing pros and cons, before writing a timid letter to The B. F. Whitney Company to ask about this opening in their sales force, and in the end he would probably have decided to play it safe and stay where he was. Miranda did not allow him time to think. She made him sit down that very night, and she stood over him dictating what he was to write, overriding his protests that the letter attributed to him qualifications he had never possessed. "You've got to blow your own horn in this world," she told him. "Nobody else is going to do it."

"I'm not sure about this working on a commission. With a pay envelope every Saturday night, you know where you are. And what's this about an automobile?"

"We'll buy one second hand. Why do you think we've been saving all these years?"

"Well, I don't know. . . ."

"What an old pessimist you are, Alfie!" Miranda sat on his knee and snuggled her cheek against his. "Don't you want to get on in the world?"

"I don't want to jump from the frying pan into the fire. What if I didn't make a go of it?"

"Why should you fail? If Mr. Baker can make a good living selling veterinary supplies, why couldn't you do just as well? Better, even?"

"Well. . . ." Alfie considered for some time. "I like to know where I'm at," he said. "I don't know about this commission business."

"Send the letter, anyway, and see what happens," Miranda said. "And don't mope about it. Look on the bright side, ducky, do! You'll never get anywhere with that long face."

She was not surprised when, after several exchanges of letters, Alfie got the job.

Headquarters for the district he would represent was a coastal town which I shall call Southport, near the mouth of the Bay of Fundy. We were preparing to move there when fortune struck again.

Great-aunt Eliza had died in Sussex during the previous winter. She left her entire estate to Alfie, and when everything was accounted for we found ourselves richer by two hundred pounds. This seemed to us an immense fortune. It was no wonder that Miranda lost her head for a while, and put on airs.

One thing that must have given her great satisfaction was telling Mrs. Saunders about our inheritance. "My husband has fallen heir to his aunt's estate in Sussex," she said, conveying a picture of a vast landed estate complete with manor house and everything that goes with it, servants and tenant farms and heirlooms. She made poor old Great-aunt Eliza, who used to wear men's boots indoors and out and took her baths standing up at the sink in the scullery, sound like an offshoot of royalty.

She was determined that, with our new wealth, we would make a proper start in Southport, become approved upper-class members of the town's society. We would live in a town house. Everyone would see that we were people of importance. She said, "We'll put everything behind us and get a fresh start. We won't make the same mistakes again."

By mistakes, she did not mean her failure to make friends. What she meant was our failure as a family to acquire standing in the community, to command the respect of the simple country people around Cheswick, and Alfie's failure to rise above a common farm laborer. His failure to *want* to be anything more than a farm hand.

"We must order some calling cards," she said.

Chapter Two

So early one April morning we left the farm and drove down the valley in the high black Overland sedan we had bought. Jess and I sat in the back seat with our feet propped on a box of new clothes. The remainder of our few belongings had been sent on by freight the previous day. Violets and yellow daffodils were blooming on the meadow banks and the sun was shining as we set out, but when we left the sheltering hills behind and neared the seacoast the weather and the landscape changed. Clouds piled up and a cold wind swept in from the ocean, over rocky ledges where the tide chafed and foamed, over stunted bushes and sandy slopes. We felt exposed. Far out on the sea, beyond help, some fishing boats were drifting toward the horizon. Jess and I were homesick for the valley before we reached Southport.

When we stopped for a picnic lunch of bread and cheese, a sad little brown dog attached himself to us. "Oh, the poor little thing, he's lost," Miranda said. She fed him bits of cheese. "Look, he's limping, too. He's been hurt." She bound up his injured leg with her own handkerchief. Then when the time came to drive on, she could not bear to leave him behind.

"He might belong to someone," Alfie reminded her.

"Then they've been neglecting him. People like that have no business keeping dogs. Why, he's only a puppy." She cradled the dog in her arms. When he licked her face, tears came into her eyes. "Oh, the poor little lost duck! Look how he's trying to make friends."

"Well, all right, then," Alfie said. "He's only a mongrel. I don't suppose he'll be missed."

For an hour or so Miranda held the little dog, which we had decided to name Brownie, on her lap. Then she handed him over to Jess and me in the back seat.

As we drew nearer to our destination we passed through seaside villages, poor little places with unpainted wooden houses, a general store, and a collection of weathered fish-houses beside a wharf. On the landward side of the road, stunted pastures sloped upward, and a few thin cattle stood about the barnyards. "It doesn't look too prosperous," Alfie remarked. These villages would be part of his district.

"These are fishing villages," Miranda said. "The farms are inland."

We tried to visualize, beyond the rocky fields, a district of rich farmlands, with orchards and fat cattle.

We could have made Southport in one day, but Miranda said it wouldn't look right for The B. F. Whitney Company's new district representative to arrive late at night, tired and travelworn. If we were to make any sort of an entrance at all, we must do it in the busy part of the day, and we must all be looking our best. So we stayed overnight at a small village, and the next morning early we rose and dressed in our best clothes, washed the dust from the car, and continued our journey.

Miranda had kept pace with the fast-changing styles. She had thrown away her knickers and chemise and now wore nothing but a pair of lace-trimmed teddies under her dress. Her coat, which she had made herself, barely covered her knees and was wrapped around her hips in the approved fashion. She wore a tight-fitting green cloche, pulled well down over her ears, and pink rayon stockings with openwork clocks up the sides.

We drove into town around eleven o'clock. Miranda had assumed that housewives would be out shopping at that hour, buying the fish for dinner and meeting one another at the tea shop for elevenses, the way they did in England. She was mistaken. Southport housewives rarely ventured out before midafternoon, as we learned later.

However, making the best of a bad entrance, we drove up and down Main Street twice, then parked the car in front of the Victoria Hotel and sauntered about looking in shop windows, feeling stylish and confident in our new clothes, conscious that we attracted attention. Miranda carried Brownie on one arm like a lap dog. Jess had given him a bath the night before, and this had improved his appearance considerably.

The sea was out of sight behind some shops, but a vigorous briny smell of salt flats came up from it, and now and then we caught glimpses of wharves down a side street. We did not venture down to the wharves—though there seemed to be a good deal of activity in that direction—for the side streets were unpaved and muddy. Slush filled the gutters, and the few women on the street wore rubbers and heavy coats. Only pride kept us from shivering in our thin spring garments.

When we had been seen and admired by everyone on the street we walked on past the post office and found a park beside the courthouse. We huddled on a bench—out of the wind and out of sight—behind the war memorial, to eat the last of the bread and cheese we had brought from the farm. Miranda sent Jess and me to look for the public conveniences. We could find none, so went behind some bushes.

Miranda's heels sank into the springy turf. "Wouldn't you know?" she grumbled, meaning wouldn't you know that this uncivilized country would expect people to go to the toilet in public. She always made derogatory remarks about Canada, never realizing how much people resented it. Actually, all she was doing was bolstering her own self-esteem by reminding everyone that in London—she still spoke as if we had just come from there—one encountered a much more advanced state of human society.

The next step in our plan to impress Southport was a visit to the local newspaper office. Alfie had to take the car around to the garage, so Miranda and Jess and I went to the *Gazette* office without him. We were met by a sandy-haired bold-eyed man of about thirty, whom we took to be the editor. His expression changed when we were ushered into his office. His eyes took Miranda in from head to toe and he smiled expansively. She introduced herself and handed him one of Alfie's business cards. (She had ordered a box—as well as some personal calling cards for herself—from the local printer before we left Cheswick. Alfie's card read "Alfred Arnold, Esq., District Representative, The B. F. Whitney Company.") The man glanced at it and laid it aside as of no consequence, but he must have noted the name. He said, "Well, Miss Arnold. . . ."

"Mrs. Arnold," Miranda corrected him.

He affected gallant disbelief. "Go on! You're not going to stand there and tell me these big girls are your daughters!"

Miranda held Brownie up to her face like a muff. "I'm afraid you're trying to flatter me, Mr.——"

"Williams. J. B. Williams. Call me Jack. No, honest, I thought you were all sisters. You really mean you're their mother? You're not kidding me?"

"I am Mrs. Alfred Arnold, of London. These are my daughters, Jessica and Rose Ann."

"I'd never believe it," Mr. Williams marveled. He moved

closer to Miranda and tickled Brownie under the chin with a freckled hand. "So you're English?" he said.

"We have recently come from London."

"I could tell right away you weren't a local girl. What brings you to this town?" He took another look at Alfie's business card. "Does this mean you're going to settle in Southport? Well, now I'm very glad to hear it. I'm a newcomer here myself. Lived in New York my whole life up to three months ago." He guided Miranda to a chair. "Take a seat and tell me what I can do for you."

Miranda sat down and crossed her legs, cradling Brownie in her arms, dropping little pouting kisses on his head.

It is difficult to remember at what point in growing up we become aware that a loved one is not necessarily perfect, but I believe it was that afternoon in the *Gazette* office that Jess and I first asked ourselves how Miranda appeared to other people, what they thought of her. Something about the way she spoke to Mr. Williams—though in her most genteel voice—and the barefaced way he looked at her, made us vaguely uneasy. I found myself wishing she would behave in a different way, though I did not know exactly how I wanted her to behave.

The gleam in Mr. Williams's eye was certainly not respectful. Miranda must have thought it was, for she warmed under his bold gaze and tilted her head sideways, giving the self-satisfied downward glance of a woman who knows she is irresistible. Jess and I looked at one another, then quickly aside, as if we had stumbled onto some guilty secret. It was the first moment of doubt, the foot-in-the-door of a bogey that we did not yet recognize, and that even later on, when we did, we refused for a time to acknowledge. We blamed other people. Certain kinds of other people. Miranda was all right when she was not with them.

We recognized Jack Williams—his type, at any rate. He was like Sidney back in London, like Dan Murphy, the salesman. We mistrusted him on sight. Jess scowled and turned her back on the room, staring through the dusty windows at the people in the street.

"Are you staying at the hotel?" Mr. Williams asked.

"Yes, the Victoria." Miranda shot a look at us. "But we wondered if you could direct us to some nice guest house —hotels are such dreary places, don't you agree?—where we could stay until we rent a house."

"I can give you the names of a couple of good boarding houses." Mr. Williams took his eyes off Miranda's knees long enough to write two addresses on a slip of paper. "Try Mrs. Calahan's first. It's over on Sycamore Street. Look, I've got a car outside. Why don't I run you over there?"

"We don't want to put you out," Miranda said, but she stood up and handed Brownie to me.

"No bother at all. It's a pleasure." He already had one hand under her elbow, guiding her through the door. He dusted off the front seat of his car for her. Jess and I, not sure what was expected of us, but unwilling to be left behind, scrambled into the back seat. The car was a dark blue sedan half a block long, with extra seats that pulled out of the floor. We had never been in such a luxurious vehicle before.

On the way to Mrs. Calahan's boarding house Mr. Williams told Miranda about Southport. It had two banks, a post office, a hospital, three schools, not to mention the County Academy, two hotels, four churches, five garages, and a golf club. Being the county seat, it also had a courthouse. Yes, and a public library, too, Mr. Williams added, and asked Miranda if she was much of a reader.

"Oh, yes, I read a great deal," she said. Sometimes she read love stories in magazines.

We met Mrs. Calahan and arranged to stay there. Mr. Williams drove us back to the *Gazette* office by a round-about way, to show us the town. All the cross streets, sloping toward the sea, were lined with chestnut and elm trees, just coming into leaf. The houses were mostly three story, quite large, with widow's walks and cupolas, set in tidy gardens behind pruned hedges. The general effect was one of neatness and prosperity.

"It's not a bad little town," Mr. Williams said. "There's a weekly boat service to New York and Boston, too, so you don't feel absolutely cut off from the rest of the world. That's the New York boat at the wharf now." Two funnels were visible over the clutter of sheds at the waterfront. "You're liable to find it pretty rustic, after London," he added, "but we'll certainly do our best to make you feel at home."

By the time we returned to the business district, more shoppers had appeared. Jess and I noted that none of the women was as fashionably dressed as Miranda. None of them wore pink stockings.

Mr. Williams said, "My grandmother owns one or two houses around town. I believe one of them is vacant right now. Shall I make inquiries?"

"Oh, please do," Miranda said.

"Just leave it to me, then. I'm sure I can find something to suit you."

"You'll want to print something in your social column." Miranda handed him the statement she had prepared. It said that Mr. Alfred Arnold, of London, had been appointed new District Representative for the B. F. Whitney Company, and that Mr. and Mrs. Arnold, with their daughters, etc. etc. She raised her eyes to his. "You will print a nice little piece about us, won't you?"

"I certainly will, Mrs. Arnold," he said.

Quite a long piece appeared in the next day's *Gazette*, when we were all settled in Mrs. Calahan's boarding house. It stated, among other things, that we were staying at the Victoria Hotel.

Mr. Williams was as good as his word. He brought his rental agent around to see us the next day, and we found a furnished house within a week. It was on Lupin Crescent, an unpaved cul-de-sac running parallel to Main Street and one block behind it. The upper side of Lupin Crescent was a solid row of aging brick houses with high front steps, trodden lawns, and great brown roots of chestnut trees heaving up under the broken walks and starving hedges.

There were no driveways; the houses were too close together for that. The old wooden carriage houses at the back which served as garages were reached by way of narrow alleys. The lower side of Lupin Crescent was taken up by the yard of the town jail, the jail itself facing Main Street. Being across from the jail yard was not as bad as it sounds. It was a well-kept graveled space edged with lawns and shrubbery, enclosed behind a high iron fence. Mr. Williams and the agent both assured us that prisoners were rarely seen behind the fence, only the jailkeeper, whose hobby was gardening. We learned later that often for weeks at a time there were no prisoners inside the jail, either.

The things that might have discouraged other tenants— the way the houses were crowded together so that all our side windows faced a neighbor's brick wall, and the jail yard across the street—were precisely what Miranda liked about the house on Lupin Crescent. One expected to be crowded in town, and the view from the front windows was lovely. You'd think it was a real park if you didn't know. Another thing that appealed to her was the fact that the house had two bathrooms, though the one on the third floor was only a toilet and a basin, what the rental agent called a half bath.

The third floor was reached by way of a flight of stairs going up from the kitchen, for the house had been built for people with servants. The district had deteriorated, was a little gone to seed, the back yards grown up in a jungle of sooty shrubbery and sagging fences. Some houses on the street had already been cut up into flats. In spite of the scars of other people's living, we thought the house was an imposing one. Certainly it was a far cry from the three-room flat we had rented from Uncle Bertie in London; and it was twice as large as the cottage at the farm.

Alfie complained that it was too big. "We'll rattle around like chips," he said. He had never lived in a house where the preparation of food and the eating of it were done in different rooms. "We don't need anything near as grand as this."

"Grand?" Miranda looked at him. "It's quite ordinary."

"It's got ten rooms, not counting that little box room. We could get lost in this big place."

"What nonsense you talk, Alfie. People will think we never lived in a decent house before."

"Well, we never had anything like this. I don't know who's going to sleep in all those beds. I like to be cozy." He would have felt much more at home in three or four small rooms. Then he would have known what he was supposed to do in each one.

The furnishings were dark and ponderous, and gave the rooms a cluttered appearance which we mistook for elegance. There were a heavy buttoned parlor suite of green plush, and gilt-framed pictures of highland glens with stags and rocky streams. Jess and I each had a bedroom to ourselves, which seemed to us the height of luxury. I would

lie in bed at night being homesick for the farm but at the
same time feeling proud of living in a big handsome town
house with central heating.

As time went along we began to suspect that Alfie was
not adjusting to his new position. He was learning—
though he had not yet told us—that the whole of his district was composed of fishing villages such as we had seen
on the drive down. There were no rich farming communi-
ties as in the valley, where Mr. Baker was doing so well.
Miranda was put out because nobody seemed to take
Alfie's job seriously. When the neighbors called and she
explained that her husband was the new District Representative (she made it sound like a diplomatic post) they
were not impressed.

Mrs. Dove, who lived next door, even went so far as to
say, "Look, why doesn't he try the fruit company where
my husband works? I heard Billy say the other day that
they were looking for a driver." Miranda took an im-
mediate and intense dislike to Mrs. Dove, which was
rather a shame, since Mrs. Dove's daughter Clara later
became my best friend. "It just shows," Miranda said to
Jess and me that night. "You can't be too careful. If I had
known we'd be forced to associate with people like that
we would never have moved to this neighborhood."

Mrs. Dove was our first caller. The second was even less
prepossessing. He was Mr. Peters, who lived at the end of
the street and kept the butcher shop on the corner of Main.
A scrawny little man with a big Adam's apple and a noisy
laugh, he dropped in one night on his way home to supper.
He had come, he said, to make certain we would trade at
his store. "You'll get A-1 service at my place," he brayed,
slapping his knee as if he had made a great joke. "I treat
my customers right."

"Such a common little man," Miranda said when he had gone.

She was very much the grand duchess, wearing the rather haughty expression one would expect from a lady whose husband has inherited an estate in Sussex. Complacent in her innocence, she believed the townspeople were slightly dazzled by her arrival. She expected to be caught up in the Southport social whirl—such as it was—almost at once, and pictured herself being just slightly bored by small-town pretensions. A silver tray was placed on the hall table to receive visiting cards, but I cannot remember that a card was ever placed there.

According to the *Gazette*, the social life of the town was very gay indeed, with dances at the golf club, tennis parties, afternoon teas, meetings of the Drama Society and the Opera Club, and many other functions. No invitations came our way.

I don't know how long it took Miranda to realize that Southport, like most small towns in what she called "the colonies," was more class conscious than any city in the world. The wife of the county judge, the wives of doctors, bank managers and the like did not go to the same teas as the wives of clerks and small businessmen, and *they* considered themselves a notch above anyone who did manual labor. To Miranda, Southport was such an unimportant dot on the map, so far removed from civilized world centers, as to be negligible. Its inhabitants, no matter what they did for a living, could not help but be provincial and undistinguished. They were colonials.

She, on the other hand, was English, and so had every right to look down her nose; in fact she would have considered it unpatriotic not to do so. Moreover, she was a Londoner, and had observed the cream of British society in Mrs. Fitzhugh's drawing room. By this time she had completely forgotten what her position in Mrs. Fitzhugh's house had been, and was creating a fantasy in which she became a sort of distant relative of her late employer's.

Another thing that Miranda did not realize was that in a small town everybody knows everybody else's business. Within a week of our arrival, the shopkeepers had a pretty accurate idea of our financial status.

When she expressed concern at not being asked to any of the important social functions of Southport, Alfie said, "Well, I'd just as soon not be asked to one of those grand affairs. I'd be a fish out of water."

Miranda hoped he wouldn't talk like that in front of Mr. Jack Williams, who had turned out to be rather more important than the mere editor of the Southport *Gazette*. He as good as owned the paper, and much more besides.

Up on the hill behind Lupin Crescent, visible from our back windows, was a great weathered stone house with five chimneys, half hidden behind tall trees. It was surrounded by parklike grounds where half a dozen sheep nibbled. Gardeners could be seen raking the smoother lawns that spread out from the wide pillared porch. This was where Jack Williams, who was a bachelor, lived with his grandmother.

Old Mrs. Williams, it appeared, owned half the town: all the houses on Lupin Crescent, a block of shops and offices on Main Street, as well as the newspaper, to mention but a few of her holdings. Jack, her only grandchild, had been living in New York and various places—sowing his wild oats, according to Mrs. Dove—and had only recently come to Southport to take over the management of his grandmother's affairs. He was her sole heir, and she was getting on. She was over eighty.

As soon as Miranda heard this she telephoned Jack Williams to thank him again for helping us to find a house.

He assured her that he was tickled to death to be of service, and added that we could send the monthly rent check to the *Gazette* office, for it was there that he conducted all his business affairs.

"I do hope your grandmother will drop around one day for a cup of tea with me," Miranda said.

He hesitated. "She doesn't get out much."

But Miranda believed that the old lady would call. She dusted the parlor every day, so as to be prepared.

Although we had never been church-goers, Miranda decided, when she learned that old Mrs. Williams and her grandson attended the Presbyterian church on High Street, that we would go there, too. She would be asked to join the Women's Institute. Someone had told her that was a sure way of getting to know everybody. She *was* asked to join the Institute, but was disappointed to learn that the most sought-after members—old Mrs. Williams and her friends—showed up at only one meeting a year, when the Christmas hampers for the poor were being prepared. However, we kept on going to church every Sunday. Jack Williams, wearing a pious expression, passed the collection plate.

As the leaves unfolded and the weather warmed, Miranda would glance up the hill toward Mrs. Williams's house, now almost hidden among the great trees, and wonder aloud if the old lady had manners enough to know it was her place to call on newcomers. The county judge's wife, too, appeared to be sadly lacking in knowledge of social customs. Miranda shrugged and said, well, what could you expect in this backward country. She had picked up enough rules of etiquette from Madam to know that it was proper for established residents to call on newcomers, not the other way around.

While she waited to be recognized, she could at least be

seen. Almost every afternoon she put on her best clothes
and her gayest lipstick and went fashion-parading up and
down Main Street. People stared at her, and I have no
doubt that as she promenaded along in her high heels, or
stood window-gazing with one hand on her hip like a fashion drawing in a magazine, she was imagining the impression they would receive. They would know at once that
she was no ordinary local product. Someone would ask,
"Who is that lovely fashionably dressed woman? Where
is she from?" And someone else would answer, "She is
Mrs. Alfred Arnold, of London."

I have no proof, of course, that Miranda indulged
in such fantasies as she tripped up and down Main Street.
I do know that after about a month she decided that since
old Mrs. Williams did not know enough to call on us, we
would call on her. She chose a Saturday afternoon, so that
Jess and I could go along, too. Dressed in our very best—
Jess and I wearing new straw sailors from the Bon Ton,
Miranda in pink crepe de Chine—we walked up the hill
to Mrs. Williams's front door. A middle-aged woman in a
maid's uniform answered our knock. Miranda presented
her calling card.

"What's this for?" The woman looked blankly at it, then
turned it over to see if anything was written on the back.

"Kindly announce us to your mistress," Miranda said.

"You're not selling anything, are you?" the woman
asked. She looked at the card again, then at us, and her
eyes alerted with recognition. "You're the new tenants,
aren't you? You ought to have gone around to the back."

"I *beg* your pardon?"

"If it's something about the house, you ought to have
gone around to the back door. And ask for one of the men,

not Mrs. Williams. Better still, phone up the office next time. Has your plumbing gone, or something?"

Miranda gave her a good stare. "This happens to be a social call, not business."

The maid looked uncertain, as if she suspected us of pulling her leg. Behind her, we caught a glimpse of a wide hall with a stairway going up.

"Did Mrs. Williams know you were coming? She never said anything to me."

Miranda said icily, "Kindly inform your mistress that Mrs. Alfred Arnold is calling."

"Well . . . I'll see if she's in." The maid went away, leaving the door ajar. We took advantage of this opening to step into the hall. Beyond an archway with double doors, a party seemed to be going on. Female voices could be heard, and the chink of teacups.

"What is it, Agnes?" A voice rose above the general conversation, which immediately died down.

Agnes said, "There's a Mrs. Arnold at the door, one of the tenants. She's got her two girls with her."

"Did she say what she wants?"

Agnes shut the double doors behind her, and we did not hear her reply. In about five minutes she reappeared.

"Mrs. Williams is taking a nap. She wants to know if you'd care to come back another day."

Beside me, I could feel Miranda tensing all over. She kept her dignity, however, and said graciously, "Thank you, Agnes." With our heads high, we walked down the broad front steps. At the bottom, I looked back and saw that Agnes was still standing in the doorway, staring after us.

"I simply cannot understand people not training their servants properly," Miranda said in a carrying voice.

Whether as a result of this encounter or not, Miranda did modify her behavior somewhat, became a little less the grand duchess. Also, the need for a friend of her own kind may have become stronger than her desire to be regarded as an aristocrat. At any rate, she made friends with Hattie Hughes, the jailkeeper's wife. Hattie was a plump careless woman with a screaming laugh. She reminded me of Florrie, Madam's old housekeeper back in London. Hattie and her husband, Roy Hughes, lived in a flat over the jail.

Her sister, Mrs. Fuller, ran the only beauty parlor in town, and every treatment in the shop had been tried out on Hattie. Her hair had been singed, dyed, bleached, and baked too long in the permanent waving machine. She had no eyebrows left to speak of, and the first time we saw her she had a crusted scab like a moustache on her upper lip, the result of a hair-removing experiment. She looked a fright, but she was sympathetic and easygoing, and had the good sense to get what fun she could out of life. Miranda was starving for Hattie's sort of companionship, someone with whom she could be herself. She had not had such a friend since she left London.

I would be doing Miranda an injustice if I suggested that she accepted Hattie because nobody else wanted her, or that she ever regarded Hattie as an inferior. Her snobbery was not the kind that looked down on people she liked. During the two years we lived in Southport, Hattie was her best friend, though they sometimes quarreled and were not on speaking terms for weeks at a time.

They would sit in our kitchen doing crossword puzzles, reading *Snappy Stories*, Dorothy Dix, and the Katzenjammer Kids, discussing Gloria Swanson, Peaches Browning, Queen Marie of Rumania, Rudolph Valentino and other celebrities of the era, fixing their hair, giving one another facials. In those days cosmetic houses were forever sending out samples of their wares to whoever cared to clip a coupon and mail it along with twenty-five cents.

Hattie and Miranda clipped every coupon they could find. Almost every day samples of powder, rouge, creams, face packs and the like would arrive at our house. Aside from Auntie Vi's monthly letter from London, this was about the only mail we ever received. Once in a while a note would come from Alfie, from wherever he was in the district trying to sell his veterinary supplies. He spent Sundays at home. Each week end he was a little quieter, and Miranda would say, "You'll do better next week, Alfie." She meant to encourage him, but it sounded more like a command.

On weekday evenings Hattie and Miranda would go to the movies or for a walk down town, strolling past the blank shop windows and the youths loitering on corners, stopping off at the ice-cream parlor to spend an hour over a ten-cent sundae. They always tried to get a seat near the window, so that they could see and be seen.

This was better than the farm, but it wasn't breaking into society. It wasn't a dance at the golf club or being asked to tea by the county judge's wife. Miranda, wistfully now, read the social notices in the *Gazette*. Hattie scoffed at her. "My God, Miranda," I heard her say one day as I came in from school, "who'd want to bother with that bunch of old coots? Personally, I wouldn't go to the backhouse with any one of them." That was the way she talked, with a down-East twang you could sharpen a knife on.

"Tell me honestly, now," she continued, "what good it would do you to get in with the so-called society of this town. Old Mrs. Williams and that bunch—I couldn't be bothered. As for Mr. Jack Williams, I'd watch my step with him if I were you."

Miranda said in a disinterested voice, "He appears to be a perfect gentleman."

"Oh, yes, he's all charming smiles and fancy manners, a regular lady-killer. No doubt he went out of his way to impress you with his city ways during your first week in town, when everybody and his dog saw you riding up and down Main Street with him four days running."

"He was kind enough to help us find this house."

"Why not? He owns the damned place, doesn't he?"

"His grandmother does."

"It comes to the same thing. . . . Not to mention stopping you on the street every other day, saying, 'Oh, Mrs. Arnold, how ravishing you look! May I call on you some evening when your husband's not there?' "

"I'll thank you not to be insulting, Hattie."

"Well, you wouldn't be the first married woman he's said that to. I've been hearing stories about him ever since he arrived here three months ago."

"What Mr. Williams says to these country women is no concern of mine. I believe he's capable of recognizing a lady when he sees one."

"I'm only warning you. You won't do yourself any good, standing around on the street talking and laughing with him the way you do." Hattie caught sight of me and exclaimed in the falsely hearty voice grown-ups use when they have been overheard saying something not intended for tender ears, "Well, who is *this* fair damsel? Don't tell me it's little Rose Ann Arnold of Sixteen Lupin Crescent! Why, so it is. I could have sworn it was Miss Mary Pickford herself." She lowered her voice to normal and said, "You know what we ought to do, Miranda? We ought to bob Rosie's hair. Make a regular little flapper out of her. Wouldn't you like that, honey? Wouldn't you like to be a regular little flapper?"

I would indeed, but did not say so, for Miranda frowned and told me to run up and do my lessons. I knew that as soon as I was out of sight she would warn Hattie about putting ideas into my head. Jess and I both longed to have our hair bobbed. Miranda would not hear of it. She thought long hair made us look younger. She could not go on giving her age as under thirty forever, but she did expect Jess and me to preserve her youth by postponing our own development as long as possible. So, though we were shooting up like weeds, we still tied our long hair back with ribbons and wore black cotton stockings and round childish hats with elastics under the chin. At home, I was addressed as "baby" more often than not.

The other day I ran across a yellowed snapshot of Jess and me taken in that year. We are standing on the street in front of our house with our arms around one another's shoulders and the shadow of the photographer—Clara Dove—slanting across us like the shadow of the invisible man. We are dressed alike, in pleated serge jumpers over white middies. The jumpers come not quite to our knees, and our bloomers show. These childish outfits caused us more than enough embarrassment. No one else we knew wore them, as we told Miranda many times. The other girls at school wore printed gingham dresses in summer and gay flannels and tartans in winter. Miranda would not listen. She wanted us to look English, and English schoolgirls wore jumpers; therefore they were correct.

I went up to my room and curled up on the windowseat overlooking the cluttered backyards. The sooty shrubbery was a tender spring green. Lilacs were coming into bloom. Brownie snuggled up beside me. He had grown into a homely awkward lovable dog with traces of beagle ancestry, sad-eyed, long-eared, affectionate. Alfie had taught him a few tricks, such as how to sit up and beg. Brownie liked to sit with me in the windowseat and watch for cats in the garden. He settled down with his nose touching the pane.

I had been writing stories on the sly for almost a year. So vivid were my impressions of those long-ago excursions about London's West End that all my stories were placed in that setting. The house in which my heroine lived was always Madam's elegant house in Park Lane. I would rough out a plot and make a list of names to fit the characters, writing in a school exercise book. But when I had described the people and the setting, the plot would seem inadequate, and I would begin all over again with a new set of characters and a new plot. I had half a dozen partly filled exercise books hidden under the mattress of my bed. As I wrote, I visualized a brilliant future. I might get my picture in a cold-cream advertisement along with Lady Diana Manners'. "Famous authoress Miss Rose Arnold guards her beauteous complexion with So-and-So's cream. 'So soothing for delicate skins' says Miss Arnold."

I was working that day on a story about an heiress who discovered that she was really the daughter of a musician who later turned out to be the rightful owner of her supposed parents' wealth—a complicated plot. I was so engrossed in it that I did not even try to hear what Hattie was saying downstairs about Jack Williams. Every once in a while she would interrupt herself—and my train of thought—with a scream of laughter. I did not mind. Unlike the elder Sitwell, I have always liked the sound of laughter in the next room.

The merriment downstairs was especially reassuring that day because I had just come from Clara Dove's house next door, where gloom hung like a curtain on the sunniest day. Clara herself managed to be at home as seldom as possible, and I did not blame her.

Mrs. Dove described herself as a good Christian woman, meaning that she had no intention of enjoying her stay here on earth, and thus endangering her chances in the next world. There was something about their house, an air of foreboding, that made you realize how foolish it was to expect anything but trouble in this world. A threatening colored motto in a polished frame hung in their dining room. "What Will You Be Doing When Jesus Comes?" it asked, and I could never look at it without a start of dismay.

I knew what Mr. Dove would be doing when Jesus came. He would be tending the one-gallon portable alky cooker in the cellar. He spent most of his evenings in the cellar with his father-in-law, Grampa Higgins, who lived with them. They had quite a thriving business going there. Besides the gin they made in the alky cooker (they even had labels printed: "Doc Billy's Cough Cure") they brewed beer. The cellar was always full of customers, many of whom drank their purchases on the spot.

Upstairs, Mrs. Dove maintained a martyr's silence. She belonged to an organization called The Sons of Temperance. I shall never forget the look on her face the first time she came to visit us, when she found Alfie and Miranda sitting in the parlor—"in the presence of innocent children," as she put it later on—drinking great mugs of our own homemade beer. Little did she know that the innocent children had made that particular batch of home brew by themselves.

Clara was the first friend I ever had. Through her, I got my first real glimpse into other people's lives. Unattractive as her home life was, I found it fascinating. Grampa Higgins soaking his corns in the kitchen, using dirty language to annoy Mrs. Dove, belching explosively even in front of company, pretending he couldn't help it, though he always shot a sly look at his daughter to see how she was taking it. She rarely disappointed him. He never took baths in winter, and seldom in summer. I think he hated Mrs. Dove, and spent hours thinking up ways to aggravate her. And I suspected that she went out of her way to present him with opportunities to abuse her, which he never failed to take advantage of.

Mr. and Mrs. Dove did not quarrel. That is, they did not flare up at one another and get things out of their systems. What they did was maintain an umbrageous silence, broken by references to one another's shortcomings. Mrs. Dove's remarks were mostly about drinking, for her husband was his own best customer. "Whatever faults I may have," I heard her say one night in her fault-finding voice, "you can't accuse me of being a drunkard." "You and your God-damned temperance league," Mr. Dove remarked without taking his eyes off the newspaper he was reading. "I'll tell you one thing you are," he continued with chilling pleasantness, "and that's a bloody bore."

At the Seavey's—James and his mother: our neighbors on the other side—I glimpsed quite another kind of home life. Mr. Seavey had died when James was nine. His widow wore an air of aimless melancholy, a staring kind of sadness. She made pies and doughnuts for one of the restaurants in town. She spoke sometimes of opening a real bake shop down town, but never did anything about it because she could not bear to think of James coming home from school to a motherless house.

James was fourteen, old enough to take care of himself, one would think. According to Clara, he was a sissy. On Saturday mornings he helped his mother with the baking. I thought he was very nice, always neat and polite, though not particularly handsome. He was a thin boy with straight yellow hair smelling of cooking fat, and the kind of face that nobody remembers.

"We do have nice times together, James and I," his mother said. "We have our little home." It had been converted into flats; they lived on the lower floor. "We're happy together, just the two of us." She gazed sadly at nothing.

We had lived in Canada for three years, and these were the first Canadian children of my own age I had really got to know. Clara, a chunky girl with her hair in a straight careless Dutch cut—she thought she resembled Colleen Moore—did not allow me to forget that we were outsiders, on probation, as it were, with the whole town watching to see how we would turn out. "Don't pay any attention if people look at you," she said kindly. "It's just because you're new in town." I developed a disconcerting—to others—habit of staring at everyone I met, trying to guess what they thought of me.

For most people in small towns, going to church is a social occasion. Mrs. Dove went to the Methodist church to praise God for making her life miserable. We went to the Presbyterian church to be seen.

Miranda had expected—quite reasonably, we thought—that the minister, Mr. Teperman, would make it his business to call on us within a week of our first appearance among his congregation. It was two months before he showed up, and by that time she had practically washed her hands of him.

He was a plump fussy little man resembling a disgusted Mr. Pickwick, and he was rigidly intolerant of anything modern. I suppose he could no more adjust the beliefs in which he had been brought up—beliefs which had been formed, set, and hardened, in his Victorian youth—or absorb new ideas, than he could change his physical appearance. "A regular old fanatic," Hattie called him. He had preached sermons denouncing bobbed hair, short skirts, playing golf on Sundays, the theory of evolution, and motion pictures. I laughed at him because Miranda did. It never occurred to me that I might do better to form opinions on my own.

When Mr. Teperman did finally come to see us, he picked a day when Miranda had been too busy to change from her cotton morning dress. A wonderful new lot of cosmetics had arrived that morning, and Hattie had come over to help her try them out. They piled the luncheon dishes in the sink while they gave themselves mud packs, plucked one another's eyebrows, and experimented with various complexion aids. By three o'clock their faces were caked with powder and rouge, they had darkened what was left of their eyebrows with black pencil, and had drawn exaggerated cupid's bow mouths.

When the doorbell rang Miranda answered it. She had just about given up expecting callers in the afternoon, and probably thought this was a magazine salesman. I was glad to see that she did not become flustered when she saw who it was, but welcomed Mr. Teperman as graciously as if she had been dressed up and waiting for him. He shook hands with everyone, including Hattie, who came in from the kitchen wearing a metal hair curler over each ear.

"You must excuse my appearance, Mr. Teperman," Miranda said, whisking Brownie off the sofa. "I'll run up and change." She meant her dress, which had a hole under one arm, but he looked at her penciled eyebrows and red mouth.

"I can't stop," he said, picking his way disgustedly past a pile of movie magazines. "I have other calls to make."

"Oh, you must have a cup of tea." Miranda gave the Bible a quick dust against her hip and placed it near him. "The kettle's on."

"No, please!" He raised his hands as if pronouncing the benediction. "I'm going on to Mrs. Raymond's. This is not my regular visiting day. The second Wednesday of each month is my day for this part of town. I called last Wednesday, but you were out, unfortunately."

"We went to the matinee," Hattie said. "We saw poor Valentino. I couldn't help crying, thinking of him dead."

Mr. Teperman pointedly ignored her. He remarked briefly on the weather, the work of the Women's Institute, and the Sunday school. Then he glanced at his watch and said he had time to read a chapter.

He drew the Bible toward him, thumbed through the pages as if he knew exactly where to look, and began to read: " 'And when Jehu had come to Jezreel, Jezebel heard of it; and she painted her face and tired her head, and looked out at the window.' " He read as if he knew the chapter by heart, but did not raise his eyes from the page. Hattie sat with her hands touching her chin and her eyes raised piously to the ceiling. I glanced at Miranda. She looked uncertain for a moment, then her face took on the excessively polite, set expression which I knew from experience meant that she was boiling inside but determined to be a lady at all costs and rise above insult. " 'Go see now this cursed woman, and bury her, for she is a king's daughter.' " Mr. Teperman read on to the end of the chapter.

When he left, Hattie pulled back the curtain to watch him down the path, then turned to us. "Well, of all the damned nerve!"

"What do you mean?" Miranda pinned her with a hard look, as though daring her to explain.

"He called us Jezebels. If that's not an insult, I don't know what is."

"I think you're mistaken, Hattie," Miranda said sharply. I could see that she was preparing to save face by feigning ignorance of Mr. Teperman's intention.

"My lord, it was as plain as the nose on your face!" Hattie cried. Her indignation was already evaporating. In a minute she would begin to laugh. "You've got to admit it was funny, though," she began as a preliminary.

"It may seem funny to you," Miranda snapped, forgetting herself. "I fail to see the humor of it myself. An ignorant little country preacher daring to cast insinuations at me! A fine state of affairs, I must say, when a lady is not safe from such vulgarity in her own home. If that's what you call manners in this country!"

"Shoot! Everyone knows old Teperman. He's forty years behind the times. No sense getting mad at him."

"Mad? I wouldn't lower myself. The only way to deal with such people is to ignore them."

Upstairs, I looked up the word Jezebel in my school dictionary. "A shameless abandoned woman," was the definition given. The faint dislike I had felt for Mr. Teperman turned to hatred. The nerve of that old man! I thought, echoing Hattie's sentiments.

Jess was in her room, reading. I stood in her doorway until she looked up. "Do you think Mr. Teperman was trying to insult Miranda?" I asked.

"How should I know? I'm not a mind reader." Jess threw her book aside and flopped face downward on the bed. "I wish to Jesus people wouldn't act so silly around this house," she grumbled. "It'll be all over town by tomorrow. Trust Hattie!" She sat up and glared at me. "For heaven's sake don't stand there like a baby with your finger in your mouth. It gets on a person's nerves."

I went downstairs. Miranda was out buying the meat for dinner, which she had forgotten to order. While I waited, I took a sip of Doc Billy's cough cure from the bottle on the sideboard, and decided I would never like the taste enough to become a drunkard; then I examined the cosmetics which had been left in a jumble on the kitchen counter. I spread rouge on my cheeks and drew a blood-red cupid's bow.

Miranda came in with a pound of sausages and a can of peaches. "Oh, baby, you look like a china doll!" She cupped my chin in her hands and kissed me. "But you're too young. You'll spoil your complexion."

I rubbed the red imprint of her lips from my forehead. "I don't like it, anyway. You've got too much on."

"Have I, ducky?" She glanced from my face to the mirror and patted her spit curls. "Don't you want me to look pretty?" She sat down and kicked off her shoes, groaning and massaging her toes. "Oh, God, these things are killing me! Be a love and fetch my slippers."

When we were leaving for church the following Sunday morning, I took special notice of her appearance. If her make-up appeared more subdued than usual, I would know that despite her denunciation of Mr. Teperman she had been influenced by his rather broad hint. As usual, we were all dressed and ready before she was. Alfie had brought the car around, and we were all grouped on the front steps waiting when she appeared. Her complexion was more vivid than ever, with the added attraction of a small black beauty spot under one eye.

She stood in the doorway to be admired. "Do I look nice, Alfie?"

"You look grand." He put away his watch, not really seeing her.

"Well, then, don't be so po-faced." She took his arm and ran him down the steps. "We're not going to a funeral."

Chapter Three

In late June we received a letter from Mr. and Mrs. Saunders, saying they were driving to Southport on business over a certain week end, would be staying at the Victoria Hotel, and if we were to be at home on the Sunday afternoon, would come to see us then.

Alfie was delighted at the prospect of seeing his friends. "Why couldn't they stay with us?" he asked. "We've got plenty of room."

"Oh, they wouldn't think it grand enough," Miranda said.

But Alfie insisted, and Miranda finally gave in. She wrote to Mr. and Mrs. Saunders, inviting them to stay at our house instead of at the hotel. As she wrote the letter she raised her eyes now and then to look about her, as if she were trying to see how the house would appear to Mrs. Saunders. The living room, when it was tidied up and dusted, had a certain class, and looked out on a town view, not a rustic country landscape. Our street was at its best at that time of the year, too, with petunias in window-boxes, the tramped-down lawns showing green in spots, and vines screening the chipped foundations. The jail yard across the street looked like the real park Miranda pretended it was, with rambler roses covering the fence.

Mr. and Mrs. Saunders accepted the invitation, and we spent the week before they arrived cleaning and airing the whole house: polishing furniture, shaking dust from curtains, sweeping carpets, waxing floors. The place had not been really cleaned since we moved in, and probably not for some time before that. Miranda grumbled a good deal, complained that she was wearing herself out and ruining her hands, but she kept at it, and when Alfie came home —on Friday night instead of Saturday—he was pleased with the work we had done. The house smelled of wax and polish, and there was an air of orderliness about it he had not seen before. "It looks grand," he said.

Miranda rubbed lemon juice into her hands to erase the stains of toil. "I wish we had something to fill up those shelves," she said, glancing toward the small room at the end of the hall. It had obviously been used as a study by the previous tenants. Open bookshelves lined one wall. They were empty, as we had no books. The room, sparsely furnished, worried Miranda because she did not know what to call it.

"Why not call it my office?" Alfie suggested. "I could move my account books in there, make it look more filled up. And what about those old magazines in the box room? Spread those around on the shelves and you won't know the place." He carried the magazines down himself and stacked them on the empty shelves. He understood her need to make an impression, and tried to be helpful. "There now, it looks quite businesslike," he said. "You don't want an office to be all cluttered up."

Mr. and Mrs. Saunders arrived on Saturday afternoon. They had a new car, a pale blue Chevrolet that made people turn and look, for colored automobiles were not seen every day.

After dinner we took Mrs. Saunders on a tour of the house. "This is Alfie's office," Miranda said, allowing only a glimpse of the room at the end of the hall. "Where he does his accounts. . . . And there's another bathroom in the servants' quarters." She meant the attic. "You go up the back stairs." She led Mrs. Saunders puffing up the narrow stairway from the kitchen, for we had cleaned up the third floor, too, so that we could show it off and prove we had two bathrooms.

"You get a nice view from here," was all Mrs. Saunders could say of this part of the house. The view was lovely. You looked over the roofs of town to the harbor and the sea beyond, saw flying gulls and fishing boats, and clouds banked on the horizon like the mountains of some distant land. Mrs. Saunders leaned her plump elbows on the sill and looked at it for some minutes. She was not much older than Miranda, but had a neglected sort of face and figure. Her clothes were years behind the styles. "Are you happy here?" she asked, still looking at the sea. "Do you never get lonesome for the valley?"

"Lonesome? Oh, no!" Miranda added, "Alfie's doing so well here. You've no idea how he's got on."

Mrs. Saunders turned to look at her. "I'm sure he'd do well anywhere," she agreed. "We were very sorry to lose him, you know. My husband would give anything to have him back at the farm."

Miranda laughed at this impossible idea and said, "These rooms are empty at the moment, since we have no help."

Whatever business had brought Mr. and Mrs. Saunders to Southport must have been attended to before they arrived at our house. They spent the remainder of Saturday and all day Sunday until four o'clock with us. Mr. Saunders and Alfie went off by themselves to talk. They seemed to have a lot to say to one another. Miranda was left to entertain Mrs. Saunders, and after a time she found that she had used up all her conversation. She was not sorry when Mrs. Saunders finally said it was time to go.

We stood on the front steps to see them off. "You let me know what you decide, then, Alfie," Mr. Saunders said in a low voice. He shook Alfie's hand and clapped him affectionately on the shoulder. We watched the new car out of sight around the corner, and all the neighbors watched it, too. We went inside, and as people often do when visitors have left, stood around aimlessly, adjusting ourselves to being alone again.

"What did Mr. Saunders mean?" Miranda asked idly, as she plumped up a cushion that Mrs. Saunders's behind had pressed flat. "Decide about what?"

"Well. . . ." Alfie looked around in a hunted way, as he always did when he was not sure of the reaction he would get, and did not go on.

"I thought they'd never go," Miranda said, yawning. "I don't know why they came in the first place."

"They're nice people." Alfie spoke with more spirit than usual. "I like Mrs. Saunders. She's got a kind heart, whatever else you might say about her." He added, "They're short-handed at the farm."

Miranda did not answer, and after a silence he took a breath as if he were about to plunge into cold water and said, "Mr. Saunders wants me back."

Miranda was studying her reflection in the gilt-framed sunburst mirror over the mantelpiece. She licked her forefinger and drew it along one eyebrow. "Naturally he wants you back," she said. "He's not as stupid as he looks. Where else could he get someone with your capabilities to work for the miserable salary he pays?"

"He's offered me more money."

Miranda turned around. "I hope you told him what he could do with it."

"I told him I'd think about it."

"Think about it? Why waste time thinking about it?"

"Well, the fact is—" Alfie hitched uncomfortably in his chair. "I'd like to go back, Miranda."

"You'd like to go *back*?" She widened her eyes at him.

"Back to shoveling manure for Mr. Saunders and plowing his bloody orchards, cleaning up after his pigs? You'd like to go back to that after I worked and slaved all those years to get away from it? I think you must be insane, Alfie. I really think you must be completely and utterly insane."

Alfie was silent for a time. He had that summer developed a habit of staring into space in a wide-eyed way. It gave him a haunted look, as if he was aware of something we could not see.

"God knows this is bad enough, without going back to that," Miranda said.

He looked up. "I thought you liked it here."

"It's all right. It will do for the time being. But we don't want to stay here forever. We want to get *on* in the world, Alfie. We want to go forward, not backward."

He thought about this. "The only thing is," he said at last, "I'm not doing so well at this job, Miranda. I don't think it's going to pan out."

"Nonsense!"

"I'm not making as much as I used to make at the farm."

"You will, as soon as you adapt yourself."

"I'm not cut out to be a salesman. I never know what to say."

"You can learn," Miranda said.

Alfie was still staring desperately at nothing. It took him a long time to make up his mind to say, "But I don't like this job. I want to go back to the farm where I know what I'm doing."

"You're not serious? You wouldn't really go back there."

"I don't know what else to do. I can't stand it here."

Seeing that he *was* serious, Miranda sat on the couch and stared, wide-eyed, at him. After a minute tears brimmed over and slipped down her cheeks. "So that's why they came here! It was all a put-up job. Saying they were coming on business when all they wanted was to put ideas into your head."

"Don't cry, there's a good girl," he begged.

Her tears came faster. "I never thought you'd be so selfish, Alfie. I never thought you'd put your own whims before the happiness of your wife and children."

"It's not a whim. I lie awake nights—"

"I thought you cared about us, and now you want to go back to that place and be a common farm hand again. It's a pity you didn't marry a fat country woman like Mrs. Saunders. I don't know why you married me, when all you can think of is looking after pigs. . . . How you can sit there so calmly!" Her voice broke. "Oh, I never expected anything like this!" She sobbed aloud, with her knuckles pressed against her eyes.

"I only thought we'd be better off."

"Asking me to give up my home!"

"We were happy in the valley," Alfie persisted. "It was more like home than this."

"Go back to your fat Mrs. Saunders, then!" Miranda cried. "Desert your wife and children! If she means more to you than we do!"

"I'd never leave you and the girls, you know that."

"Oh, no, you'd never leave us. You'd only drag us back to that farm, wreck our lives so you can be near Mrs. Saunders."

Alfie was a little slow in grasping the form of Miranda's accusations. "Look here, I never said anything about *Mrs.* Saunders," he protested. "I never even thought of her."

Miranda threw herself full length on the couch. "I wish to God I had never asked that woman to come here. I wish I had never set eyes on her. Going behind my back, making you dissatisfied with your job. Oh, I never heard of anything so deceitful!"

"Well, I only mentioned it. I never thought you'd get so upset."

"Coming down here, putting on airs, showing off her new car!"

"Don't cry, Miranda. You'll give yourself a headache."

"Trying to take you away from your wife and children!"

"Look here, it wasn't anything like that. You know I'd never look twice at Mrs. Saunders." Alfie hovered anxiously over the couch. "Sit up, Miranda, do!" he pleaded. "If I'd known you were going to carry on like this, I'd never have mentioned the farm."

"Breaking up my home!"

"Look, I won't say anything more about the farm. I won't mention it again."

Miranda sobbed on and on as if her heart would break.

"I won't say another word. Shall I make you a nice cup of tea? Or what about a nice drink of Doc Billy's Cough Cure? Let's have a drink of cough cure and forget all about the farm." Glancing despairingly around the room, seeking a way to placate her, his eyes fell on a parcel Mrs. Saunders had left on the table. It was wrapped in tissue paper and tied with blue ribbon. "Look here, Mrs. Saunders has left you a present." He put one hand on Miranda's shoulder. "Don't you want to open it?"

She hunched away from him and went on crying.

"Here, Jess, you open it," he said. "Show your mother."

Jess untied the blue ribbon and folded back the tissue paper. Inside the box, in a nest of excelsior, was a cup and saucer of fine china.

"Look at the nice present from Mrs. Saunders," Alfie coaxed. "A nice cup and saucer."

Miranda raised herself on one elbow. Her face was streaked with mascara and her eyebrows had rubbed off. "I don't want her damned present," she said.

"It's real English china. Look." He tried to thrust the cup into her hand.

"I don't care if it's got diamonds in it." She flung his arm aside and the cup fell to the floor and broke.

"Oh, Alfie!" She raised her hands to shut out the sight and burst into fresh tears. "That was a good cup!"

"It cost three-fifty. Here's the price still on the box." He knelt on the floor to scoop up the pieces.

"I never had a cup that cost so much!" Miranda sobbed.

"Never mind. I'll glue it together and we'll put it on the sideboard for show."

During the remainder of the afternoon Miranda lay on the couch in a state of convalescence. Jess and I got the supper.

"You're so good to me, Alfie," she said, when he carried her meal in on a tray. She gave him the brave smile of an invalid who has just come safely through a bad time.

"I only want you to be happy."

"And you won't make us go back to that farm?"

"We're going to forget the whole thing. Forget I mentioned it, even. Are you out of cigarettes? Shall I get you some?"

"The girls can go." Miranda held his hand against her cheek.

Jess and I walked down to the little store on Main Street where cigarettes were sold. It was a warm scented summer evening. We loitered along without speaking, hearing the squeak of porch hammocks where couples sat hidden behind the vines, and someone practicing piano scales in a house on the next street. Nearer at hand a victrola was playing *There's a New Star in Heaven Tonight*. The air was blue and wispy as chiffon, and all the trees were still, waiting for rain. "I lie awake nights," Alfie had said, and I pictured him lying awake in the dark as I often did, longing for the trees and meadows and the summer skies of the valley.

Chapter Four

Miranda kept hoping that Alfie would get the hang of selling veterinary supplies. The knack would come, she encouraged him, if he really made an effort to adapt himself.
In the meantime, she could not ignore the fact that he was
not making enough to live on. If it had not been for Great-
aunt Eliza's two hundred pounds, we might have starved.

To help out, Miranda got a part-time job with Hattie's
sister, Mrs. Betty Fuller, who ran the beauty shop, the only
one in town. Betty's Beauty Parlor, it was called. There
was no lack of business *there*. And Miranda, after all her
practicing at home, certainly had a flair for that sort of
work.

Left to ourselves, Jess and I were often bored, unable to
decide how to pass the time. At the farm, those summer
months during the long vacation had been a time of idle-
ness, too, but we were never at a loss for something to do.
We could spend whole days paddling in the river shal-
lows or wandering through the woods searching for wild
berries, and straggle home in time for supper feeling well
satisfied with our day. In Southport there were no woods
or meadows within walking distance, only cinder sidewalks
and cluttered back yards. I have an idea, though, that we
would have been bored no matter where we were, that it
was really a matter of outgrowing childish pastimes.

Miranda grew impatient with us. "I wish you'd stop saying 'What shall we do?' like that," she complained. "Are
you trying to be difficult, or what? It isn't as if we were
still at the farm, where there was nowhere to go. You're

not such babies that you have to be told what to do every minute of the day. Why don't you visit your friends?"

All the girls we knew, including Clara, were at the Campfire Girls' camp about twenty miles up-country.

"Well, if all the girls go to camp, then you must go too, next year," Miranda said. "I can't have you hanging about like this. Why don't you go swimming in the park? Or you could walk down to the shop with me," she offered, "but you mustn't hang about making nuisances of yourselves." She worked certain afternoons, from one to six.

We would walk down to the shop with her, and Mrs. Fuller would allow us to do small jobs, such as washing out combs and sweeping up hair clippings. Mrs. Fuller was a bit more dignified than Hattie, and abundantly conscious of her position as a successful businesswoman. She was stout, with a round face arranged into an expression of such unchanging affability that you wondered if she held it that way with pins. Her hair, dyed or bleached to a gleaming copper tone, was marceled into careful scallops over her forehead and shingled closely behind.

As soon as Miranda had changed into her starched white beautician's uniform she became a different person. In the steamy warmth of the beauty parlor, heavy with the scent of cold cream and permanent-waving lotion, all three of Mrs. Fuller's girls—there were two besides Miranda: a dark-eyed French girl named Selena, and a bleached blonde named Gertie who wore so much mascara on her eyelashes that it seemed an effort for her to hold them up—looked like my conception of pagan priestesses; voluptuous, perfumed, with creamy pale-green eyelids and polished nails. I even got the feeling that they were about to perform some mystic rite. The first time I saw one of the town matrons strung up in the tortuous permanent-waving machine of the day, I thought for a minute that she was about to be sacrificed.

"Your mother's the best operator I ever had," Mrs. Fuller said. "I never saw anyone catch on so quick. She can marcel better than I can, and wind up a perm in half the time it takes the others."

Miranda never allowed us to hang about for more than ten minutes. "Off you go now, girls," she would say. "Run along and play." We would leave that exotic world reluctantly.

Sometimes we went swimming in the park, which was situated at the end of the single-track trolley line that ran the length of Main Street. The creaking red wooden trolleys have long since disappeared from Southport, but in those days they provided the only public transportation from one end of town to the other. At the park, there was a roller-skating rink, a rustic bandstand, a place to rent canoes, one or two refreshment stands, and a scattering of picnic tables.

Evenings and week ends, young men wearing bell-bottomed trousers and toting ukeleles took their girls canoeing on the lake. It was *the* thing to do. On Saturday nights in summer the roller-skating rink was turned into a dancehall. It cost ten cents to get into the park, and twenty-five cents for one of the damp and dirty little bathhouses that screened the cove where swimming was allowed. Jess and I soon learned that renting a bathhouse was a waste of money. We could undress in the woods, the same as everyone else.

We wore one-piece bathing suits of cotton jersey. These garments did nothing for us, only made us realize that we had not inherited Miranda's looks or figure. We were turning out more like Alfie: somber-faced, stolid, a bit on the heavy side. Jess was dark like Miranda, but without her flashing beauty. I was fair.

In a year or so both of us began to slim down and acquire curves, but that summer we were going through a stage of development that plagues most young girls. We were absolutely shapeless, bearing no resemblance whatsoever to the bathing beauties pictured in magazines. We lay awake at night wondering if we would ever acquire sex appeal. It was the fashion to be flat-chested, but not as flat as we were. Jess must have rubbed a gallon of Lubriform into her chest that summer. At the same time, she was taking reducing pills on the sly, trying to slim down the rest of her.

The lake waters were muddy and weedgrown, and only the convenience of getting there appealed to us. We would much rather swim in the clean salt water at Piper's Beach. This was two miles beyond the other end of the trolley line. We took lunches and made an all-day excursion of our trips there, since to reach it we had to walk the full two miles, along a sandy unshaded road. The beach swept away in a long curve between the sea and the dunes; miles of white sand and hardly a person to be seen. The ebbtide exposed great black rocks covered with seaweed, and pebbly pools filled with barnacles and blue snails.

We took Brownie with us, and had to carry him home, usually, because he got so hot and tired. He frolicked in the surf and raced along the tide-washed sand. We followed him barefoot over the dunes, among the scratchy sea grass, and returned to cool our feet in the pools, stirring the bladdery seaweed with our toes. Since there was no one to see us, we could forget that we were awkward and unlovely, all unmanageable arms and legs. Idle, preoccupied, we gazed at the lapping waves. This was the first summer we had spent near the sea and it was, besides, our

last summer of childhood. In a year's time we had lost the
knack of being carefree.

On Sundays, when we invited a few neighbors—Hattie
and her husband, James and his mother, or, after she returned from camp, Clara—to drive down with us and
spend the afternoon, the beach lost some of its weekday
enchantment. Everybody in town was there, undressing
under tented towels, shouting and splashing and broiling
under the summer sun. An ice-cream vendor would appear
and set up for business in the most crowded spot. The lost
enchantment was more than offset, for me, by the enjoyment of being there with people we knew. It was a new
and pleasant sensation for us not to be alone in a crowd.

Mrs. Scavcy, fully dressed, would sit on the sand with a
newspaper over her head against the sun, keeping an eye on
James. He wore a bathing suit that hung on his thin figure
like something in a cartoon. It must have been ten years
old, at least, handed down from some relative. "I'm
ashamed to be seen near him," Clara once confided to me.
"Wouldn't you think he'd have more pride than to wear a
thing like that?"

James appeared completely unself-conscious. "Now,
don't go past the rocks, James," his mother would warn.

"No, I won't, mother," he'd promise. "I'll be careful."

"Listen to him!" Clara once muttered. "It's a wonder
he doesn't call her Mumsie-wumsie."

Miranda would lounge against a pile of cushions leafing
through magazines, conscious of the picture she made.
Once or twice Jack Williams came sauntering by, wearing
a silk shirt and white flannels, and stopped to chat with
Alfie about business conditions and the weather.

"The way he stared at you in that bathing suit, I expected his eyes to pop out any minute," Hattie told
Miranda. "You ought to feel flattered, I suppose. He

doesn't usually condescend to associate with common people. He brings his ritzy friends over from New York. The house has been full of them all summer, so I've heard. Not that anyone's been given a chance to meet them; they're much too stuck-up to hobnob with the natives. . . . And when they're not visiting him, he's running off to New York to see them."

Miranda had smiled and looked at the sea.

One morning I overheard a conversation between Miranda and Mrs. Dove. Clara's mother had come over to report that a young woman who rented a flat on our street, a Miss Watson, was having an affair with a married man. He came to see her late at night, and had been observed slipping away at dawn.

Mrs. Dove went on to discuss the evils of our modern age, a subject which interested her. "In my opinion, it's all the picture shows the young people see nowadays that's ruining their morals. *Flaming Youth*, and pictures like that. I don't allow Clara to go to movies. I don't go myself, but I've heard about them. And when the young people aren't going to movies, they're out sitting in parked cars, or sitting up half the night listening to the radio. We were a lot better off before we got all these modern inventions. . . .

"Another thing I disapprove of is this modern idea of telling young girls the facts of life. I've never said anything to Clara, and I don't intend to. Such things should not be discussed with children. It puts ideas into their heads, is all it does. I'm an old-fashioned mother," she proclaimed in her righteous voice. "I'm going to bring my girl up properly. Then if she does get into trouble, at least I'll have done my duty."

"Won't she find out, anyway?" Miranda asked. "I thought all young girls discussed sex among themselves."

"Do *your* girls?" Mrs. Dove asked in a threatening voice.

There was a pause during which Miranda decided to laugh this off, not happily. "Perhaps they *are* too young," she conceded.

"I should hope so. It's no laughing matter, either. Isn't it our duty as parents to bring up our children in a decent Christian atmosphere?"

"Yes, of course."

"This is a respectable neighborhood. We don't tolerate people like that Miss Watson here."

"Oh, well, perhaps she'll leave," Miranda said idly.

"We intend to see that she does leave."

"How can you do that?"

"We intend to take the law into our own hands."

Miranda laughed. "But there's no *law* against two people sleeping together."

Mrs. Dove's voice sharpened. "It may be different where you come from, but we don't tolerate things like that in this town. I've written a letter to Miss Watson, and got everybody on the street to sign their names to it, asking her to leave town."

Miranda said, aghast, "Oh, the poor thing!"

"Poor thing? She's got nobody but herself to blame."

"But she may be in love with him."

"Love? What's that got to do with it? She's a wicked immoral woman, and it's time she was taught a lesson. Here's the letter. Your name will be the twenty-fifth signature."

"I've seen that poor woman going by the house on her way to work," Miranda said. "She seems such a sad little thing. And surely what she does in her own home is nobody else's business?"

"We have our children to think of," Mrs. Dove reminded sharply.

"Oh, poo! They'll run into that sort of thing sooner or later. Don't ask me to sign your nasty letter. I couldn't be so cruel to that poor woman."

After a long cold silence Mrs. Dove said, "Well, suit yourself. No doubt, being new to this country, you have your own ideas. Things are done differently where you come from, no doubt. Here we pride ourselves on knowing right from wrong."

After Mrs. Dove had gone Miranda discovered me in the next room. She did not scold me for listening, but said, "Did you hear what that awful woman is up to? As if it's any of her business! I don't know how people can be so mean."

A week later Mr. and Mrs. Dove went to Boston to visit relatives. Grampa Higgins was sent to his sister's place in the country, and Clara stayed with us. These arrangements had been made before the conversation I have recorded above took place, and no doubt Mrs. Dove experienced some qualms about leaving her daughter in the hands of a woman who condoned adultery. As if in defense of her own recklessness, she pointed out that they could not afford to take Clara with them; they really couldn't afford the trip themselves, they were only going as a duty, because Mr. Dove had not seen his only sister for eight years.

She could not, with a clear conscience, go off to Boston simply to have a good time, for the only pleasures she enjoyed were those she denied herself. By giving the trip the name of duty—and providing a little extra worry over Clara's welfare as an added damper—she made sure that her husband would not be tempted to enjoy his holiday, either.

Clara slept with Brownie and me. She tried to make him stay under the sheets with us, but he wriggled out and slept on the floor. "I wish I could have a dog," she said wistfully. "Beverley Bayne has three, did you know?" Beverley Bayne was a little-known motion picture actress whom Clara had once, while visiting her aunt in Boston, seen in person. Clara knew all the movie stars and, regardless of what her mother allowed, managed to see at least two picture shows a week. She kept a scrapbook collection of stars' pictures cut from magazines.

We sat up in bed until long after midnight, talking, eating, reading old copies of *College Humor* and various movie magazines. Jess stayed in her own room reading *The Private Life of Helen of Troy*, which she had got from the library. One night we walked in on her just as she was fishing her bottle of Marmola Reducing Tablets from its hiding place under the mattress. She lost her temper and ordered us out, but later relented and allowed us to sample the pills.

Dissatisfaction with her home life, and the restraints placed upon her there, made Clara want to attract attention when she was out. She *collected* attention, was always on the lookout for it, like a bargain-hunter; then, having captured someone's notice, she would say in a hissing whisper, "Don't look now, but that man is simply staring at us. I think it's really you he's looking at."

She still thought of us as newcomers, which made me suppose that everyone else did, too. I tried to guess how we looked to others, whether we were likely to pass whatever tests newcomers were supposed to pass before they were judged acceptable. When I walked downtown with Clara I felt the eyes of the whole town on me.

Clara also hoped someday to have a movie career, and was continually practicing how she would act then. Down town, as we loitered along the aisles of the five-and-ten, she talked in a carrying voice, waved her hands dramatically, and posed in graceful but unnatural attitudes. She swore a good deal, too, because she thought it sounded sophisticated. I found none of these traits objectionable. On the contrary, I admired everything she did. The mere fact that she liked me was enough to make me like her.

She admired Miranda. "My God, Rose," she said, "you don't know how lucky you are, having a mother like Miranda. She's more like one of you girls. And imagine you calling your parents by their first names. I do think that sounds sophisticated. My mother says it doesn't show proper respect, but I never listen to her. You and Jess aren't a bit like Miranda, are you? Who do you wish you were?"

I had dreamed of being Edna St. Vincent Millay, Bessie Love, a changeling daughter of royalty, and Gertrude Ederle.

"Jesus, I wouldn't mind being anybody but me," Clara said. "Do you want to know something? I've never told this to a living soul before, but they're not really my father and mother. They stole me from my real parents. Do you want to hear about it?"

I said I did.

"It was one time we were visiting Aunt Emma in Boston." Clara gazed at the ceiling and raised her hands tragically to her face, the tips of her fingers just touching her rounded cheeks. "I mean, *they* were visiting, the two of them and their revolting child. I already lived there. I was out in the park one day with my nursemaid, in a white carriage lined with satin, when they came along and dressed their own ugly brat in my clothes, and put her in my carriage, and made me wear their own baby's cheap clothes, and took me home with them."

"What about the nursemaid? She would have gone to the police."

"She was in on the plot, too," Clara said solemnly.

"Who told you? You couldn't remember that far back."

Clara scowled. "Can't you tell by *looking* at me that I'm not theirs?"

"Did you ever tell them that you know?"

Clara shook her head. "I'm not going to, either. I wouldn't give them the satisfaction. But as soon as I finish school I'm going away. I'll change my name and they'll never see me again."

"What will you call yourself?"

"You won't tell? I'm going to call myself Lucille Harrington." She closed her eyes and said in a dreamy voice, "Miss Lucille Harrington, Hollywood, California."

I felt sad. In my wildest imaginings I had never wanted different parents.

"Oh, Brownie, I love you!" Clara hugged him to her chest. When he jumped down she lay on the floor with her head on the rug beside him. "Look how he's kissing me! You love Lucille, don't you, precious?"

Clara stayed with us for two weeks. The first week end she was there Alfie arrived home on Saturday morning. He drove up the narrow alley that led to the garages, and came in through the back door. We were all in the kitchen helping Miranda with a dress she was making. We did not hear Alfie coming, and when he opened the back door Miranda was in her teddies, having just stepped out of the dress she was trying on.

"It's the Fuller Brush man!" she cried in mock panic. She grabbed the unfinished dress from the floor and held it over her bosom like the virtuous heroine in a play. "Sir, how dare you intrude! How dare you come spying on a lady in her underwear!"

Alfie gave his slow smile. He placed his sample case on the drainboard and waited to be kissed.

"Oh, Alfie, it's you!" Miranda tossed the dress aside and threw her arms around him. "You did give me a fright." She kissed him over and over, and when he sat down she perched on his knee, hugging him and rumpling his hair. She was showing off a little for Clara's benefit, being the passionate and playful young wife she had seen in some movie.

I glanced at Clara and was surprised to note that she had turned a dull red. She carefully did not look at my parents. I suppose she had never witnessed such extravagant love-making outside of movies before—certainly not in her own home.

"I'll get you a nice drink, Alfie," Miranda said. She sent Jess to the cellar to draw off a pint of home brew. She did not bother to put her dress back on, but fox-trotted around the kitchen singing *Valencia*. Her legs, tapering down to slim ankles, were tanned from our Sunday afternoons at the beach. She looked young and pretty and full of beans. When Jess came up with the beer she poured a drink for herself as well. "God, I'm thirsty!" she said, throwing a great draught down her throat.

"Put your dress on, there's a good girl," Alfie said.

She wriggled into her dress obediently. "Guess how much money I made this week, Alfie."

He thought for a minute. "Five dollars."

"*Ten* dollars!"

"Ten dollars?" His face fell. In all probability he had not earned that much himself. He brightened almost immediately and said, "That's grand!"

"It's nice to have a little extra," Miranda said.

The extra money bought new dresses of fine flannel for Jess and me when school reopened in September. These dresses were for best wear, not for school. I still wore my jumpers on weekdays, while Jess, as a concession to her entering the county academy, was allowed to wear middies and pleated skirts.

"I think I can say without fear of contradiction that I know a little more about what a girl should or should not wear to school than the mothers of your friends," Miranda said, when we complained that our clothes looked odd in comparison with those worn by other girls. "I might remind you that I have not always lived in a backward colonial town such as this. I have seen something of the world."

There was no reply to this sort of argument. We felt that she did know more of the world and what should be worn in it than any of the town ladies, but this was no comfort. We did not care whether we were correctly dressed or not, so long as we looked the same as everyone else.

"Why in God's name would you want to look like everyone else?" Miranda asked once. "Are you sheep, or what? Sometimes I wonder about you girls, I really do."

When she spoke like this, we blamed ourselves for not turning out as she had hoped we would. We were plain, straight-haired, serious-eyed, not cute and vivacious as she would have liked her daughters to be. We would have changed ourselves if we could. We did not expect her to understand our need to sit by ourselves sometimes and dream. "Always mooning about," she complained. "Sitting around like puddings."

I could not tell her about the stories I wrote. She was already alarmed because we read too much. Jess and I had discovered the public library, where, with what we considered wonderful generosity, books were stacked for the benefit of anyone who cared to borrow them. We spent hours going up and down the shelved partitions, selecting and rejecting, inhaling the inspiring pasteboard smell.

"Always sitting around with your noses in a book," Miranda said. "You'll ruin your eyes. You'll turn into old maids wearing horn-rimmed glasses." She had the lower-class mistrust of bookworms. "Where are all your friends?" she would ask. "You ought to be going to parties and enjoying yourselves instead of moping around indoors."

We knew any number of girls, but were not sure enough of ourselves to make friends easily, so they remained acquaintances only. The only real friend we had was Clara. We did, however, join the Campfire Girls troop at the Methodist church that autumn, and went to the meetings once a week. We spent a good part of these evenings doing rhythmic exercises with Indian clubs, to music played by Miss Harriet Anderson, the troop leader.

Miss Anderson was also good at arts and crafts. At the summer camp to which all the girls went in July—and Jess and I had only signed up for the winter meetings so we could get in on the camp deal—she taught the girls how to make pincushions filled with pine needles, birchbark frames for snapshots, picture arrangements of pressed wildflowers under glass, and many other useful items.

Miss Anderson was a gentle dovelike woman. The girls were slavish in their adoration of her. Jess and I did not allow ourselves to become too enthusiastic, for we could not regard as perfect anyone who was so unlike Miranda. We searched for faults and found a few. Miss Anderson was a spinster, she did not wear enough make-up, or have her hair shingled, and she wore lisle stockings. Though her clothes were moderately up-to-date, she managed to wear them with a sort of Edwardian grace—no mean feat, when you consider the styles of the day. She was high-breasted and slim-waisted (she wore corsets, a custom we considered not only antiquated but injurious to the health as well). Her long pale hair was drawn smoothly across her forehead and done in a sort of fan behind, high up, so that little ringlets escaped at the neckline. She moved unhurriedly, wearing an expression of impartial loving kindness. I never heard her laugh aloud, and of course she never lost her temper.

She was a good influence, most of the mothers agreed. The Campfire Girls would do well to follow her example in all things. Mrs. Dove's fondest wish, often spoken aloud, was for Clara to be like Miss Anderson when she grew up. This made Clara want to be the exact opposite. "I would rather die than be an old maid," she told me.

Jess, though she pretended to laugh at Miss Anderson, began to adopt some of her mannerisms—her way of clasping her hands together when she was pleased, for example —until I told her not to be a copy cat. Then she stated too emphatically that if she wanted to imitate anyone, it would not be a person as behind the times as Miss Anderson.

When he came home each week end Alfie put on a cheerful face, but it was obvious that he was not prospering. "Things are bound to be slow at this time of year," he excused himself. When no one was looking the haunted expression crept over his face again.

The autumn days were cool, with morning fog sometimes, and every afternoon someone along the street burned a pile of leaves. The smoke seemed to hang forever in the thinning trees. The shabbiness of Lupin Crescent showed most at that time of year, with the leaves being stripped away and the tired chrysanthemums around front doors getting some sun at last. Spiky husks of horse chestnuts littered the lawns and sidewalks. In mid-September

Miss Watson gave up her flat and moved away, nobody knew where.

October was damp, and the monotonous groan of the foghorn sounded for days on end. Then Indian summer, giving everyone a false lift, carried over into November. Afternoons were filled with the sort of clear translucent light that sifts through piled-up clouds. The air was warm, and winter seemed far away. It came soon enough, however. Overnight the temperature fell, and fine snow like sand drove down from the darkening sky and settled in the grass. The wind began a businesslike creeping into corners and under coat collars. There was nothing crisp or invigorating about the weather, so near the sea. The wind came straight off the water. Damp settled on everything.

In the dreariest part of the year, in mid-December, Alfie came home one night so cold and wet and tired that Miranda made him go to bed at once with a hot-water bottle. Something had gone wrong with the car, he said, and after trying for a long time to locate the trouble himself, he had been forced to walk miles to a farmhouse for help, then spend more hours in a chilly little crossroads garage waiting for the car to be repaired.

He lay in bed shivering. "Try this nice soup, Alfie," Miranda coaxed, but he could not stop shaking. She took off her clothes and got into bed with him, trying to warm him with her body. In the morning he was flushed and feverish, and the doctor was sent for. He was a long time coming. He would not neglect his regular patients for someone who had never been to him before.

"We must get your husband to a hospital," he said when the examination was over.

Miranda looked at him suspiciously. Some childhood association made her afraid of doctors and hospitals.

He added in a kind voice, "I wouldn't worry about the

expense. He needn't have a private room. He'll be well taken care of in the ward."

"What nonsense!" Miranda tossed her head. She would not allow Dr. Gilbert to see her fear, and to throw him off the scent took exception to his inference that a private room was beyond our means. "I know your hospitals," she said. "Those dreary rooms, and the nurses standing about gossiping, the food not fit to eat. I can give Alfie better care than that."

"I'm afraid he's got pneumonia, Mrs. Arnold."

"I will look after him," Miranda said.

"We don't want to take chances," Dr. Gilbert said. He waited for a moment, then gave in. "Perhaps it would be best not to move him, then."

"Furthermore, I'm not at all satisfied with your diagnosis. I intend to call a specialist."

"I'm afraid you won't find many specialists in Southport. However, if it will ease your mind, I can get Dr. Forbes to look at him."

"Please do, then."

"In the meantime, will you do exactly as I tell you?"

"I believe I'm capable of following simple instructions," Miranda said haughtily. She began to dislike Dr. Gilbert, and to wonder if he knew his business.

Dr. Forbes, delayed by a difficult maternity case, did not arrive until the following morning, and by that time Miranda had lost faith in him, too. "If they neglect their patients like this at home, what would they do to them in that hospital?" she said. Alfie was worse, and she began to be really frightened. She left his side only to prepare trays of food which he would not eat, and medicine which she could not always make him take.

"You must *try*, Alfie," she pleaded, as if he were a refractory child and could help himself if he would.

Jess and I stayed home from school all that week, feeling banished and useless in the downstairs rooms while Miranda kept watch upstairs. She would not lie down to rest even for an hour. "Alfie needs *me*," she said, when Hattie came and begged to be allowed to take over for a time. "I can do without sleep." At night she sat upright in a chair beside his bed, keeping herself awake with strong tea, watching him, ready to reassure him when he became restless or woke up in terror, not knowing where he was. "*I'm* here, Alfie," she would say, drawing him into her arms, rocking him back and forth as if he were an infant. "You mustn't be afraid."

None of us considered for one minute the possibility that he might die. We knew that he was very ill, and might have to spend a long time convalescing, but death was something that happened to old people, in other families. It could not happen to us, we thought. By the middle of the week Alfie seemed a little better, and we were concerned only with getting him well quickly, and with how we should manage until he was on his feet again.

Downstairs, Jess and I found something to do. We cleaned and polished all the rooms so that everything would look nice on his first day up. Miranda spoke about going back to the beauty parlor on the following Monday. Jess and I could take turns staying with Alfie, she said. It wouldn't hurt us to miss a few days from school while she earned enough to keep the household going.

By Friday night we had all reached a stage of convalescence from anxiety. Miranda moved a cot into Alfie's room and slept there, quite certain that he had passed the crisis and was on the road to recovery. She thought that if he did need attention during the night, she would hear him. When, toward morning, his tossings and mutterings finally wakened her, she was so dazed from exhaustion that she could not at first grasp what was happening.

"But he was *better!*" she cried piteously, as if she could not believe what she saw. Jess called the doctor.

Try as I will, I can evoke only a hazy recollection of the events of that night, though a number of little things—impressions, moods—come back quite clearly. After the doctor came Jess and I sat in my room with the lights out. A ray from the ceiling fixture in the hall threw a yellow triangle on the wallpaper near the door, and this was caught up by pale objects on the dark side of the room: the thrown-back bedclothes, our sprigged cotton nightgowns, and our faces. Jess looked as pale as a ghost, with great black shadows for eyes. Brownie crept close to me and looked up, asking me to explain what we were doing. "What's going on?" he seemed to be saying. "What are we waiting for?"

Outside, the night took on that strange quality that is evident when our senses are heightened or disturbed—after nightmares, for instance. A faint grayness crept down the alley and revealed the dark tossing trees; then snowflakes came like a horde of tiny meteors out of space and hit the window as if knocking to be let in.

I don't think Jess and I talked much, but when it was almost morning we went down to the kitchen and boiled a kettle of water for tea, thinking that both Miranda and the doctor would need a pick-up. Hattie, seeing our light from her window, came knocking on the front door. A rush of cold air came in with her, and her face without make-up looked pinched and naked. Just about the time she came, Alfie died.

Hattie took charge. I don't know what we would have done without her, for Miranda went to pieces completely.

She wept hysterically and had, finally, to be carried from the room so that the undertakers' men could get in. Hattie carried her, the tears streaming down her own face in a blinding flood. Miranda was put to bed in the spare room, where she stayed until the morning of the funeral.

The funeral service was held in the little chapel in the cemetery, with less than a dozen people attending: Hattie and Roy Hughes, Mrs. Fuller and the two girls from the beauty parlor, James's mother, and Mrs. Dove. Mr. and Mrs. Saunders did not come because nobody had remembered to tell them. Miss Anderson sent flowers.

Miranda wore a black veil that hung to her shoulders and partially concealed her dark-rimmed eyes and swollen cheeks. She was apathetic, worn out with weeping, and would have gone to the funeral with her hair tangled from two days of lying in bed if Jess had not brushed it for her. Mr. Teperman, disdaining so small an audience, read the briefest possible service, and refrained from eulogizing. He could not extol the virtues of someone he scarcely knew, his manner implied.

The coffin was lowered into a crypt for burial later on, when the ground was less flinty. Then Mr. Teperman shook hands with everyone and, perhaps wondering if he had offered enough in the way of comfort, said to Miranda, "He is not dead; he is sleeping." Then he hurried off to keep another appointment.

We drove through the wintry streets to our empty house.

Chapter Five

For more than a week after the funeral Miranda was pathetically listless and quiet, looking so woebegone that Jess and I grew anxious about her health. We began to worry lest we should have to give up school and go to work ourselves, for she seemed unable to rouse herself, and we had read enough stories about people going into a decline over some great grief to know what could happen.

At night we lay awake recalling such oppressed children of fiction as the poor little match girl and Oliver Twist. We pictured Jack Williams, like the villain of an old movie, turning us out of the house because we could not pay the rent. Mrs. Fuller had called the day after the funeral to offer Miranda a full-time job in the beauty parlor, but Miranda seemed incapable of deciding whether or not she would accept it.

Christmas was almost at hand and we had made no preparations for it. The bill from the funeral parlor was unpaid. There was very little money in the house and we did not know how much was in the bank, for all year we had been dipping into Great-aunt Eliza's two hundred pounds to help pay the household expenses, and we had no idea how much of it was left.

"Don't bother me now, please," Miranda said when we asked her about it. "I have a headache. I'll see about it tomorrow." But the next day her headache was no better. I think this was the only time in her life that she was not trying to be something or somebody else. She was lost because she did not know how to be herself.

Hattie came every day with food—a meat loaf or a pot

of stew; she was a very good cook—and tried her best to cheer us up, but the minute she left the house seemed bleak and empty again.

James's mother brought food, too. Her idea of giving comfort was to tell the story of her own bereavement. "When Arthur died. . . ." She repeated the long story of his last illness and death in her sad, sad voice. When Miranda cried, she nodded and said, "I know. I've been through it." Mrs. Dove came, and we could not help feeling, though she was so ready with sympathy, that she felt any misfortune we had suffered served us right.

On Friday, two days before Christmas, Mr. and Mrs. Saunders arrived. They had come by train. "The very second we heard," Mrs. Saunders told Jess, who answered the door. Miranda was upstairs. It was just past lunchtime, and she had been downstairs, dressed, minutes before, had in fact been attempting a little sewing, but when I went up to fetch her I found her undressed and in bed.

"Oh, ducky, I can't see anyone." She turned away from the light and drew the sheet up around her face. "Tell them I'm ill. Tell them I can't come down."

"But they've come all this way! And we didn't even let them know; they had to read it in the papers."

I could not understand why Miranda was reluctant to see Mr. and Mrs. Saunders. It seemed to me that the atmosphere of the house had changed, become less threatening, the minute they stepped inside. They were Alfie's best friends, really the only friends he had in this country. I could see that they were saddened by his death and greatly concerned for us. Here is someone who will know what to do, I thought. I was immensely comforted.

"Shall I send them up, then?" I asked.

"Oh, I suppose so. You'll have to tidy up a bit first. Can you find my wrap?"

I helped her into a Chinese kimono of flowered pongee. Her dress and teddies lay on the floor where she had dropped them. I hung them in the closet and straightened up the bureau. Miranda piled pillows against the headboard and sat up in bed with her arms thrust into the wide sleeves of the kimono, her eyes closed, looking helpless and appealing, with not a trace of make-up to hide the dark smudges under her eyes or brighten her pale mouth. Perhaps she thought Mr. and Mrs. Saunders would blame her for Alfie's death, for if she had allowed him to go back to the farm he might still be alive.

Mr. and Mrs. Saunders went upstairs by themselves, while Jess and I held a conference in the kitchen. "We must ask them to stay for dinner," Jess said. "We can't let them go hungry after coming all this way. And they'll have to stay the night, too. There's only one train a day to the valley."

"Then we'll need something for breakfast tomorrow as well as dinner tonight."

"Yes." Jess took stock of the food on hand. "We'll have to buy something." She fished in Miranda's handbag, which yielded less than a dollar. We found two dollars in the piggy bank, and some discolored nickels and dimes in a broken sugar bowl. Jess made out a list—a pound of minced beef, a loaf of bread, half a dozen eggs, a can of pears, a jar of jam—and sent me off to the grocery store to have it filled. When I returned she had a batch of biscuits in the oven and was making tea. "Oh, lord, are they burning?" she worried, peering into the oven every few minutes. She had made biscuits before, but not for company.

When Mr. and Mrs. Saunders came downstairs we had tea ready in the living room. "How lovely!" Mrs. Saunders exclaimed, as if she had never expected anything so delightful. Jess, sitting behind the tray, flushed with pleasure. The biscuits were not burned after all, and we had not forgotten spoons or napkins.

Jess lifted the teapot with both hands, her elbows stuck out like wings and her lower lip caught between her teeth as she watched the wobbly stream descend into the cups. Her relief was so great when she had passed the cups without slopping tea into the saucers that she lost her head and said, "This is the first time I've poured tea for anyone, because we've never had company before."

"You do it beautifully, dear," Mrs. Saunders said. "As if you'd been doing it for years. And don't tell me you made these biscuits, too! I've never tasted anything so good."

"Are they really all right?"

"Oh, delicious!" Mrs. Saunders took another bite and rolled her eyes.

"How old are you?" Mr. Saunders asked.

"Fourteen and a half."

"Could *you* make biscuits like this when you were fourteen and a half?" Mr. Saunders asked his wife.

"I can't *yet!*" She shook her head ruefully. "And the lovely way you've fixed the tray, too!"

"Rose fixed the tray," Jess said.

"Then you're both to be congratulated."

"Yes, indeed," Mr. Saunders agreed quickly.

We knew they were overdoing it, but Jess and I stole glances at one another. We were warmed by such flattery, and hoped to earn more of it before the day was done.

We did not forget that Miranda was upstairs shamming illness, but avoided mentioning her name, for we were afraid of letting slip the fact that she had been up and around less than five minutes before our visitors arrived. When we were clearing away the tea things, Mrs. Saunders said, "I wonder if your mother could manage one of these nice biscuits, dear, and a cup of tea?" If she suspected anything, she did not show it. We breathed a little easier and I took a tray up to Miranda.

Mr. and Mrs. Saunders had a talk with Jess while I was upstairs. They did not, as most people are tempted to do in times of bereavement, go on about being brave and not losing courage. Instead, so Jess told me later, they made her promise to let them know if we ever needed help.

"You must never be too proud to accept help from friends," Mrs. Saunders said. "It's what friends are for, you know; and one day we may need *your* help. There are ups and downs in every life." Mr. Saunders tucked an envelope into the pocket of Jess's middy. "A little Christmas present," he said. "Buy yourselves something pretty."

As I came downstairs, Mrs. Saunders began to pull on her galoshes.

"Are you leaving now?" Jess asked.

"Yes, dear. We've stayed too long as it is."

"But there's no train until tomorrow."

"We've left our bags at the hotel. We'll stay there tonight and be off first thing in the morning."

Jess could not control her disappointment. She turned away to hide the tears that sprang to her eyes, and said, "We thought you'd stay here, with us."

Mr. and Mrs. Saunders looked at one another. Mrs. Saunders took half a step forward, and for a minute I thought she was going to put her arms around Jess. I knew that if she did, Jess's carefully built-up adult pose would collapse, and she would burst into tears. And if she cried, I would, too.

But Mrs. Saunders checked herself and said, "Oh, *could* we tuck up in your spare room? We'd love that. As a matter of fact, we were hoping you'd ask us. I don't know what it is about hotel rooms—they're the dreariest places on earth. You're sure we won't be a bother?" Though not normally a talkative woman, she rattled on for several minutes about the inconvenience of staying in hotels, and how much nicer it was to stay with friends, giving Jess time to regain her composure.

"But I don't want to sit around feeling useless," she said. "You must let me help." She sent Mr. Saunders off to the hotel to get their bags, found an apron in the kitchen and sat down to peel vegetables for dinner. "Meat cakes—my favorite!" she said when she saw what we were going to have. "Do you make them with or without gravy?"

"I think we always have gravy," Jess said uncertainly.

"Yes, that's the way I like them, too." Mrs. Saunders nodded.

While we were working in the kitchen, and seeing to it that the spare-room bed had clean sheets, Mr. Saunders sat in the living room in his shirtsleeves, reading the paper. His presence there, the rustle of his newspaper as he turned the pages, the smell of his pipe, gave the whole house an atmosphere of warmth and stability. Brownie lay at his feet.

"See if Miranda is coming down," Jess whispered to me when the dinner was ready.

Miranda pretended to be asleep, but when I spoke to her she rolled over and opened her eyes, then sat up and whispered, "Have they gone?"

"No, they're staying the night. Dinner's ready. Are you coming down?"

She closed her eyes again and pushed the hair back from her forehead. "Just bring me up some little thing on a tray, will you, lovie? I don't care what."

The dinner was a success, in spite of the empty chair. "I had no idea you were such accomplished cooks," Mrs.

Saunders said. After dinner Hattie came over and gave us
a bad few minutes by demanding bluntly, "What the devil
is Miranda doing in bed?"

"She's got a headache, poor thing," Mrs. Saunders answered. "I'm sure she'll be all right tomorrow." She slid
the conversation smoothly along to something else.

Hattie stayed until after nine. I don't remember what
all we found to talk about, but I do know that there were
no silences that had to be filled up. We felt relaxed and,
if not exactly happy, at least we put worry behind us for
the time being.

We went to bed early because Mr. and Mrs. Saunders
had to catch the seven o'clock train to the valley the next
morning. Jess and I were downstairs before six, preparing
breakfast. Miranda's door was closed. Mr. and Mrs. Saunders left without seeing her. About an hour after they had
gone, Jess suddenly remembered the envelope in the pocket
of her middy. When we opened it, we found that it contained one hundred dollars.

To Jess and me, a hundred dollars seemed like a fortune. Although it was Christmas Eve, it did not enter our
heads to spend any of the money on gifts or holiday food
—we had been invited to Hattie's house for Christmas
dinner, anyway—but sat down and tried to figure out how
far it would go if we were careful. We knew so little about
financial matters that we thought it might do us for years.
It might have to, for Miranda was still in bed, and we did
not know when she intended to get up, if ever.

Then, perhaps because the Saunders's visit had cheered
us up—people in despair are apt to overlook opportunities, I have found—we hit upon a way to *make* money. We
could sell the car. It was sitting out in the garage, abso-

lutely useless, since Miranda did not drive. When Hattie came over later that morning with a pot of beans for our lunch, we asked her advice about this.

"Oh, you poor babies!" she cried, bursting into tears. "To have all this worry at your age!" When she had calmed down she promised that Roy would send a man up from the garage to look at the car and give us an estimate of its worth. Then she went upstairs and gave Miranda a piece of her mind. Miranda had been shamming illness for almost twenty-four hours by this time, and must have been getting tired of it. She probably welcomed Hattie's lecture, which went something like this:

"Crying won't bring Alfie back. All the tears in the world won't alter what's happened. In the meantime, what about the girls? You've a duty to them, too."

"You think I'm selfish," Miranda said listlessly.

"Yes, I do. I call it a bloody crime, the way you're carrying on, as if there was no one else in the world. Damned selfishness, that's what it is. What would Alfie say if he could see you now? He'd be ashamed, that's what. Now, I've had my say—" Hattie was crying so hard she had difficulty speaking—"and you're free to take offense, but I won't stand by and see innocent children suffer. Standing around down there looking like homeless waifs, wondering where their next meal is coming from. Asking about selling the car to buy a crust of bread for themselves. It's enough to break a person's heart."

"I *am* trying, Hattie," Miranda said.

"Then try harder."

"I don't know where to begin," Miranda said pathetically.

"You might try getting your backside up off that bed for a start. And comb your hair, for God's sake! If anyone should come and see you looking like that!"

They did not know it, but somebody *was* coming, and it was this visitor who succeeded in snapping Miranda out of her depression. Hattie, feeling relieved at having spoken her mind at last, and encouraged by the way Miranda had taken her scolding, bullied her into coming downstairs for lunch, with her hair combed and even a little lipstick on. Hattie stayed for the meal, eating her own beans and keeping up a relentless flow of cheerful conversation.

Half an hour later a knock came on the front door. When I opened it, old Mrs. Williams entered, followed by her chauffeur carrying a large wicker clothes hamper. "Put it here, George," she said, tapping a spot on the hall rug with her cane. George placed the hamper where she had indicated. "Wait outside," she told him. "I won't be long." He went out and sat in the car, which was a very old-fashioned model of a kind that is seen nowadays only in museums, with a glass shield between the front and back seats.

Mrs. Williams said, "There, I've brought you a lovely hamper, Mrs. Arnold!"

Miranda did not know what she was talking about, but she said, "Won't you come in?"

"I might sit down for a minute," Mrs. Williams conceded, throwing back her furs—she wore a great shawl of black fox—and creaking into a chair. "Such a cozy room," she said, looking around with a benign smile.

"A nice cup of tea, Mrs. Williams?" Hattie asked. I suppose she thought Miranda was incapable of showing proper hospitality. "There's some still in the pot."

"Oh, dear, no. You mustn't put yourself out. Besides, I can't stop. I've got eight more hampers in the car."

Miranda looked at her in a dazed way. "I don't understand," she said.

"There, I know how you feel. I'm sure it was a great shock, losing your husband. I always feel it's such a tragedy, when it's the breadwinner, and growing children to feed. You have the sympathy of all the ladies, Mrs. Arnold. When we were making up the baskets, I don't know how many of them said, "Whatever we do, we mustn't forget poor Mrs. Arnold."

"What ladies?"

"Why, the ladies from the church, dear. Didn't I mention it was from the church? I *am* getting absent-minded."

All of us suddenly realized what she had brought with her. It was one of the Christmas hampers for the poor, or, as Mr. Teperman put it when he was asking for contributions, the indigent of the parish; those who, but for the generosity of the church ladies, might go hungry on Christmas day. We knew that each poor-basket, as it was called, contained a ten-pound goose, a jar of homemade relish, a plum pudding, a wedge of fruit cake, two dozen cookies, nuts, oranges, apples, and, as a crowning touch, some little gift such as a potholder or a pincushion. We knew this because Miranda had been given a list earlier in the year and had promised to contribute six dozen sugar cookies and two potholders, but had forgotten.

Miranda stood up and her eyes began to flash. "Am I to understand, Mrs. Williams, that you have brought me one of your poor-baskets?"

"Such lovely fat geese we got this year!" Mrs. Williams was so filled with beneficence that she did not notice Miranda's tone. Perhaps she did not hear what was said. She gave us all a warm smile and adjusted her furs, preparing to leave. "I mustn't linger," she said.

Miranda followed her into the hall. She said in a dangerously polite voice, "I think you had better take your hamper, too, Mrs. Williams."

"Oh, the hamper's part of our little gift, dear." Mrs. Williams laughed. "We don't want it back. It'll make a lovely clothes basket."

"Are you suggesting that I am incapable of providing food for my family?" Miranda asked.

"Oh, dear!" Mrs. Williams began to suspect that something was wrong.

"Take your damned poor-basket and give it to someone who needs it," Miranda said. "And tell your friends what I think of their insolence. Offering charity to me! To *me!*" she repeated, her voice rising as if she could scarcely believe her own words.

"I never dreamed. . . ." Mrs. Williams had turned a deep red. She was an old woman, greatly overweight, with wattled cheeks and bulging ankles.

"Sitting around on your fat bottoms gossiping about 'poor Mrs. Arnold!'" Miranda went on. "You may tell them—and that vulgar little preacher, too—that Mrs. Arnold is quite capable of buying her own food."

"Oh, dear!" Mrs. Williams said again. She fumbled with the doorknob as if she feared Miranda might attack her bodily, and finally succeeded in getting the door open.

"Get this damned thing out of my house!" Miranda pointed threateningly at the hamper.

"I can't lift . . . I'll have to get George. . . ." Mrs. Williams was dropping her cane and handbag in her agitation. As she stooped to lift the basket, one end of her fur shawl touched the floor and she trod on a foxtail, which ripped away with a vicious little snarl; then, hanging by a thread, trailed after her like a live animal. She managed finally to retrieve everything, and hoisted herself and the hamper through the front door. George saw her coming and ran up the walk to meet her. When he had deposited the hamper in the car, and settled her in the back seat, he had to come back as far as the steps to gather up the handbag and cane she had dropped.

Hattie stood at the window with her hands pressed to her face, afraid to laugh until she saw how Miranda was going to react.

"Don't stand there like an idiot gaping at the passersby!" Miranda snapped at her.

Hattie let herself go. She plumped onto the sofa, wheezing and huffing like an engine getting up steam, then began to shriek with laughter. "Oh, I never heard anything so funny in my life!" she gasped. "Oh, the look of her! 'I've brought you a lovely hamper, Mrs. Arnold,' all smiles and loving kindness. . . . 'Take your damned charity and give it to someone who needs it. . . .' Oh, the look on her face! 'Why, Mrs. Arnold, I never *dreamed*. . . .'" She tried to give a mincing imitation of Mrs. Williams's bewilderment, but failed.

"The look on her *face!*" she screamed, collapsing over the end of the sofa and beating the cushions with her fist. "'It'll make a lovely clothes basket, Mrs. Arnold. So handy if you want to take in washing.'" Hattie gasped and sputtered and wiped her streaming eyes, enjoying the first good laugh she had had in weeks.

Miranda ignored her. She stood thinking for a minute, then went into the kitchen.

Having lost part of her audience, Hattie gained some control of herself. She followed Miranda into the kitchen and leaned against the drainboard, moaning and patting her face with a sodden handkerchief, ready, with a little encouragement, to begin laughing all over again. When no encouragement was offered, she said, "*Now* what?" in a complaining voice.

Miranda was searching in the cupboard, opening and closing drawers. "I'm looking for the key to the car," she said. "I don't know where Alfie kept it. Would this be it, do you think?"

"Yes, that's it. But you can't drive."

"I know *how* to drive. All I need is practice." Miranda sent me to get her coat and galoshes, glanced at herself in the mirror beside the window, and picked up the lipstick she always kept on the sill. "Bring my hat and gloves, too, ducky," she called after me, and bent forward to make up her mouth.

"Now, look, don't tell me you're thinking of taking that car out and *driving* it!" Hattie's blotched face registered alarm. "You'll kill yourself."

"Do you want to come with me?"

"I'm not a complete idiot! All right then, I'll come, if only to protect you from your own foolishness. . . . One minute lying around in bed looking like God knows what, the next out driving a car when you don't even know how! Why *now?*" Hattie grumbled. "You know how crowded the streets are on Saturdays. Christmas Eve, too."

Miranda looked up, frowning. "Is the bank closed?"

"Of course it's closed. What did you think?"

"Oh, damn! I need money for shopping."

"It's a pity you didn't think of that earlier. Lying around in bed like the last rose of summer! A person never knows what you'll do next. Honestly, Miranda, I just don't know what to make of you."

"Are you coming?" Miranda asked.

They got the car backed out of the garage without mishap and went jerking off down the alley. They turned into the street and that was the last we saw of them for an hour. Perhaps it was ignorance that prevented Jess and me from worrying about them. We had perfect faith in Miranda's ability to drive a car if she put her mind to it. After all, it was only a simple matter of being able to start and stop and steer around corners, and despite Hattie's warning about crowds, Southport had no real traffic problem even on the busiest days. What we did worry about was whether or not to tell Miranda, when she returned, about the hundred dollars Mr. Saunders had given us.

We suspected—a suspicion strengthened by the little talk Mrs. Saunders had had with Jess about the folly of being too proud to accept help from friends—that when Mr. and Mrs. Saunders had been upstairs with Miranda the day before they had offered assistance and she had turned them down in much the same way as she had turned down Mrs. Williams's hamper. She might even have used words like "insolence"—one of her favorites—and accused them of insulting her.

"Perhaps she wouldn't mind if it was only fifty dollars," Jess worried.

"Could we say he gave us each twenty-five?" I suggested. "That doesn't sound quite as bad as fifty. Do people ever give one another fifty-dollar Christmas presents?"

Jess could not imagine such a thing, and neither could I. "Millionaires, maybe," she conceded.

"Mr. Saunders might be a millionaire."

"I think he must be."

We decided, finally, to tell Miranda that Mr. Saunders had given us each twenty-five dollars. "We can put the other fifty away somewhere until we get hard up," Jess said. She wrapped the extra money—five tens—in brown paper and hid the package behind her favorite picture, "Madame LeBrun and Daughter," which hung in her room.

"Back in one piece," Hattie announced, "though God knows how we managed it. We went clear up to the end of the car line and back again, and along every side street in town. Your mother is a perfect wonder, girls. She drove that damned car, though it fought her all the way—bucking and trying to climb up onto the sidewalk—a total distance of fifteen miles. And then, would you believe it, she drove right through town, along Main Street, with everybody in the county milling around there like sheep, out doing their Christmas shopping. We almost ran over old Mr. Gilroy, hobbling across to the post office on his cane, but he got out of the way in time. Your mother blew the horn at him. You've got to admire her nerve, if nothing else. I feel weak!" Hattie sagged into a chair.

Miranda rummaged in her handbag. "Is this all the money in the house, girls?"

We thought that might be a good time, with Hattie there, to tell her about Mr. Saunders's gift. We had placed the money in two envelopes, which Jess now brought forth. "Mr. Saunders left these," she said, trying to speak casually. Then, with what I thought was a really wonderful burst of inspiration, she added, "He said it was money he owed us, for back wages or something."

Miranda's face underwent a swift change as she adjusted to this. Then she said, "So he's finally decided to pay back the money he borrowed from poor Alfie. Now, when it's too late for him to enjoy it."

She threw a side glance at Hattie to see if she was accepting this story. Hattie, of course, looked back at her with bland innocence. Miranda was wise enough to say no more, and by suppertime even Jess and I were beginning to believe that Mr. Saunders's gift was not really a gift at all, but something that had been owing to us for a long time. We never did tell Miranda about the other fifty dollars hidden behind "Madame LeBrun and Daughter" in Jess's room.

At intervals during the following winter we removed one

of the ten-dollar bills from its hiding place, had it changed
at the bank into bills of smaller denomination, and whenever we got a chance, slipped one or two of these into the
household money. I cannot remember that we ever wrote
Mr. and Mrs. Saunders to thank them. I know we talked
about it—Jess and I, that is; we could not very well con-
sult Miranda after the lie we had told—and decided that
we should write.

We *intended* to write, but time went by and soon it was
weeks, months. We would have to apologize for the delay
in writing, as well as thank them. It weighed on our con-
sciences for a long time, but the longer we put off writing
the less it worried us, and by spring we had decided that it
was too late. We never saw Mr. and Mrs. Saunders again.

"Come, girls," Miranda said that evening. "Get your
things on. We're going shopping."

We could have walked the few blocks to the business district—we had always done so before—but that night Miranda insisted upon driving. She managed very well, too.
You would never have guessed that she had driven a car
for the first time only a few hours earlier. On the way down
we stopped at the garage and bought two gallons of gas.

In those days, all the shops stayed open until ten o'clock
on Saturday nights. This was Christmas Eve as well. Every
window was hung with wreaths and bells and festoons of
crepe paper, and a tree with colored lights stood beside the
post-office steps. The Salvation Army was singing carols.
Everybody in town was out, tramping up and down in the
slush—for the weather had turned mild again—calling out
greetings, not really going anywhere or doing anything, but
simply herding together as at a carnival, enjoying the feeling of being part of a crowd. Very few were actually shopping.

At the Chez Marie Hat Shop Mrs. LeBlanc, the stout French-Canadian proprietor, was entertaining some friends. She continued to converse with them in French while she reluctantly selected a few of the cheaper hats to show us. Miranda had been in her shop before, to check on the latest styles and try on everything in sight before going around to the Bon Ton, where it was cheaper. It was quite natural for Mrs. LeBlanc to suppose we were simply killing time.

"Six ninety-eight," she said, when Miranda sat down before a mirror and tried on a black felt trimmed with satin bows. "Very good on you," she added carelessly.

Miranda pulled off the hat and threw it aside. "I'd like to see something better, please."

Mrs. LeBlanc shrugged and reached for a green turban. The conversation of her friends lulled a bit, and they too shrugged and glanced at one another.

"Ten ninety-eight," Mrs. LeBlanc said patiently.

Miranda tossed the turban aside, too. "I can't wear green. I am in mourning. Let me see that one." She indicated a bell-shaped helmet of black velvet, beautifully draped and tucked, with a single pink velvet rose in full bloom atop the crown, which was displayed in a glass case in the window, on a plaster head with round painted eyes.

"That one is twenty dollars." Mrs. LeBlanc did not move.

We knew it was. The price was printed on a card for all the passersby to see.

"I'd like to try it on, please," Miranda said.

Grudgingly, fastidiously, as if to impress upon us that such a hat was not to be handled carelessly, Mrs. LeBlanc opened the glass door and lifted out the black velvet. She placed it on Miranda's head, then stood with her hands half raised, ready to snatch it off again.

Miranda picked up a hand mirror and viewed herself from all sides. Ignoring Mrs. LeBlanc's protective flutterings, she removed the hat from her head and examined the lining, stretched back a draped fold to check the stitching, held it out at arm's length in a considering way, then tried it on again, pulling it down well over her ears, pushing it this way and that to get the best effect.

"Twenty dollars," Mrs. LeBlanc reminded sharply.

Miranda raised the mirror again and tilted her head from side to side, taking her time. Finally she gave a condescending nod. "Yes, I'll take it. I'd like it boxed, please."

"You want to buy *this* hat?"

"Yes, I think it will do."

Mrs. LeBlanc did not begin to thaw out until Miranda had paid her, and then she did not make the transition to affability gracefully, being angry with herself for misjudging our intentions, and angry with us, too, holding us responsible for her mistake. "This style suits you," she said, trying to smile as she wrapped the hat in tissue paper and placed it in a box. "Very becoming, with your eyes."

"Now I'd like to see something for the girls," Miranda said.

"Ah, yes, I have just the thing!" Mrs. LeBlanc was warming up. From a drawer at the back of the shop she selected a tissue-swathed bundle, folded back the wrappings with an air of mystery, and held up two identical hat-and-muff sets of white fur. "Ermine!" she pronounced. "Only ten dollars a set. The very latest fashion. I have only two in the shop. You will be exclusive."

The fur was really rabbit. Never having seen ermine, we did not know the difference. I felt that I would undergo any privation to possess such luxury, and by the look on Jess's face, I could tell she felt the same way. Mrs. LeBlanc placed the hats on our heads and made us walk up and down the shop while her friends admired us. "Hold the muffs up—so," she admonished, lacing her fingers under her chin and rolling her eyes flirtatiously. "So much nicer than black," she told Miranda, "and quite the thing for young girls in mourning. All the magazines say so." We held the muffs up to our chins and stole glances at ourselves in the mirror, then looked anxiously at Miranda.

"Well, girls?" Miranda sat back and waited for us to decide.

"Perhaps they're too expensive," Jess said finally.

"Nonsense!" Miranda spoke as if spending forty dollars for hats was an everyday thing with her. "Do you like them? Very well." She motioned to Mrs. LeBlanc, indicating that the sale had been completed.

Clutching our boxes, we went out into the chilly dampness of the street. We were halfway home before Jess came down to earth and reminded Miranda that there was no food in the house. We stopped at the corner store and bought four dollars' worth of groceries. We had five dollars left.

We wore our new hats to church the next morning. Since it was Christmas Day as well as Sunday, the church was packed. Jack Williams and his grandmother were in their usual seats, the old lady wearing a fusty Queen Mary turban trimmed with violets. We sat well up front, and put four dollars in the collection plate.

While Jack Williams stood at the end of the pew waiting for the plate to be passed along, Miranda, with a great air of indifference, extracted three one-dollar bills from her handbag, spread them fanwise and dropped them on top of the assorted silver pieces other people had contributed. Jess and I each dropped in fifty cents.

I glanced at Jack Williams. He was looking at Miranda's profile, and though his face was set in the sanctimonious expression he always wore in church, his eyes sparkled with admiration. I didn't blame him. Her black velvet was far and away the most stylish hat there, and we felt quite sure that everybody knew how much she had paid for it.

After the service Mr. Teperman stood in the vestry to shake hands with each member of his congregation. Miranda avoided his outstretched hand by pretending not to see it. She could not so easily avoid Jack Williams, who stationed himself at the foot of the steps and blocked our path. He took off his hat and said, "May I offer you a lift home, Mrs. Arnold?"

"Thank you, I have my own car." Miranda gave a cool nod and swept past him.

Chapter Six

Trying to recall the past is like looking into one of those glass paperweights inside which memories instead of artificial snowflakes lie imprisoned and asleep. Tip the globe upside down and people, events, places, come to life, begin to drift and circle, magnified behind the curving glass surface, demanding recognition. One memory leads to another, too. Recall one long-forgotten incident and half a dozen others spring up behind, presenting themselves as clearly as if they had happened yesterday.

"Don't sit around mooning, girls; we can't afford the time," Miranda said to us many times that winter. I must say that she followed her own advice. After that one week of utter despair she never allowed herself to sink back into despondency again, though at the least reminder of her loss she would have a good cry. She did not mourn in private, however, and her tears did us all good. She might find some little keepsake in the button box—a rosette of tarnished gold set with imitation pearls, for example—and she would hold it up to the light and look at it with swimming eyes.

"There's the little brooch Alfie gave me on our first anniversary. I thought it was lost. We went up to London to spend the day and I saw it in a shop window. . . ." Tears would run down her cheeks as she recounted the story of that holiday in London. Jess and I would listen, crying even harder than she did, and after a time Miranda would wipe her eyes and say, "Now let's have a cup of tea." Refreshed and comforted, we would mop up the last of our tears and put the kettle on to boil.

The day after Christmas was a holiday. When Jess and I

went downstairs at eight-thirty Miranda had already eaten breakfast, and was sitting at the kitchen table composing an advertisement for the *Gazette*. She said, "Tell me how this sounds, girls. 'To let: furnished lodgings in refined English home.'"

"Are we going to take in boarders?" Jess asked.

"Not boarders, lodgers. I won't have time to feed people. I'll be working at the beauty shop all day. They can arrange with Mrs. Seavey to take their meals at her house, if they like. I've already spoken to her about it. We'll move our things up to the third floor—you girls won't mind sharing a room—and we'll rent the bedrooms on the second floor. How much do people pay for rooms in a town like this, I wonder? I'll telephone the *Gazette* office and find out."

We spent the morning moving our personal belongings to the bare little rooms on the third floor. Jess and I had the larger of the two rooms, the front one that overlooked the town and the sea. The chipped iron bed had wooden slats instead of springs, and the painted floor creaked at every step, but I grew to like that room. I liked being tucked up under the eaves, so high up that in bed at night we could put out a hand and touch the sloping ceiling. From the jutting window that opened onto a steep roof with chimneys—like a casement in a fairy tale—we could watch the sea.

Though I was still at times homesick for the valley, I was developing a grudging fondness for the harsher climate of the coast. Already the valley was taking on the remoteness of a dream world. In dreams I longed to go back to that enchanted place behind the mountains where we had been happy, where childhood belonged; awake, I wanted a wider world than that. So when the wind blew from the sea and the storm warnings were up and the gulls were driven inland, I dreamed of wild distant places, for the wind came from a long way off, and the waves that crashed against our shores had touched the coast of Spain, the Cape Verde Islands, even some African beach. Anyone who has lived near the sea has experienced this awareness of other lands, of strange worlds beyond the horizon.

Around three o'clock in the afternoon Miranda rang up the *Gazette* office. In those days, when you wanted to telephone anyone, you took the receiver off the hook and waited for the operator's voice, then gave her the number. Nine times out of ten she listened in on your conversation. "The *Gazette* office is closed today," she informed Miranda, "but I saw Mr. Williams going in half an hour ago." She rang the number and after a minute Jack Williams answered. When Miranda told him what she wanted he said he would drop around to see her, then rang off before she could protest that she didn't expect him to go to all that trouble.

She replaced the receiver and glanced down at the dress she was wearing, then ran upstairs and changed into a better one. She touched up her face and fixed her hair.

Jack Williams arrived within ten minutes. He must have come straight up from the *Gazette* office. He shook hands with Miranda and murmured some words of condolence. His manner was formal and exceedingly respectful. He might have been a visiting clergyman or an elderly uncle, the way he sat on the couch and smiled benignly, rather sadly, at us all. It impressed Miranda—I could see her being impressed, could see that she was marshaling up some gentility of her own to match his—but I wondered if he was overdoing it.

The expression on his face was a bit too pious, I thought, and for a minute I wondered if he might be trying in some subtle way to make fun of us. Then I decided he was only trying to be helpful, for he listened with grave attention while Miranda outlined her plans for supporting her family. He assured her that she was not to worry for one minute if she could not pay the rent that month. In fact, rather than cause her embarrassment, he had already marked the account "paid" in his books.

She stiffened. "That's very kind of you, Mr. Williams, but I think we can manage."

He saw his mistake and tried to rectify it. "Yes, I'm sure you will. I do admire your courage, Mrs. Arnold. Not many women would be so plucky about a thing like this. You're going to manage very well, I can see that."

"Your grandmother apparently thinks I am incapable of fending for myself."

He laughed apologetically. "Poor old Gran. You mustn't mind her. She gets carried away. Every Christmas she fancies herself a Lady Bountiful. She means well, but I'm afraid she may have offended you with that hamper. . . ."

"I told her what she could do with it, too," Miranda said hotly, forgetting herself.

"Good for you!"

"The insolence of these women!" She regained her composure and arranged her features. "Your grandmother reminds me of a woman I knew once in London. Lady Barton. She used to visit my aunt at our house in Park Lane. Do you know London at all?" Her eyes took on a faraway expression. "I lived with my aunt, Mrs. Fitzhugh—oh, an enormous great house in Park Lane. . . . Then there was our country place in Sussex; Alfie's old home."

"You still own property in England?"

She shook her head sadly. "My aunt's house went to someone else, and the estate in Sussex was sold." She looked around the room as if she had suddenly found herself in a strange place. "I never dreamed, in those days, that I'd be reduced to this—working for a living, taking in lodgers." She made an effort to smile. "But I mustn't go on about the past. It's the future I must think about. You do agree, then, Mr. Williams, that if I advertise I might get some nice refined people for my rooms?"

"No doubt about it. In fact, I can put you in touch with a couple of very nice women right away—schoolteachers."

There was a quick knock at the front door and Hattie let herself in. She was in her best dress, with her old seal-skin coat thrown around her shoulders. She paused in the hallway long enough to catch her breath and throw her coat on the settee. "Why, Mr. Williams!" She stood transfixed in the doorway. "Imagine seeing you here!"

I wondered why she was pretending she had not seen his car out front.

"I had no idea you were entertaining company," she told Miranda.

When Jess and I went out to the kitchen to make tea, she followed us. "What is *he* doing here?" she whispered.

We told her that he had come to see Miranda about placing an advertisement in the *Gazette*.

"I suppose she couldn't have telephoned."

"She did telephone, but he said he wanted to come up. We're going to rent the rooms on the second floor. Miranda wanted to ask him how much to charge."

"So he said, 'Oh, Mrs. Arnold, you poor thing, *do* let me help you. Let me offer my manly shoulder for you to cry on.' I know his ways."

"He's been very nice," Jess said.

"Oh, no doubt! Butter wouldn't melt in his mouth. I was doing a bit of washing when I looked out and saw him prancing up your front walk. Believe me, I hustled into my good clothes and came on the double. Look, I didn't even change my stockings." She thrust out one sturdy leg to show a run.

"He's got more than renting rooms on his mind," she warned darkly, and went back into the living room, where she monopolized the conversation until Jack Williams took his leave. She even saw him out, as if it were her house and not ours, and walked a little way along the path with him.

She left the door open to the frosty air for so long that Miranda called impatiently, "What are you *doing* out there?"

"I'm showing myself to the neighbors, that's what." Hattie came in and banged the door behind her, rubbing her chilled hands up and down her arms to warm herself. "I don't want them getting ideas."

"I'm sure I don't know what you mean," Miranda said.

"If you don't, you ought to."

Miranda gave her a hostile stare. "This is my house, if I may say so. I'm well aware that you dislike Mr. Williams for some unknown reason, though he's always been a perfect gentleman in my presence. I must say I consider it nothing less than damned impertinence on your part, barging in here when I'm entertaining callers, making vulgar insinuations."

"I'm not insinuating anything. I'm saying right out. He had no business coming here."

"And why not, might I inquire?"

"Because people will talk, that's why."

Miranda raised her eyebrows. "And what do you mean by that remark, pray?"

"Oh, you know damned well what I mean."

"I must confess that I do not."

"Hell, I was only trying to warn you. People are going to think it's pretty funny, you getting chummy with Jack Williams before Alfie's hardly cold in his grave, when everyone knows he's been eying you like an old roué since the first day he saw you. This isn't London."

Miranda drew herself up and thrust out her chin. "I'll thank you not to be insulting, Hattie. It so happens that I know how to conduct myself."

"But does *he?*" Hattie interposed.

"—in a manner befitting a lady. You may insinuate until you're blue in the face, it won't butter any parsnips with me. I know how to behave, thank you very much. As for the neighbors, do you think I for one minute give a damn for their opinions? Quite the reverse, I assure you. I did not come to this uncivilized country to be taught manners. Things have come to a pretty pass, I must say, when a lady can't receive a gentleman caller in her own home without a lot of vulgar country women gawping out windows."

"All right, then. It's none of my business. If you're going to get uppity about it. . . ." Hattie thrust her arms into her coat and flounced out.

Half an hour later she was back to apologize. She and Miranda had a good cry, and nothing more was said about Jack Williams.

I noticed, however, that for some time after that Miranda appeared unusually dignified when we happened to meet Jack Williams on the street. He would be all kind encouragement and solicitous inquiries about our welfare, and there was certainly nothing in his manner to suggest that he had anything else on his mind. Our first two roomers, Ernestine Harris and Myrtle King, came on his recommendation. They taught at the central grade school. They shared the big front bedroom.

Then Mr. Parker, a commercial traveler, took my old room at the back of the house, near the attic stairs, and Paul Brooks, the bank teller, took Jess's room. Miss Kennedy, an elderly female who kept the books at the township office, rented the remaining bedroom. We even furnished the little box room on the second floor and put someone in there. This was Mrs. Walsh, a widow who sold tickets at the Palace Theater. She was not, strictly speaking, a roomer. She got her room and board free for helping around the house.

Except for the Wednesday and Saturday matinees, the Palace was open only in the evenings, so Mrs. Walsh had plenty of time to make the beds and tidy up the house, look after the furnace and help with the meals. She ate with us. The rest of the roomers went next door to Mrs. Seavey's for their meals. Having Mrs. Walsh there was a good arrangement, since Miranda was working full time at the beauty shop, and Jess and I were in school all day. On Saturdays we helped Mrs. Walsh with the weekly cleaning and the laundry.

By the end of January we were, as Jack Williams had predicted, managing very well. We were, in fact, much better off financially than we had been when Alfie was living. I was glad that we were able to take care of ourselves, but at the same time I could not help feeling that we were in some obscure way letting him down by managing so well without him. We were able to afford luxuries we had considered beyond our means before: a radio, one of the new electric washing machines, and also a standing lamp with a silk shade, an accessory which was just coming into vogue.

Our roomers were all, to use Miranda's words, refined people. She had no cause for complaint there. Mr. Parker, the commercial traveler, was one of the saddest looking men I ever saw. I told Miranda he looked like Brownie, and this made her laugh, until she discovered what made him sad. Then she went out of her way to be nice to him. His wife was dying of tuberculosis in the sanitarium. He owned a house in another part of town, but had rented it out to other people because he could not bear being alone.

Tears came into Miranda's eyes when he told her this, and he had to lend her his handkerchief. He was so shy, so lost looking, that we all felt sorry for him. We wondered how he ever got up enough courage to sell anything, which proves that appearances can be deceiving, for he was doing very well. His line was caskets and undertakers' supplies. He was out on his rounds all week, returning on Fridays.

Paul Brooks, the bank teller, had been transferred to Southport from another small town, though he gave the impression of coming from somewhere much more worldly. He was fairly young, around twenty-five. In those days, going into the bank was considered the next best thing to going to college, for tellers eventually became managers, and the bank manager in any town was and I suppose still is a person of some importance. Mr. Brooks was much sought after. He was asked to join the golf club and the tennis club and the opera group, and was invited to parties and teas.

All the girls went mad over him, though it was well known that banking rules would not allow him to marry for some years. He had three or four girls on the string at one time. It was really the parents he was courting. What he wanted was free meals, and he got plenty of those. He was invited out to dinner almost every night.

Miss Harris and Miss King were the sort of nice girls you see busying themselves in community work for other people's good. They were unattractive in an undefinable way. Miss Harris was a square dark-haired woman with an enormous mouth and big teeth, intensely neuter rather than masculine. Miss King was neuter, too, but not intensely so. A bit of femininity struggled to the surface and peeped through now and then.

She was smaller than Miss Harris, more rounded at the corners, quieter, and most of her face was hidden behind horn-rimmed glasses. The two were constant companions. When not playing badminton or attending committee meetings, they read poetry to one another in their room. Miss King kept a much-read copy of Rupert Brooke's *Collected Poems* on the night-table at her side of the bed.

Miss Kennedy, the clerk in the township office, wore the rather vacant expression often seen on the faces of lonely people; as if all her thoughts, turning inward, presented their backs to the world. She had no friends, no interests, nothing but her job, which must have been rather a dull one. Evenings, she puttered in her room, rinsed out her stockings in the bathroom, made tea on a little alcohol stove, and gazed sadly at a smiling portrait of the Prince of Wales on her dresser.

She was quite unlike Mrs. Walsh, who was so determinedly cheerful that even I knew she was whistling in the dark, trying desperately to ignore the bogeymen of despair and loneliness that haunted her. Once she had had a husband and a home of her own, and though it seemed improbable that she would ever have these things again, she clung with unreasoning tenacity to the belief that something just as good was bound to come along. Her optimism was more pathetic than Miss Kennedy's resignation.

I was naturally interested in these strangers who had come to live with us. Observing them, I could not help but realize that growing to maturity does not necessarily mean that all life's problems have been solved. It surprised me to learn that adults can be lonely, too, and unsure of themselves. I had been waiting impatiently for the day when I would grow up and put all the cares of childhood behind me, when I would become serenely self-assured, having discovered the answers to all the questions that troubled me. Now I began to wonder if the climate of thirteen was so bad after all.

If growing up meant that I would have to stave off bogeys, like Mrs. Walsh, or live within a bleak world of myself, like Miss Kennedy, I would just as soon stay where I was. For a time I found comfort in reading books I thought I had outgrown. One day Jess saw me reading *The Wind in the Willows.* "For heaven's sake, are you going to be an infant all your life?" she demanded. "Reading those childish books! Just because you're the youngest you needn't think we're going to keep on babying you forever."

It was a time of adjustment for her, too, and no doubt she could have done with a little babying herself. Our home had been a normal happy one, and then suddenly it was a semipublic place, no more depressing than any other rooming house, perhaps, but to anyone who valued privacy, as Jess and I did, the atmosphere was not exactly congenial. I have always considered privacy one of the necessities of life. It seems to me that life would be unbearable without a room of one's own, a place to shut out the world.

I pity the poor, not so much because they cannot afford good food as because they are forced to live in one another's pockets. I cannot change my convictions, even though I learned long ago that what people fear most is being left alone with themselves. They feel safer in one another's pockets.

Miranda liked having other people around. She was working all day, and when she came home at six o'clock on those winter evenings it cheered her up to see all the lights on, to know that the house was full of people, that she would not be able to sit in her own living room for half an hour without some interruption: someone wanting to iron a slip, or asking for clean towels, or simply wanting to talk.

She welcomed such intrusions, found the roomers' problems entertaining, not depressing. She would sit and listen, while they talked about themselves, as if she were hearing the most intriguing gossip, and then she would tell them about her own life.

With no one there to question whether or not she was getting the facts straight, she let her imagination run wild, and built up an entirely new past for herself, presenting herself as an only child who, having lost her high-born parents when she was fifteen, had been taken in by a wealthy aunt. The aunt was of course Madam—Mrs. Fitzhugh. Miranda did not make the mistake of getting carried away with her own story. She did not overdo it.

She let fall casual remarks about the sort of life she had once been privileged to observe—only now she placed herself in the position of a participant instead of a spectator—and allowed her listeners to fill in the larger picture. I wondered what Auntie Vi would say if she could hear her.

Sometimes Miranda did not even have to lie. It was true, in a way, that she had been married from the house in Park Lane. Alfie had called for her at the servants' entrance and driven her off in a hired carriage to the registry office. And she had spent a good part of her life in Madam's house. A place to which you return again and again *sounds* like home.

Even Hattie's saying, "It's funny you never told me all this before," did not disconcert Miranda. She said, "Alfie never liked to hear me talk about home. He didn't get along with Auntie."

Loyalty drove Jess and me to go along as best we could with Miranda's inventions, though we could not rid ourselves of the suspicion that everyone knew or guessed she was lying. We would watch her listeners' faces and imagine that we caught glimpses of amusement or disbelief. There was always the danger, too, that we might make a slip and give her away. To protect her, we were forced into lies ourselves, and since we had both inherited a good share of Alfie's veracity, guilt weighed us down.

Guilt was not a thing that bothered Miranda. However, she did avoid any reference to or reminder of her real past. Perhaps, like poor Clara, she found her present lot bearable only when she could embroider it with make-believe. She had hoped, when we left England, to take a step up in the world. Since this had not happened, she rearranged her dreams to fit. If she could not go up, she would pretend to have come down.

She entered so thoroughly into the role of a lady of rank in reduced circumstances—but with typical British pluck marshaling the ingenuity and daring to work for a living, and take in roomers to boot—that she almost forgot who she really was. Sometimes when a letter came from Auntie Vi she would frown at it in a puzzled way as if she did not recognize the handwriting, then stick it in a corner of the kitchen mirror for a day or so before reading it.

When Auntie Vi hinted that she and Uncle Bertie might blow the little nestegg they had been saving for their old age on a trip to Canada, Miranda wrote back at once urging them on no account to contemplate such folly. They would be disappointed, she warned. The climate was bad, and besides, we had no room to put them up.

I must admit that the climate was not always agreeable. We had never spent a winter so near the sea, and we found it trying at times. Storms swept in from the Atlantic, herding great rolling whitecaps which exploded in fury against the rocks of the outer harbor. Fishing boats with ice-covered shrouds clung shivering to the wharves. In town, the wind was everywhere, buffeting around corners, tossing the pigeons, searching down coat collars. The foghorn, like some giant animal, woke now and then with a shuddering urgently repeated groan that shook the very air. Up in our third-floor bedroom at night we could hear the wind crying around the chimneys, a restless disturbing sound that did nothing to dispel the feeling of sadness and uncertainty I had been experiencing since Christmas.

The sadness was normal, and perhaps the uncertainty was, too. I was growing out of childhood, going on thirteen. No doubt all girls of that age go through periods when they feel confused and a little apprehensive, not knowing quite what is expected of them or what the future holds. I was undergoing a physical change, too. "Oh, not my baby!" Miranda exclaimed when I went to her with my first adult problem. "You're growing up too fast. You're making me feel old." She glanced in the mirror to reassure herself.

What bothered me, I suppose, was that I had been made aware so suddenly of how inconstant life is, and though I had always accepted the belief that death is not final, that when people die they go to heaven, I now began to question the fairness of this arrangement. Alfie had been snatched away, protesting, into what I could not help but think of as some sort of exile. It seemed to me that a great mistake had been made somewhere.

During troubled nights I dreamed that the mistake had been rectified. Waking, still on the edge of such a dream,

I was confident that Alfie was back with us where he belonged. Full wakefulness brought disillusionment and despair. How could he be happy anywhere without his family? He knew how much we needed him. Now there was no one to tell us what to do or how to be, no one to bring Miranda back to earth when she got ideas that were too grand, or when she got carried away with her own inventiveness.

Jess gathered together all the snapshots of Alfie she could find, and pasted them into an album. "Haven't we got any real photographs of Dad?" she asked. We had always called him by his Christian name. That winter—perhaps because we felt it would better explain who he was—we began to speak of him as Dad. Rummaging through trunks, Miranda found a sepia likeness of him in uniform, and their wedding picture. "Is this you?" Jess asked. Miranda looked at the woman in the photograph as if she could not believe that she had ever worn such old-fashioned clothes, or combed her hair in those ridiculous puffs. She raised her hands to her eyes to shut out the sight.

"Put it away. I can't bear to look at it."

One thing Jess and I found reassuring. Miranda became a regular homebody that winter. Every night she sat in the living room in her somber mourning dress—she had put away all her colored clothes and wore black garments everywhere—listening to the radio. Anyone going by on the street outside could look in and see that she was spending a quiet evening at home, as was proper for a woman so recently widowed. She was never alone, for the roomers were invited to share the radio, too.

Poor Miss Kennedy sat with her ears cocked, staring with intense longing at whatever picture the voices and sound effects produced in her mind. Miss Harris and Miss

King liked musical programs which were often too classical for the others to enjoy. Mr. Parker joined the group on week ends, saying apologetically that he hoped he wasn't being a nuisance, offering boxes of chocolates to stave off criticism in case he was. Miranda knew how to make him smile, but this had the effect of making him look more sad.

Her conduct made a good impression on the neighbors. Even Mrs. Dove warmed somewhat, and took to dropping in occasionally to recount endless stories about the goings-on of the townspeople. She was a chronic gossip, and made it worse by convincing herself that she was not a gossip at all, but a good woman whose duty it was to know and correct every deviation from her own standard of human behavior. She made me realize more than ever how small-town people watch one another, and with what suspicion the nonconformist is viewed.

Mrs. Seavey and James also helped to while away the winter evenings. James brought his books along and studied with me on the dining table while his mother and Miranda talked in the next room. Jess was usually studying in the attic. Mrs. Seavey told sad stories about her past. "But James and I are happy now," she concluded. "We have each another. We have our home, and the bit of insurance Arthur left us. We do have nice times together."

James and I worked at opposite ends of the table. When we spoke, it was to discuss some problem. We could think of nothing else to talk about. Looking faintly mauve and pinched, for cold weather did not agree with him, smelling of doughnuts, he sat hunched over his books, concentrating earnestly. He was better at mathematics than I was, and kindly explained difficult problems. Sometimes when he had been silent for a time I would look up and catch him listening intently to his mother's voice in the next room, and I thought that he deliberately made his face expressionless so I would not guess what he was thinking.

James seemed to work at being average in all things. At school—he was in my class—he was neither popular nor unpopular. He was not much noticed, in fact. His grades were not good enough to win praise, nor poor enough to draw censure. He sent me a valentine that winter, a lace-trimmed heart bearing the inscription "Be My Valentine." Under this he had signed himself, "Yours truly, James Seavey."

The next time I saw him I thanked him for the valentine. He shrugged and said, "Oh, that's all right," in an embarrassed voice. It made me wonder whether it was proper for a girl to acknowledge such a gift. It was the custom, then, when a boy sent a valentine to a girl, to sign it "Guess Who?" or something equally anonymous.

Someone sent Miranda a valentine, too, a quite expensive-looking card with garlands of hearts and flowers, and a verse:

> "Roses are red,
> Violets are blue,
> Be my sugar,
> I'm sweet on you."

It was signed "An Admirer" in a scrawling masculine hand. Miranda said she could not for the life of her imagine who had sent it.

I suspected Jack Williams. He came around once a month to collect the rent. It was not his custom to do this. All his other tenants sent their rent checks to the *Gazette* office. If he had an ulterior motive in collecting ours in person, he must have been disconcerted, for every time he came he found Miranda surrounded by people. She would send someone else to the door to let him in. As she wrote out the check, she made genteel remarks about the weather, while he looked at her with a faint smile as if he knew she was up to something and admired her for it. He was not urged to stay.

That she was up to something Jess and I did not realize for some time. We had no way of knowing that during those late-winter evenings when she sat at home doing what was expected of her, she was making plans for the future, scheming as craftily as a Victorian mother selecting a husband for a marriageable daughter, the only difference being that it was herself she was planning to marry off.

As I reconstructed it later, her thoughts went something like this: Here she was, a lovely young widow whom any man would jump at the chance of marrying. Naturally, she would be content with nothing but the best, and the best catch in town was Mr. Jack Williams. Through the winter trees she could see that big house of his up there on the hill, with its five chimneys and the white columns beside the front door, and no doubt she spent many an hour dreaming of the day when she would become mistress of it, with country girls to wait on her hand and foot, and a big closed car with a chauffeur. It would be like the stories she had read back home in London, about people who had gone out to the colonies and made their fortunes.

Jack Williams was head over heels in love with her already—he had been since the day they met—but it wouldn't do to encourage him too soon. She must observe a proper period of mourning—perhaps six months, like the Royal Family—before she allowed him to call on her. She must be dignified, show him that she was not the sort of woman to be trifled with, make herself a little hard to get. She knew his kind. If he thought the conquest was too easy, he'd lose interest.

She had no doubt that she could lure him to the altar, though. Was she not the irresistible Mrs. Arnold, who had broken half the male hearts in London when she married Alfie? Perhaps she made tentative plans for a Christmas wedding. In the meantime—for she believed in miracles —Jack Williams's hateful old grandmother would die. She was well past eighty, and really had no business hanging on so long.

That was how, later on, I imagined Miranda's thoughts went. I don't think I was far wrong.

Chapter Seven

Jess changed a lot that year. Physically, she grew almost overnight from a flat-chested adolescent to a rather well-developed young maiden. (I was about to say woman, but she was only going on fifteen.) All that cream she had rubbed into her chest must have finally taken effect. She was really quite pretty, in what I can best describe as a well-rounded way, with plump cheeks and those big brown eyes—cow eyes, we called them, teasing her. I mean it as a compliment when I say that her eyes did have that same liquid innocent wide-eyed look that a well-behaved cow turns on you, mildly reproachful and dubious. She blushed easily, and once she had started, her inability to control the pink flood mortified her so much that her eyes got dewy.

During the winter she gradually took over the care of the house, and with Mrs. Walsh's help kept it cleaner than it had ever been before. She did the shopping and prepared the meals, too, leaving Miranda entirely free of the bother of household routine.

When the last of the home brew Alfie had made was finished, Jess and I walked down to Elliot's Feed and Grain store near the waterfront to buy the ingredients for a new batch. Elliot's had somewhat the air of a saloon in an old Western, with men lounging against the counters and a perpetual card game going on in one corner.

We did not know that the bales of hay and bags of corn stacked in the front shop were simply there for effect. Elliot's real business was supplying the raw materials for bootleg liquor. At that time, in every Maritime port, bootlegging was a thriving business.

The big operators transported contraband in fishing schooners from the French islands of St. Pierre and Miquelon to somewhere outside the three-mile limit of the U.S. coast, where it was transferred to American cutters; while small operators like Mr. Dove set up illicit distilleries in cellars, to supply the local trade.

Mr. Elliot himself served us, and if his manner suggested that the sight of two demure schoolgirls buying "makings" tickled him, we put it down to bad manners. "You girls been in the business long?" he inquired facetiously as he wrapped up the malt. At the door he called after us, "Don't drink it all in one sitting, now!"

This being the first time Jess and I had made beer without supervision, Miranda thought it would be a good idea to ask Mr. Dove to check on the mash and give an opinion as to its quality. He gave us a funny look as he replaced the cover on the earthenware crock. "Quite a professional job," he remarked. "You girls make this stuff by yourselves?"

"Alfie taught them," Miranda explained. "They've been doing it for years."

"Hmm . . ." Mr. Dove looked aside and drew one hand over his mouth as if trying to erase a smile. "Mind you, I'm not saying there's anything wrong with making beer, but if I was you I don't think I'd mention it to anyone—my wife, for instance. If she ever told that Sons of Temperance crowd she hangs around with that you'd put your girls to work making beer in the cellar—well, you know what they'd say."

"It's not against the law, is it?"

"Well, no, not if it's for home consumption; but it's against their principles. Comes to the same thing, in this town."

"I simply cannot understand the attitude of such people," Miranda complained.

"That's the way they are." Mr. Dove shrugged resignedly. "No sense giving them anything to talk about."

"I don't know what they'll think of next in this uncivilized country."

"Well, I only mentioned it. People are different in England, I guess."

"I should hope so," Miranda said.

When Mr. Dove had gone she said, "Did you ever hear anything so ridiculous? These country people really make me laugh."

Jess was a thrifty housekeeper. She shopped by telephone, as did everyone else, for there were no supermarkets. You ordered meat from the butcher, groceries from the grocer, fish from the fish shop, fruit from the fruit market, and they delivered once a day. Jess soon got to know which tradesmen could be trusted, and could tell at a glance when the butcher had palmed off one of his poorer cuts on us.

One Saturday when Mr. Peters, who lived on our street and ran the butcher shop on Main, had delivered what she considered a particularly inferior roast of beef, she decided to return it and demand a better one. She did not relish such an errand, for Mr. Peters was known around town as a great kidder, a man who liked to have a bit of fun at someone else's expense.

His jokes were more often malicious than funny; such as the time he borrowed the hearse from the undertaking parlors and persuaded a friend to drive up to his house in it. When Mrs. Peters answered the door, the friend, wearing a stovepipe hat and black cutaway coat, put on a long face and said, "We've come for poor old Fred, Mrs. Peters." The fact that Mrs. Peters fainted dead away did not seem to lessen her husband's enjoyment of this prank. When talking to Miranda, he employed a Cockney accent. You could see that he thought this was very clever and humorous.

I went along with Jess that afternoon to lend support. Mr. Peters and his assistant, a boy of about nineteen, were alone in the shop, which had sawdust on the floor and smelled horribly of old bones. Jess laid the parcel on the counter and folded back the bloody paper. She was agonizingly embarrassed, her cheeks crimson, but she said, "I'm afraid this roast is not up to scratch, Mr. Peters, so I'd like to exchange it for a better one."

Mr. Peters seemed taken aback for a minute; then he wiped his hands on his apron and threw a glance at his assistant. Both arranged their faces into solemn lines and leaned on the counter, staring at the roast as if they had never seen anything like it before. Mr. Peters poked at it with his forefinger.

"You see anything wrong with this roast, Sam?" Sam turned it over, examined it from all sides, and after a good deal of squinting and considering, admitted that he couldn't say, offhand. "Wait till I get my glasses on," Mr. Peters said. He adjusted his glasses and bent over the counter again, poking and prodding and shaking his head, saying "Hmm," and "Well, now," in a baffled voice.

"It doesn't smell good," Jess explained.

Mr. Peters bent down and sniffed. "It don't smell like attar of roses," he admitted, "but I never knew a piece of beef that did." He straightened. "What do you think we ought to do, Sam? These ladies claim this roast stinks."

It was pretty obvious by this time that they were ragging us. Mr. Peters said, Well now, he'd just have to find us a roast that smelled good. He didn't want dissatisfied customers. "A-1 service, that's my motto." Sam went into the back shop and staggered out with a whole quarter of beef, which he laid on the counter. "Now then, ladies, take your choice." Mr. Peters waved a giant cleaver. "Which part of this animal do you fancy?"

They made such a to-do about selecting the one perfect cut to please us that we felt like complete fools. I know Jess wanted to die. She stared with moist eyes at a spot just above their heads, trying desperately to retain some dignity, conscious that her blushes gave her away.

But as we were leaving, when Mr. Peters and his assistant both scurried to open the door for us, bowing and scraping and saying they did hope there'd be no further cause for complaint—Mr. Peters using his British accent—Jess suddenly got control of herself.

She said in a perfect imitation of Miranda, "Perhaps you wouldn't find it so amusing, Mr. Peters, if we took our business elsewhere." We swept out. I imagined that as soon as the door closed behind us they fell in a heap on the counter, beside the hacked-up carcass, and laughed themselves sick.

Jess wasn't fooling. She did take her business elsewhere until, several weeks later, Mr. Peters came in on his way home one night to make peace. Miranda was there. He peeked around the half-open kitchen door, pretending to be afraid of Jess. "You still mad at me?" he asked. Of course Jess blushed. "Aw, come on, don't be mad," he coaxed. "Look, I've brought you a peace offering, a nice pot of head cheese. . . . She's been buying her meat from that crook up the street," he complained to Miranda, looking injured. "Guess she doesn't care if my wife and kids starve. . . . No, honest, I was real cut up about losing your business. You try me again and I'll personally see to it that you get A-1 service."

He hung around for a while talking to Miranda. When Jess went upstairs to do her lessons, he said, "That girl of yours is the cutest little dickens I've seen in a month of

Sundays. She's cute. She's real cute. Getting to be a real corker for looks, too."

"She's nothing but a child," Miranda said sharply.

Miranda might protest that Jess was still a child, but when spring came she taught her to drive the car. Jess drove very carefully, with intense concentration, up and down town on various errands. I cannot remember that she ever had a license to drive. Perhaps none was required in those days. In any case, nobody questioned her ability.

Everything she did, in fact, earned such applause from all sides that it was a wonder it didn't go to her head. It would have gone to mine. The roomers had special commendatory smiles for her. They marveled at what a good little housekeeper she was, running the house practically single-handed, and keeping up her school work besides. Such praise only made her more conscientious in her efforts to be helpful, and this endeared her still further to all and sundry. "You're a little wonder," Mr. Parker told her. "A regular little wonder." Miss Harris and Miss King invited her to play badminton with them.

"Well, they're good wholesome girls," Hattie remarked. She and Miranda both laughed. "Wholesome" was not a flattering adjective to apply to a woman. It meant something a little queer. I did not understand this attitude at the time, but later on I realized that it was the thing just then to scoff at virtue. A good girl was either so inhibited that her mental health was in danger, or else she was letting off steam in some other, less normal, way.

By the end of the decade the trend had reversed, and chastity was in vogue again. The change came rather abruptly. One fine morning a great many girls woke to the realization that they had sacrificed themselves, so to speak, to a fashion which was already passé. It was most disconcerting; not quite fair, really. As one girl of my acquaintance put it, "How could I know it was going to become the rage all of a sudden to be a prude?"

Though Jess and I had no way of knowing what plans Miranda was dreaming up for the future, we should have realized, if we had stopped to think about it, that since she was the sort of woman who attracted men, and was attracted to them, it would not be long before she wanted more companionship than we could give her. She might even consider marriage. Somewhere in the back of our minds was the knowledge that we might one day have to face this problem. But not for two or three years, at least. When you are young, even next year seems far away, and it was quite easy to put off thinking, to assure ourselves that there was no need to worry for a long long time.

As the spring days lengthened, Miranda began to go out sometimes in the evenings, and though she still wore black, and returned home early enough to suit the most exacting Mrs. Grundy, people assumed that the mourning period was over and they could behave naturally again. When she went down town with Jess and me on Saturday nights, certain of the middle-aged shopkeepers came out of their offices at the back to assure us in a jocular way that our credit was good.

They tried to sound merely affable, for the benefit of listening clerks, but there was more than affability in their eyes. Even the milkman who came around each morning at eight o'clock began bringing the bottles inside instead of leaving them on the back porch. He lingered inside the kitchen where Miranda was eating, cracking feeble jokes and threatening to invite himself for breakfast.

Mr. Peters was more of a nuisance. In order to insure that we got A-1 service, he delivered the day's meat himself, on the way home from his shop around seven o'clock, when he knew Miranda would be there. He too lingered in the doorway, being witty, talking with a Cockney accent for her benefit.

"Ere you are, now, your 'ighness. Ere's tuppence thruppence worth of pig's trotters, marked down special for the h'anniversary sale." He hinted that he wouldn't turn down a good drink of home brew if someone offered it.

I knew perfectly well that Miranda was capable of dealing with such people. What I did wonder was whether there was something in her appearance or manner that suggested she would not resent being given what Hattie called the glad eye. I could not imagine the milkman trying to get fresh with, for example, Miss Anderson.

Jess must have been thinking the same thing. She remarked, "Miss Anderson says it depends on people themselves whether other people respect them."

Miranda, not recognizing this as a hint, said, "I could have told you that. Who is this Miss Anderson you're always talking about?"

"You know, our Campfire Girls leader. I've told you about her."

"Well, I wish you wouldn't keep quoting her as if she were God. What does she know, a simple country woman who's never been anywhere or done anything?"

One day in June, as Clara and I walked home from school together, she gave me the first inkling that Miranda might in truth be looking for a different kind of companionship.

There had been fog around all day. By midafternoon the sun had almost come through, giving the air a pearly underwater glow like the inside of a seashell. In all the gardens along the street, honeysuckle was blooming. The foghorn groaned every few minutes, warning ships of rocks in the outer harbor. People who had lived in Southport all their lives never really listened to the foghorn, any more than they would listen to a clock ticking. When the weather closed in, the doleful sound reassured them. I never grew accustomed to it. Once it had started I would wait and listen for the next drawn-out boom that seemed to come from everywhere at once, like the voice of the fog itself.

As we lagged along, Jack Williams passed us in his car. "There goes Miranda's boy friend," Clara said.

"Her boy friend? What makes you say that?"

"Well, isn't he?"

"He certainly is not. Miranda wouldn't be caught dead with him." I quickened my steps. Undaunted, Clara hurried to keep pace with me. Having brought up this subject, which was to engross her attention for months to come, she had no intention of dropping it so quickly.

"Then how come they have lunch together every day at the Coffee Pot?"

"They do not!"

"Honest. I wouldn't lie to you. They sit in the back booth, and he pays the check for both of them. He drives her home some nights, too."

The old feeling of anxiety that I had first known back in London when I thought Miranda was going to be stolen away, came over me. "You don't know for sure," I said. You never saw them."

"My mother knows everything," Clara said. "The thing she's wondering now is: what's going to come of it? Is he going to marry her?"

I walked on without speaking, while the foghorn groaned dismally.

Clara studied my face. Her bangs and eyelashes were

beaded with mist. "Would you really mind if they got married?" she asked. "He's got lots of money, you know."

"I don't care. I don't like him."

"Well, I wouldn't have told you if I'd known you were going to get upset. Don't cry here on the street, will you? We don't want to attract attention." Clara obligingly changed the subject. "Do you know what my mother made me do the other day? She made me take the pledge. I had to sign a paper saying I would never touch beer, wine, or alcohol in any form as long as I live. Did you ever hear of anything so silly?"

"Did your father sign it, too?"

Clara doubled up with laughter. "Did my father sign it! Oh, that's a scream!" James and three other boys from our class overtook us and crowded past without speaking. "Oh, you are an absolute scream, Rose!" Clara cried in a high affected voice. The boys paid no attention, though they loitered just ahead.

"No, but talking about being upset, how would you like it if you had a mother like mine?" Clara continued, lowering her voice to a confidential mutter. "Always talking as if God was sitting up there ready to pounce the minute I do something wrong. And how would you like to put up with a dirty old man like Grampa Higgins swearing around the house? He hasn't taken a bath since Christmas. Sometimes I hate to go home. I wouldn't be surprised if I came down with a nervous breakdown any day. Honestly, my nerves are on edge all the time. You know what we ought to do? We ought to take a drink of Pa's liquor. I know where he keeps the key to the cellar.

"You've signed the pledge."

"I signed it Clara Dove, which doesn't happen to be my real name."

"What if your mother caught us?"

"She's taken Grampa Higgins out to his sister's place for the day. My uncle called for them this morning. They won't be back until suppertime."

One by one the boys ahead of us had turned off. James was the last. He waited for us at the end of the lane that ran behind the houses on Lupin Crescent. He did not mind being seen with girls, but there was a time and a place for everything.

"How'd you like a drink of Pa's liquor?" Clara asked him.

He considered. "I wouldn't mind."

We went to Clara's house and found the key to the cellar behind the kitchen clock. "I want to practice drinking so I'll be good and sophisticated when I go to Hollywood," Clara explained, as we went down the cellar steps and stumbled past the coal pile in the half dark. "I think there's nothing more disgusting than a girl who acts like a hick in sophisticated company."

Bottles of various shapes and sizes, all labeled "Doc Billy's Cough Cure," were lined up on the shelf. Clara selected one and rearranged the others so that the gap didn't show. We filed upstairs and sat at the dining-room table while Clara dusted three jelly glasses.

James read aloud the framed motto that hung between the windows. " 'What Will You Be Doing When Jesus Comes?' " He added with a straight face, "All I hope is I'm not under the table." Clara and I went into fits of laughter, but soon we felt uneasy.

"What if your mother comes back unexpectedly?" I asked.

"She'd kill me. Why can't we go to your house?"

"All right. But we'll have to stay in the cellar. Mrs. Walsh is there, and you never know who might come in."

James stuffed the bottle and the three jelly glasses into

his school bag. We walked behind the garages to our house and sat on packing boxes in the cellar, behind the partition where Alfie had kept his samples. A few bottles of leather polish and horse liniment still gathered dust on the shelves.

"Here's mud in your eye!" Clara filled the glasses, dribbled in a little water from the laundry taps, and handed them around. "Down the hatch!" We threw back our heads as if we were taking medicine and gulped down a great swallow apiece. It was minutes before we could stop gasping and choking, and pretend that we liked it.

"You wouldn't by any chance have a cigarette?" Clara asked James. "Never mind, I've probably got some myself." She opened the battered imitation leather handbag she carried everywhere she went. Inside, wrapped in toilet paper, was one crushed cigarette, two kitchen matches, and a six-inch jade-green holder she had found one day on the floor of the five-and-ten. "Sorry I can't offer you one," she said, lighting up, "but have a drag anyway." She passed the holder around like a peace pipe.

Under the influence of alcohol James exhibited a dry owlish humor that sent Clara and me into stitches. We pretended to sip from our glasses, staggered around like drunks we had seen in movies, exchanged quips that struck us as the epitome of wit. Then, before we knew what was happening, exhilaration vanished and we felt sick. James was the first. He went white around the mouth. "I've got to go!" He flung his schoolbag over his shoulder and made for the stairs, trying not to hurry, but frantic to escape.

Clara stopped posing as a movie star to glare at him. "Damn it, the party's not *over*."

But James raced up the stairs and banged out the back door.

"There's a sissy for you!" Clara grumbled. Minutes later

we were both sick in the laundry tubs. When it was over Clara sat on the floor, tears of rage and disappointment running down her cheeks. "Oh, damn, damn, *damn!*" She beat her hands against her forehead in a gesture of extreme frustration. How would she ever be a success at a Hollywood party? "Can I stay at your house tonight?" she asked.

"Only until bedtime. There's nowhere for you to sleep."

"I can't go home. My mother will kill me, and anyway I'm going to be sick again. Oh, can't we go somewhere and lie down? I think I'm going to die."

We helped one another up the three flights of stairs to my bedroom, and fell into bed with our clothes on. Mrs. Walsh heard us, and came up to see what was wrong. She got such a fright that she telephoned Miranda to come home at once.

One look at us was enough for Miranda. She knew what to do. Whatever emetic she gave us was thorough. In an hour or so we were propped up in bed with pillows, purged, shaken, weak as cats, but clearheaded. "Now, then," Miranda said. "What happened?"

We told her. She listened, keeping a straight face until Clara said, "I wanted to learn how to be sophisticated." Then she began to laugh in the way that people do when they have been trying not to for a long time. She laughed so hard that her mascara ran.

"I don't see what's so funny." Clara was ready to take offense.

"Oh, honeybunch, I'm not laughing *at* you!" Miranda hugged her and brushed back her untidy bangs.

"My mother won't think it's funny, either. She'll skin me alive."

"Or James's mother," I reminded.

Miranda sobered at once. "We mustn't let them know."

She thought for a minute. "We must say that you ate something. You all came back here after school and opened a tin of something—sardines?"

"My mother knows I hate sardines."

"Well, then, corned beef. You opened a tin of corned beef and made sandwiches, but the beef must have been bad and you got food poisoning. How does that sound?" Miranda waited for our approval, then said, "I'll nip around and spread the word. I'd better go to James's mother first—I hope to God he hasn't spilled the beans. Then I'll go to your house, Clara. Would you like to spend the night here, lovie? Jess won't mind sleeping in the study. I'll explain to your mother that you're too ill to be moved. I suppose she'll want to see you. If she comes here, you'll remember what to say, won't you?"

"Yes. Corned beef."

"Right you are!" Miranda said cheerily. "Wish me luck, girls."

Luck was with her all the way. James's mother had been too busy in the kitchen to pay much attention to what her son was doing, and by the time she did get around to noting his condition, he had achieved on his own about the same state of convalescence as Clara and I were enjoying.

Mrs. Seavey was just about to send for the doctor when Miranda arrived. She couldn't think what had happened to James; he must have picked up a germ. She was glad to learn that it was nothing but a touch of food poisoning. Didn't Miranda agree that a good dose of Epsom salts would set him on his feet? Miranda reported all this to us later. She said with a laugh, "Poor James, he looked so funny and pathetic, like a sick sparrow, lying there with the bedclothes up around his chin."

Clara's mother was dealt with just as easily. Miranda caught her ten minutes after she returned home from visiting, before she had had time to wonder where Clara was. Of course she came right over. She, too, suggested Epsom salts—a favorite remedy for almost anything in those days —but Miranda managed to talk her out of it.

After she had gone Clara and I lay in bed pretending we enjoyed the novelty of convalescing together, of being the center of attention. Jess was sent up with hot soup. She was the only one who expressed disapproval. "You kids ought to be ashamed of yourselves," she said.

"You'd think *she* was your mother," Clara said when we were alone. "Miranda didn't carry on. She's too good a sport."

We tried to re-create the fun of getting drunk in the cellar, but our laughter was all on the surface. Looking back, I can see clearly what we only sensed then, the vague feeling of incompleteness. We had done wrong, and instead of being scolded or punished, our crime had been belittled, laughed off as a minor prank.

Unrebuked, we felt burdened with the great bottled-up reservoir of tears that should have been shed to prove our repentance and earn forgiveness; and the knowledge that since our escapade had not received the censure it deserved, there was nothing for it but to try something more blameworthy next time.

Around ten o'clock Clara decided that she felt well enough to go home and spend the night in her own bed.

So Jess was able to sleep in her own bed, too. She was still rather disapproving. To show it, she complained about the way the sheets were rumpled and pulled out at the bottom, from Clara's having been there. When she had put out the light I lay awake for a time staring at the ceiling. There was a leafy smell in the night air and then the fog had settled in again, thicker than ever. I listened to the mournful boom coming from the sea; then, though I realized I was not picking the best time to exchange confidences, I told Jess what Clara had said about Miranda and Jack Williams.

"You tell Clara to mind her own business," Jess said, and turned over, composing herself for sleep.

She was growing away from me. Instead of confiding in me, she now wrote secrets in her diary. On weekday evenings she did her homework in our bedroom, and I had to agree not to disturb her between the hours of seven and nine. When I went up after doing my own lessons in the dining room I would have to wait in the hall while she went through some furtive rustlings and tiptoeing. She was hiding her diary. A waste of time, since I knew perfectly well where she kept it, and she knew that I knew. It was under a pile of her schoolbooks in the windowseat that was also a chest for storing things, with a lid that lifted up.

Jess knew where I kept my stories, too—in a low shelved closet under the eaves. All the hiding of papers, the pretense of mistrust, was a sort of ritual we observed. We respected one another's privacy. Jess would no more dream of snooping into my secret papers than I would dream of reading hers. Writing anything, whether it was a diary or something you made up, was a private thing. It had to be done when you were alone. And it had to be done for yourself, not for anyone else to see. If you were suddenly interrupted, it was like being caught without your clothes on.

Jess had not gone to sleep. She had been lying in the darkness thinking. She said suddenly, "If she married him, what would become of us?"

"I don't know. . . . Would we have to live in his house, with that old grandmother?"

"I wouldn't live there."

"Neither would I."

"I don't like him. I don't like that old woman, either. They needn't think they can make me live with her."

"They'd have to do something with us. Miranda wouldn't just go off and leave us, would she?"

Jess thought about this for a time. "They might send us away to some school," she said. She turned over with an angry jerk of the bedclothes. "If he thinks he's going to take Miranda away from us, he can damned well think again."

"What could we do? We couldn't stop him."

"I'm going to think of something." Jess lay tense, concentrating. "I've *got* to think of something."

After a time I suggested, "We could drive down in the car and pick Miranda up after work. Then he wouldn't be able to drive her home."

"Yes, that's one thing we could do. We could wait outside the shop."

The next night we were waiting outside the beauty parlor when Miranda came out at six o'clock. "I'm going to drive you home every night after this," Jess told her. "It's too tiring for you, having to walk, after working all day."

"Oh, honey, that's lovely of you," Miranda said, "but I've been doing it for months and it hasn't killed me yet. Who's getting the dinner?"

"It's all ready. Mrs. Walsh is keeping it warm."

After dinner we began a bombardment of casual questions and suggestions. "I think I'll pick you up at noon, too," Jess said, "so that you can have lunch at home with Rose and me. You don't like the food in those restaurants."

Miranda looked up, suspicious of so much attention. "I like eating down town," she said.

"It won't be any trouble for me," Jess said. "At school we have a whole hour and a half for lunch."

"Well, I don't. Sometimes I only take half an hour."

"You really ought to have a good meal at noon, to keep you going the rest of the day," Jess persisted.

Miranda frowned at her. "Why this sudden concern for my welfare? What are you up to?"

Jess was wise enough to drop the subject for the time being. A little later she said, "Couldn't we buy a stone for Dad's grave?"

We had spoken of this before. As soon as the ground was workable in the spring, Alfie's coffin had been moved from the crypt under the chapel to a plot in the newer part of the cemetery. We went out on Sundays to lay flowers on the unmarked grave.

"Yes, I've been meaning to buy a stone," Miranda said.

"It looks so bare without one," Jess went on. "As if we didn't care. How will people know he belongs to us if his name isn't there?"

"I'll see about it, dear," Miranda said.

"When? Shall I telephone the stonecutter tomorrow and make an appointment?"

"Well, all right, if you like. I suppose it should have been done before."

We began to watch Miranda the way a young mother watches a child whose behavior is unpredictable. If she went out in the evening, perhaps to a movie with Hattie, we noted the time she returned, and asked what we hoped sounded like offhand questions—"What was the movie about? Who else did you see down town?"—to make certain that she really had been where she said she was.

Chapter Eight

In July, Clara and I spent two weeks at Camp Minnehaha. Jess stayed at home. She said she could not possibly go off and leave the house to run by itself, but this was not the real reason. She stayed at home to watch Miranda.

The camp was not the Sherwood Forest sort of place I had imagined it would be. It was simply a collection of tents in a clearing, grouped around a central unpainted wooden building that we called the assembly hall, beside a small lake. There were woods all around, and a shaky pier jutting into the water.

Miss Anderson, with her fair hair parted down the middle and done in two braids over her shoulders like an Indian maiden, was the camp leader. We all wore voluminous pleated gym bloomers of navy serge—the Campfire Girls' uniform, they hung well below the knees like baggy plus fours—with white middies, black stockings, white tennis shoes, and bands around our foreheads, Indian fashion, with a feather sticking up behind.

The girls, members of various troops, had all met in previous years. I was the only one who did not know everybody. On the first day they ran around greeting one another with cries of delight, comparing notes, forming cliques. I fervently hoped that I would make a good enough impression to become a member of a clique, and not be left on the sidelines, as were one or two of the least popular girls.

We had no time to wonder whether or not we were enjoying ourselves. At seven in the morning Miss Anderson sounded reveille, and from then on until taps we were kept busy every minute. So much time for eating, so much for making beds, for inspection, swimming, hiking, arts and crafts, canoe practice, singing songs around the campfire, and so on. It was all very jolly and outdoorsy. My main recollection, though, is of wet sneakers and damp bedding. It rained only three times during the two weeks, but nothing dried out completely.

On visitors' day, Sunday, all the parents drove up to spend the afternoon, and the girls entertained them with exhibitions of gymnastics and canoe racing, followed by lemonade and cookies in the assembly hall. Miranda and Jess came. They were late arriving, and I had time to observe that all the other mothers wore casual cotton prints or tweeds, and country shoes.

When our car drove up, half a dozen girls were standing in a group, waiting. "Hey, kids, get a load of the vamp!" one girl said. Another nudged her and told her to shut up. Miranda ran to me and hugged me as if we had been separated for months. "Oh, baby, we have missed you!" she cried. There were tears in her eyes.

She had left off wearing mourning at the end of June, and had on a green dress with a silk fringe going round and round in spirals from the neckline to the hem, and a garden-party hat. Her high heels sank into the ground at every step as I led her off to be introduced to Miss Anderson. She was completely at ease. She was the only one who was properly dressed, she thought.

Jess and I had a few minutes alone. "Anything new?" I asked her.

She shook her head. "Nothing, except that you-know-who telephoned the other night."

"What did he want?"

"He didn't say. I told him Miranda was out."

"Where was she?"

"She was only upstairs. I didn't tell her he phoned." She looked across to where Miranda was chatting with Miss Anderson, and muttered, "I *said* she ought to wear country things. . . ."

Miranda and Miss Anderson strolled toward us. "Jessica won the gold star for leadership this year, as you know," Miss Anderson was saying. She gave Jess a warm smile. "We hope she'll lead a troop of her own when she's older."

The visitors left around five. After such a busy day, the girls were given the evening off. Some walked to the village, a mile away. The rest hung around the assembly hall talking.

"Rose, is it true that you and Jess know how to make beer?" a girl from our troop asked me.

"Oh, shut up," Clara said.

"Shut up yourself. I only wanted Rose to give us her recipe."

I looked suspiciously at the girl, wondering whether she was trying to start something. Her eyes were friendly, and I was reassured.

She said, "What I thought was, we might make some out behind the binney some night."

"You can't make it in one night. Anyway, we haven't got anything to make it in."

"Oh, well. I thought it would be fun to try. Where did you learn to make it?"

"My father taught me." I told a small lie. "He used to own a pub over home, in England."

I saw my mistake at once. The girls thought of a pub as a disreputable place, like the saloons they had seen in movies.

"I thought your parents were rich," another girl said, not in a hostile way. I decided she was merely being curious. "I thought you lived next door to Buckingham Palace."

I felt that the answer I gave would determine whether I was accepted or rejected. The girls had heard Miranda's fanciful stories about her life in London, and were testing me to see whether or not they were true. "It wasn't next door to Buckingham Palace," I said. "Not quite. Anyway, that was where my mother lived before she was married."

"Was that your mother, the one with the English accent?" a girl from another troop asked. "Goodness, you could tell *she* wasn't Canadian."

"She lived in London, with her aunt." I described Madam's house in detail, while the girls sat forward with their chins in their hands, being impressed.

"Was her aunt very wealthy? She must have been."

"Oh, yes." I thought the girls would wonder why Miranda had to work for a living, and added, "You mustn't mention this, because my mother doesn't want anyone to know, but when she fell in love with my father, her aunt wouldn't accept him because he wasn't rich enough. So they ran away and got married, and then her people disinherited her."

The girls widened their eyes and murmured. This was the sort of story they liked. "Didn't her family ever forgive her?"

"No, they cut her off without a cent. And if they hadn't been so mean, that's where we'd be living today, in that big house with all those servants. . . ."

I caught sight of Miss Anderson in the doorway, and realized that she had been standing there for some minutes. She walked through the room without speaking. I felt that she saw right through my falsehoods and could scarcely contain her repugnance.

Miss Anderson had cast aside enough of her Edwardian dignity to be a good sport, but not enough to encourage undue familiarity. Though the girls went to her with some rather intimate problems, they did not forget to address her as "Ma'am." The next morning she asked me rather casually to walk through the woods with her to a spot where we had some days earlier discovered a plover's nest.

She did not as a rule play favorites in this way, and I dreaded what she might have to say. We found the plover's nest, and saw that the eggs were still unhatched. Then, as we walked back along the shore of the lake together, she remarked that one of the reasons girls went to camp was of course to enjoy themselves in the open air and learn how to paddle a canoe and so on. But she did feel that manners and deportment were terribly important, too, because people judged us by our speech and actions, not by where we came from or how much money we had. "It's what you are yourself that matters," she said earnestly.

So she always tried to instill the importance of right conduct into her girls. She did hope they would be truthful at all times, and not pretend to be something they weren't, and so on and so on. She tried to sound as if she were discussing people in general, but I knew what she was driving at. I was wondering miserably how I should react, when she switched to another subject, calling my attention to the view across the lake, the dark line of the shore and the still reflections. She said it made her wish she could write poetry.

Being spared the ordeal of either admitting I had been

lying the night before, or maintaining indignantly that I had never told a lie in my life—for I could not decide which course to take—was such a relief that I forgot myself and admitted I sometimes wrote stories. Miss Anderson was intensely interested. I might be a great writer some day. I must work hard, and study, and read all the great books, and never lose sight of my goal.

"You can be anything you want to be," she said. "Remember that. Nothing is impossible." She hoped I would allow her to read some of my stories. In the meantime, would I care to borrow her copy of Emerson? She had run across the most beautiful sentence in it just the other day: "Sleep lingers all our lifetime about our eyes, as night hovers all day in the boughs of the fir trees."

She was about to go on with more quotations when a group of girls came running to meet us. The mail, which was sent up each morning from the village, had arrived. I did not see Miss Anderson alone again until the day we were leaving, when she came to my tent with her copy of Emerson and a book of poems by Bliss Carman. By this time, having mulled things over and come to the conclusion that she had really been criticizing Miranda when she spoke of other people judging us by our speech and actions, I regretted having confided in her. I told her politely that we had both Emerson and Bliss Carman at home. "In our library," I said, hoping to convey a picture of a vast room stocked with the world's finest literature.

Chapter Nine

Clara and I returned home from camp around noon. Jess drove up to fetch us. Although it was Saturday, Miranda had the day off. The beauty parlor had been closed for three days because Mrs. Fuller's husband had died. Miranda went to the funeral in the afternoon, returning around four o'clock.

"Did you have a nice time at camp, lovie?" she asked me.

"Oh, yes. . . ."

"That Miss Anderson—what is she like?"

"She's very nice. All the girls like her."

"Jess seems to have a crush on her. I can't think why. She's such an old-maid thing. I never did trust that goody-goody type. Jess ought to have more friends her own age."

After supper Miranda went to her room. Jess and I followed to see what she was doing. "Are you going out?" we asked, seeing the clothes laid out on the bed.

"I may go out later," Miranda said evasively, fixing her face before the mirror. "Run along now. I'm busy."

She spent an hour dressing. When she came downstairs she said, "Do I look nice, girls?" and twirled on her toes to be admired. She wore a sleeveless dress of red satin with a lot of chiffon panels fastened to the skirt. The satin was cut in a straight line from shoulder to hem, but clung to her hips and showed her round stomach, even the hollow of her navel. A long string of glass beads hung down to her waist.

"Is that a new dress?" Jess asked.

Miranda looked at her. "Don't you like it?"

"It's all right, I guess."

"All right? It's the latest style."

"It looks as if you haven't got anything on under it. I can see your button."

Miranda glanced downward and pulled in her stomach. She bunched the glittering beads in her hand and played with them as she wandered about the room. "I don't know what time I'll be home," she said abruptly. "I'm going for a drive in the country with Mr. Williams." She peered into the mirror over the mantelpiece, but it was not her reflection that interested her. She was looking at us. "What are you girls planning to do this evening?" she asked.

We had no plans. We exchanged despairing glances.

Miranda turned around. "Don't bite your nails, Rose," she said sharply. She made an impatient gesture that included us both. "For heaven's sake don't sit there looking like lumps of pudding. Surely you can find something to do with yourselves. You're not babies. You don't have to be led around by the hand and told what to do. Why don't you go to the movies? Here." She opened her bag and handed us two dollars. "I don't care where you go, but for heaven's sake do *something.* Don't sit around in here mooning."

She plumped up the cushions on the couch and shoved a pile of magazines behind a chair. We understood that she wanted to be alone when Jack Williams arrived.

We went to the kitchen, feeling banished. Jess looked in the paper to see what was playing at the Palace. The advertisement promised "Midnight kisses . . . pleasure-mad women . . . the bold naked truth." Not the sort of entertainment we were looking for that night.

It was exactly the sort of entertainment Clara was looking for, she said when she came in a few minutes later.

The bold naked truth; she really owed it to her future to bone up on that. And *why* didn't Jess and I want to see it? How would we know how to act when we started going out with boys if we ignored such an opportunity to learn about life?

When the doorbell rang and she discovered who was calling, she was all agog. "Is Miranda actually going out on a real date with him? Did she say where they're going? There's a dance at the tennis club. Is he taking her there?"

She strained her ears toward the hall, but all she heard was Miranda saying what a lovely evening, and asking was it cool enough for a wrap. Jack Williams's reply was given in such a low voice that we missed it.

As soon as the door closed, we went into the living room to watch out the front windows. Across the street, clearly visible beyond the jail yard, Hattie was planted in a window, watching, too.

Jack Williams took Miranda's arm and helped her into his long blue sedan. He walked around and got in himself, then drove to the end of the street, made a U turn, and drove back again. He and Miranda were both laughing, looking at one another, not in a way that suggested they were oblivious of the people sitting on porches all down the street, but rather as if they were doing a scene in a play before an audience, portraying a sophisticated couple setting out for an evening of gaiety. Mrs. Peters, out for a stroll, stopped in her tracks and watched until the car had rounded the corner. "Did you see that?" she sang out to some invisible watcher—Mrs. Dove, probably—on the porch next door.

We went to the movies with Clara after all. The feature picture—nothing like the eye-opener promised by the advertisements—was half over, and when the lights came on for intermission Jess and I decided to go home. At some time during the film the thought had struck both of us that Miranda and Jack Williams might have returned from their drive in the country and would be alone in the house.

Clara elected to stay. She found that she was sitting next to a boy she knew slightly, an older boy of about eighteen, a clerk in the hardware store. She began a conversation with him, hoping, when we left, that people would think he was with her. She put her mouth close to my ear and whispered, "If he asks me, I'm going to let him walk home with me."

There was no one in the house when we got home, only Mr. Parker sitting on the back steps in the dark, looking terribly lonesome. He had picked up a quart of ice cream at the corner store, expecting to find someone to share it with him. Of all the roomers, he was our favorite, a poor homeless man with a sick wife, grateful for small attentions. It was a new thing for us to see in someone else such an eagerness to be liked, to be thought well of. It placed Mr. Parker on our side, and we went out of our way to assure him that *we* liked him. Jess mended his socks for him.

"Perhaps your mother is visiting a neighbor," he said. "I noticed your car is in the garage."

"No, she's gone out for a drive with someone."

"Oh . . . well . . ." He looked dejectedly at the melting ice cream. "I suppose we'd better eat this."

As we spooned it into saucers, someone came in the front door. Mr. Parker looked up hopefully, but it was only Miss Kennedy. She joined us in the kitchen and we had a sad little party.

A memory of London came back to me, of the days when we used to go to Madam's house on Miranda's afternoon off; of Miranda slapping the chauffeur's wrist and saying, "Now, you behave yourself, Sidney." I imagined her sitting in some lovers' lane with Jack Williams, laughing and saying, "Now, you behave yourself, Jack."

Children do not acknowledge the subtler emotions. If anyone had told me that I was jealous, that I was indulging in self-pity, I would have denied it emphatically. But the truth is that I saw both Jess and myself as poor neglected things, with the prospect ahead of being even more neglected, even discarded and left to face on our own whatever lay beyond childhood.

While I was thus preoccupied with myself, Clara was having her own troubles. The boy who had sat beside her at the movies—his name was Elward Adams—*had* offered to walk home with her, and a little later Mrs. Dove caught them kissing on the front porch. Clara told me afterward that she thought Elward was an awful drip, but he had asked for a kiss and she had consented because she felt she needed the experience.

Mrs. Dove raised a terrible fuss. It struck me later that all through Clara's teens her mother seemed to be waiting for her to go wrong, *knew* she would go wrong sooner or later, so it might as well happen quickly and be done with. Each time Clara was caught in some misdemeanor—if you can call a thing like kissing a boy on the front porch a misdemeanor—her mother pounced on it almost gratefully, one would think, as if she were saying to herself, "Ah, at last!"

I don't know what all she said to Clara that night. Plenty, I imagine. Mr. Dove and Grampa Higgins added their opinions, but all Clara did was look stubborn. She wouldn't cry and she wouldn't promise to reform. When they had all said their say she went up to her room, locked herself in, dressed in her best clothes, packed a suitcase, and left home by way of the kitchen roof. Wearing lipstick and powder, her eyelashes bristling with mascara, dragging her old cardboard suitcase, and with two dollars and fifty cents in her handbag, she came to our door to ask if she could spend the night with us before embarking for Hollywood, which was where she had decided to go.

She had not cried at home, but as soon as she stepped inside our kitchen she burst into such a flood of tears that all the make-up she had put on to impress the world washed away in a minute, and we could hardly make out what she was saying. Miss Kennedy had gone to her room by this time. Mr. Parker was still in the kitchen.

He reacted to Clara's tears the way shy men usually do. He said, "Oh, dear, dear! Oh, look now, you mustn't!" and stood around with his handkerchief ready for when she decided to mop up. Looking back at him from this distance, it seems to me that he was always consoling, though so in need of consolation himself; always standing around with a handkerchief ready for when the tears stopped.

Clara was mopping up when Miranda arrived.

"Oh, honey, what is it?" Miranda cried. "What have they been doing to you?" She drew Clara into her arms. Of course Clara began to weep all over again. She repeated her sad story. "They're so God-damned narrow-minded," she hiccupped. "All I did was let this jerk kiss me, and you'd think from the way they carried on that he'd raped me in broad daylight on the courthouse steps. My mother quoting the Bible. . . ."

"But I don't understand," Miranda said. "What did happen? Surely your mother wouldn't make a fuss because some boy kissed you. Haven't you been kissed before?"

Clara mumbled, "No."

"At your age?" Miranda exclaimed. "What have you been doing all these years?"

Clara giggled hysterically, and confessed, "I never had a chance before. I wanted to find out what it was like."

"All this to-do about a little kiss," Miranda said. "I simply cannot understand your mother. I hope you enjoyed it."

"No, I didn't," Clara said. "It was all teeth. I don't think he'd had any practice, either."

"Now, no more crying," Miranda said. "Look what you've done to Mr. Parker's nice handkerchief, too. Just remember the next time you want to kiss a boy, do it where your mother can't see you, not on the front porch. If I were you I'd go home and forget the whole thing."

"I'm not going home. I'm going away. I've got my suitcase."

"You're under age, you know. Your parents could have you brought back."

"I won't be treated like a baby. I'm going to Hollywood."

"But think how silly you'd feel if they sent someone after you," Miranda coaxed. "Your mother might blame me, too."

"Yes, it would place Mrs. Arnold in an awkward position if you went to Hollywood from here," Mr. Parker sided in. "Your parents might say she aided and abetted you."

"Well, I wouldn't want to get you in wrong." Clara was wavering. All the crying had done her good.

In the end, she decided to go home. Smothering giggles, we crept across the back yards and boosted her onto the kitchen roof, which formed a balcony outside her bedroom window. Mr. Parker handed up her suitcase. He kept putting one finger to his lips and saying "Shh!" in a voice that was louder than anyone else's whisper, and glancing over his shoulder. He was suppressing laughter,

too, and for the first time since I had known him, he forgot to look sad.

In bed, later, Jess said, "Have you noticed the way he
looks at Miranda?"

You would have to be blind not to. When Miranda
came into a room where he was his look of melancholy,
though it did not fade altogether, was overlaid with a sort
of wistful tenderness. His eyes followed her about.

"He's the person she ought to marry," Jess said.

I did not remind her that he already had a wife.

Mr. Parker's wife was no more real to us than a myth.
We had visited her once at the sanatorium—only once, because Miranda felt it was unwise to expose ourselves to
germs—and found, not the frail wasted creature we had
expected to see, but a plump woman with rosy cheeks. Her
substantial appearance could not dispel our conviction
that she little more than haunted the room she was in; she
would fade away soon. A person who had spent a whole
year in a sanatorium never came out of it alive.

Miranda's drive in the country with Jack Williams
marked the beginning of a courtship that was attentively
watched by the townspeople. They liked to keep up to
date on who was courting whom, and to speculate as to
the probable outcome. Jack and Miranda furnished live-
lier gossip than usual, because neither conformed to local
standards of conventionality.

She had been a widow just over six months; she should
not be running around with men so soon, especially with
such a gay blade as he was. He had piqued a number of
town matrons by ignoring their nice daughters. Mothers
and daughters both could have forgiven him for being a
gay blade, even—considering his money and position—
for occasionally preferring the company of loose women,

as he was said to do, as long as he showed some indication of eventually intending to settle down. It was a bachelor's privilege to sow a few wild oats.

The thing was, did he intend to settle down, or why was he courting Miranda? She was neither a loose woman nor one of the town's nice girls. She was somewhere in between —though just where, nobody knew for sure. She had not been in Southport long enough to be placed in a definite category. Her appearance sometimes gave rise to the conjecture that she might be a bit too worldly for local tastes, but it was difficult to tell about outsiders.

For all the town ladies knew, she might turn out to *be* a loose woman; on the other hand, her rather flamboyant appearance might, in London, be considered merely fashionable. "We shall have to wait and see," the ladies probably told one another. "Remember, she is an outsider. It's so hard to tell about them." Jack was a newcomer, which was quite a different thing from being an outsider. His family had been known and respected in the town for more than half a century.

In the beginning, he sent Miranda flowers and candy, and telephoned well beforehand when he wanted to call; but his way of entertaining her was to take her for a drive somewhere, and after a time this began to give the affair a clandestine appearance, as if there was some reason why they could not be seen together in public. I find it impossible to imagine what they talked about when they were alone. Before other people, the few they did see, they exchanged bantering small talk. They could not keep that up when they were alone, surely, yet I can imagine them behaving in no other way. Their laughter always bypassed someone else.

"I notice he doesn't invite you to one of those brawls at the golf club," Hattie sniffed. "I daresay he thinks you're not good enough for that bunch. Where *do* you go? And don't give me that old song about a drive in the country. You can't keep on driving for five hours straight. I understand he's got a nice little cottage at the beach," she hinted. "A regular hideaway."

Miranda scarcely listened. The excitement of being courted, of being showered with gifts, of sporting about in the most expensive car in town, made her blind to any little fly in the ointment, such as when Jack made excuses for not taking her where his friends were. She thought she was irresistible, she could twist any man around her little finger.

After a few weeks of being the perfect suitor, Jack relaxed a bit. He forgot to telephone beforehand, and took to dropping in unannounced. Jess and I easily convinced ourselves that he called on Miranda only when he had nothing better to do, and told her so. We spent quite a lot of time collecting and cataloging anything about him that could be regarded as a fault.

If he suspected that we did not like him, he gave no sign. He was always friendly and lighthearted. We could not deny that he had a way of livening up a room when he stepped into it. Sometimes when Jess or I answered his knock at the front door he would pretend he was a salesman selling some improbable item, such as fur-lined tennis shoes. We smiled frostily.

Inside, he would lounge in an upholstered chair, flicking cigarette butts into the empty fireplace, joking, flattering Jess and me. He called us Princess Dark-eyes and Goldilocks, or the beautiful Arnold girls, but no amount of flattery could make us like him.

Miranda scolded us for not appreciating his jokes. "Where are your manners?" she asked.

"Well, I don't like him," Jess said, glowering. "I don't know why he keeps coming here."

"He comes to see me, as you very well know," Miranda said, "and I'll thank you to treat him with respect. Is it unreasonable of me to expect a little happiness? I'm young. I have my life to live, the same as other people."

"You're past thirty-five," Jess reminded.

Miranda's eyes filled with angry tears. "I'll thank you to keep your opinions to yourself," she snapped. A little later she said, "*Why* don't you like him?"

"It's only that he drives other people away sometimes. Like Mr. Parker the other night. He got up and left the room. He thought he was in the way."

"I'm not in my dotage," Miranda said, not listening.

We were greatly relieved when, in August, Jack stopped coming for several weeks. Hattie did not allow Miranda to forget that he was entertaining what she called "his ritzy New York friends." As he had already explained to Miranda that these were his grandmother's friends and must be entertained by him no matter how much it displeased him, Hattie's hints and innuendos had little effect. During this period she read Dorothy Dix letters aloud to Miranda. " 'Dear Miss Dix: My boy friend says he loves me, but never takes me anywhere. All he wants us to do is be by ourselves and neck. What do you advise? Perplexed.' 'Dear Perplexed: It is obvious that your boy friend's intentions are not honorable. You would be well advised to terminate this affair. Dorothy Dix.' "

"If there is one thing I cannot abide," Miranda said, "it's people poking and prying into other people's affairs."

"I don't expect you to take advice from me," Hattie said, "but just remember this: Dorothy Dix is the world's greatest authority on affairs of the heart. And if what I've just read isn't your problem to a T, then I don't know what is. As I said to Roy the other night, it does seem funny the way Mr. Williams keeps those friends of his to himself. A person would think he was ashamed."

"They are his grandmother's friends, not his."

"That's not what I meant," Hattie said.

Miranda flared up. "Will you kindly take your insinuations elsewhere?"

When old Mrs. Williams's visitors had gone, Jack began coming to our house again. He gave Miranda a solid-silver bracelet and earrings to match.

It was not a conventional courtship, by Southport standards. People didn't quite know what to make of it. "Is he going with her, or isn't he?" Clara asked me. Obviously, she had heard this question asked at home. Mrs. Dove and Mrs. Scavey both began to stay away from our house, rather pointedly, giving the impression that they did not wish to intrude.

Mr. Peters, coming around each night with the day's meat, left no doubt in anyone's mind that he was watching the affair with interest. "I've got to admit it agrees with you," he said to Miranda one night. "Yes, sir. Never saw you looking better."

"What do you mean?" Miranda glared at him...

He edged closer and jogged her with his elbow. "How about you stepping out with me some night?" He pretended to dodge away from her sudden fury, and went off laughing.

Miss Kennedy gave up her room for a cheaper one nearer her office. This was a matter of convenience for her, and had nothing to do with Jack Williams's repeated visits. Luckily, another roomer was found almost at once. This was Mr. Stuart, a new teacher at the county academy. He came in September.

I went to my first dance that summer, with James. The event is worth mentioning because it taught me that you cannot always judge a person by the face he presents to the world. People are many-sided, and the clever ones know which side to show.

I had never thought of James as being particularly clever. Everyone agreed that he was a nice boy, meaning that he was quiet and polite. I liked him well enough, but when he invited me to go to the Saturday-night dance in the park with him, I did not look forward to the event with anything resembling pleasurable anticipation. What did please me was that I had got ahead of Jess and Clara. They had never been invited to a dance. Clara pointed out that it was only James who had asked me, after all, and no doubt he had picked on me because nobody else would go with him.

James was clever enough to make sure that my dancing would pass muster before inviting me to the dance, at any rate. We practiced in our kitchen, to music from the radio, trotting sedately back and forth with set solemn faces. At the end of each piece James would throw in a few extra steps, as if he were trying to catch me unawares, and occasionally he would show off by executing the more intricate steps of the Charleston or the Black Bottom by himself. These two dances, though probably out of date in other parts of the world, were still fashionable in our neighborhood. James's professional demonstration surprised me no end, but more surprises were to come.

I have since concluded that James wanted to go to the dance by himself, but his mother wouldn't let him. I can imagine her reaction when, earlier, he had asked permission to go. "What is this dance, dear? Is it a school dance?"

"No, it's just the Saturday-night dance at the roller-

skating rink in the park. It's the last one of the summer.
Everybody goes."

"Not boys as young as you, I'm sure."

He would spend some time convincing her that all his
friends went. She would ask whom he intended to take as
a partner, and he would say, "I wasn't thinking of *taking*
anyone."

"But you can't go to a dance alone."

That was exactly what James wanted to do, to go by
himself and dance with the waitresses and the girls from
the canning factory who went to the park in pairs, hoping
to be picked up. "A lot of boys go alone," he told his
mother.

"But if you went by yourself there would be nobody to
dance with. If you're sure it's a nice place, you could ask
Rose's mother if Rose can go with you."

James would assure his mother that it was really a very
nice dance, well chaperoned, quite safe for young inno-
cents like himself, and in the end Mrs. Seavey gave her
consent. She herself asked Miranda if I might accompany
James.

On Saturday night, James called for me around seven
o'clock. Jess had gone off to play badminton with Miss
Harris and Miss King. Miranda and Mr. Parker were listening to the radio. Miranda was at loose ends that week
end, for Jack Williams was off somewhere else, on one of
his many trips.

"What a grown-up young lady!" Mr. Parker exclaimed.
"You look like Cinderella herself. You'll be the belle of
the ball."

This was sheer nonsense, but it pleased me. My dress, a
sprigged muslin with a blue sash, was embarrassingly childish. James wore white flannels, very smart, though obviously handed down from some uncle, and a blue blazer.

He had washed his yellow hair and darkened it down with brilliantine, so that it smelled of lavender instead of cooking fat.

"Now have a good time, lovies." Miranda kissed us both. Tears sprang into her eyes. "I can't believe it's my baby, going off to a dance with a young man!"

She straightened James's tie and rested her hands on his shoulders for a minute. "Why, you're taller than I am! You look so handsome. I wish you were *my* beau."

He shuffled back a few steps as if he had been thrown off balance, and gave an embarrassed laugh. "Well, gee, I wouldn't mind that, either!"

Mr. Parker pulled a roll of bills from his pocket and made James take two dollars. "This is a great occasion," he said. "A big night."

We walked all the way to the park. This was James's idea. What we saved on carfare we could spend on ice cream and drinks, he said. We arrived at the roller-skating rink where the dance was held a good hour before the orchestra started tuning up and the early birds ventured onto the floor. We were the first of the early birds. "Might as well get our money's worth," James said as we stepped out.

Presently the hall began to fill up, not so much with couples as with unattached men and women intent upon making new friends. The girls formed an animated group near the door, laughing, chewing gum, powdering their noses. The men, lounging in careless attitudes at the opposite side of the entrance, eyed them judiciously. Occasionally two girls danced together to show how good they were. I recognized several of them: a waitress from the ice-cream parlor, her sister who worked in the five-and-ten, and the older sister of a girl in our class at school. Half a dozen boys of James's age loitered nearby.

After about the fourth dance James said, "You wait here. I'll get a drink." He darted off, leaving me alone at the back of the hall, returning after an interval with two bottles of ginger beer and a friend whom he introduced as Charlie Somebody. "Charlie wants to dance with you," he said, and rushed off again.

Charlie and I finished our drinks, and as he foxtrotted me through the next number I looked over his shoulder and saw James dancing with the waitress. They were doing a fast Charleston, a spectacular performance that made everybody turn and look. It made people avoid them, too. Some couples stopped dancing to watch.

I didn't dance with James again that evening. Each time the music stopped he sought me out with a drink of pop, a hot dog, or an ice-cream cone, plus a new partner he had recruited from the stag line. These recruits, it dawned on me after a time, were not all boys he knew, even. Before the evening was over I had learned, too, that he was palming me off as his sister. Presumably he said to them, the boys he didn't know, "Listen, bud, I'm stuck with my sister. Be a sport and dance with her, will you?" In return for this favor they got free drinks or hot dogs or whatever James was passing out in the way of refreshments at the moment.

Late in the evening I looked up to see Hattie and Miranda standing among the girls near the door. They had dropped in to look on for a minute, I knew, but seeing them there, standing around as if they were waiting to be picked up, gave me a funny feeling.

"Is that someone waving at you?" the boy I was dancing with asked.

I deliberately looked in the wrong place, and shook my head. "I don't see anyone."

Just before we left the dance, while I visited the ladies'

room, James slipped back for one last whirl with the waitress from the ice-cream parlor. She was a pretty, flashy girl of about twenty, with dark hair arranged in little half-moon spit curls against her cheeks, and dark flirtatious eyes. She wore a beaded dress with a bow on one shoulder. Her sister, the one who worked in the five-and-ten, was not so pretty, but much sought after as a dancing partner. These two girls were rumored to be very fast. Clara had told me that they went out with traveling salesmen. Their name was Hunter. I never learned their first names. Everybody called them the Hunter girls.

As we rode home in the trolley, James's face assumed its usual expressionless expression. "Did you have a good time?" he asked.

"Oh, yes, lovely!" I said. Actually, I felt that I hadn't done too badly. I had danced with ten different boys, which would sound well when I casually mentioned it to Jess and Clara. "Did you?" I asked.

He gave me an appraising look. "Oh, it was all right." He added with a straight face, "You were so popular I never got a chance to dance with you again. All the boys kept pestering me to meet you."

I did not flatter myself. I knew he was warning me not to give him away. We sat side by side and could think of nothing to say. Already he had reverted back to the James I had known before, a nice boy you could see half a dozen times without remembering what he looked like. I had never been up so late before, and besides being tired I was uncomfortably aware that I had had too much to eat and drink. The lateness of the hour, my discomfort, and the letdown after the excitement of the dance, combined to give the ride home an illusional quality. I felt as if I had left the real James back at the dance, and it was only his ghost sitting there beside me.

I had avoided thinking about the Hunter girls, but as we walked up from the trolley stop on Main Street, our footsteps echoing back from the darkened houses—for it was now past midnight—something I had been running away from in my mind caught up with me. The pretty Hunter girl, the waitress, was an indefinable caricature of Miranda. As if they were two figures on display my mind circled around them, comparing features, hoping to reject any likeness. There was no discernible physical resemblance, yet something about them—something not seen, but sensed—was the same. One was a disconcerting echo of the other.

Our house was in darkness. In the Seavey's house, a light burned in the front window and Mrs. Seavey's head was outlined against it. The angle of her head against the light suggested that she had one eye on the clock, one ear cocked toward the door. Seeing her there made James quicken his steps. He opened our front door for me, said good night, and scurried off across the lawn. I felt my way through the sleeping house and up the back stairs. Jess and Miranda were both asleep. I undressed and got into bed without disturbing either of them.

I dreamed that I was back at the dance, this time standing on the sidelines, watching. The Hunter girl was there, doing a wild whirling dance. Everybody stepped back into the shadows to make room for her, and soon she was in a space by herself, with a changing partner whose face I could not see. Then she turned into Miranda, and against the looming shadows filled with eyes I saw, suddenly, that she was in her teddies. Someone leaned close to me and said in a loud ventriloquist's voice, "Is that your mother?" My denial went echoing around the hall. I tried to find a door out, but there were walls behind me and people on all sides.

Miranda came running from her room across the hall. "Oh, baby, what is it?" She turned on the light. "What's frightened you?"

"I thought I was somewhere else."

"I'm here, lovie, you mustn't be afraid. Did you have a bad old dream?" She took me in her arms and nestled my head in the warm hollow of her shoulder. "Look, you're right here in your own bed, safe and sound, and you've waked up Jess."

"You almost kicked me out of bed, too." Jess screwed up her eyes against the light. "Where did you think you were, sitting up yelling like that? Was something after you? It's one o'clock in the morning, too."

"Would you like to come in with me for a bit, ducky?" Miranda asked, lifting my head to lay her cheek against mine. "I won't let any old bogeys get you. . . . Then go to sleep, like a good girl." She turned out the light and went back to her own room.

"I suppose you've been eating all sorts of trash," Jess said, but she threw one arm across my shoulder. "Now, don't have any more silly nightmares."

"I'm afraid to sleep," I said. I was still within the haunted perimeter of my dream. If I closed my eyes I would be drawn back to the dark center of it in a minute.

"Oh, well . . . I'll stay awake for a while, too, then," Jess said. "It won't kill me."

"Oh, it's all sunshine and roses at this stage of the game, no doubt," Hattie said. "All sunshine and roses, tra-la-la. It'll be a different story later on."

With such remarks, and dark hints about the future, she helped Jess and me to dislike Jack Williams more and more. "You poor children," she said more than once, standing looking at us with a heavy sigh and a dismal shake of her head, as if she had a foreknowledge of some dire fate in store for us.

We grumbled, "Are you going out with him *again?*" so many times that Miranda said she was sick of hearing it.

"Well, I wish he wouldn't hang around here. Nobody wants him."

Jess finally said outright, "Are you going to marry him?"

"Would you mind?" Miranda asked.

"Yes, I would," Jess said. "If you're so set on getting married—though I don't see why—there are plenty of other men in the world."

"I believe I'm capable of choosing my own husband," Miranda told her.

One day just before school started in September Jack walked in on a Sunday afternoon and surprised Hattie in the kitchen with her feet on the table. She left at once. "My God, does he live here now?" she grumbled. "Popping in and out at all hours of the day without so much as knocking!

He had come that day to discuss a business proposition with Miranda. He had heard that Mrs. Fuller wanted to sell her beauty shop and move to Boston, where she had another sister, also widowed. He proposed—or his grandmother proposed; it amounted to the same thing—to buy the shop and install Miranda as manageress. Miranda accepted at once. She thought he was offering her this position as a first step in acquainting her with his business affairs. The salary quoted was much more than Mrs. Fuller was paying her, and this, too, she interpreted as an indication that Jack had plans for elevating her to a rather more important post than that of a mere employee.

The sale of the shop was completed during the following week, and shortly afterward Mrs. Fuller and her son moved to Boston.

Chapter Ten

Clara and James and I had passed the high-school entrance examinations, and when school opened in September we enrolled at the county academy. This was a large converted dwelling, one of the old mansions built around the middle of the last century. There were perhaps half a dozen houses in Southport which could properly be called mansions—the Williams's house was one of them—and they had been built, according to local historians, by men who had made their fortunes in the whaling industry.

The whaling ships had gone out from this Canadian port, too, we were told, though not in such numbers as from Nantucket and New Bedford. Only the Williams's house and one other were still used as dwellings. The high cost of living—how often we heard *that* phrase in the twenties!—had forced other owners to move into less expensive quarters. One house had been turned into a convent, another into a sanatorium for tubercular patients (where poor Mrs. Parker was), another into a home for old people.

The academy was set in parklike grounds with lawns and trees all around, but no flowers. Shrubs inside an iron paling secluded it from the street. A wide cinder drive curved in one gateway and out the other. The stone walls of the building were covered with ivy. Inside, enormous halls were paneled with dark wood, and a wide stairway went up and up to the roof, where a stained-glass dome let down a rainbow of light. The classrooms had bay windows of curved glass, and fireplaces that were never lit.

The old pantries had been made over into offices, the

servants' sleeping quarters into cloakrooms for the girls. The boys' washrooms were somewhere in the cavernous basement, the front rooms of which had been turned into laboratories where, under a threatening maze of furnace pipes, we experimented with litmus paper and glass tubes.

With all the changes, the old house managed to retain a certain air. I could easily imagine what it had been like before the Turkish carpets were ripped up and the floors varnished, before the chandeliers were taken down, and the rows of scarred desks bolted to the classroom floors. The red velvet curtains and the books in glass cases might have been taken out the day before. The rooms waited for them to come back.

Looking around on my first day, I decided that I liked the scholarly, ivy-walled atmosphere of the school. This would be a safe place to spend the next four years. (Jess and I had agreed that if Miranda married Jack Williams we would ask Mr. Parker if we could live with him.) During the opening-day speech of Mr. Stanley, the principal, I sat with rapt attention while he went on about the great vista opening up before us, the road to knowledge, and so on. My enthusiasm was not dimmed by the fact that all the while he was talking he wore the look of a man who has by some misfortune found himself in undesirable company.

This expression of distaste was habitual with him. During classes he would sometimes lay down his chalk, give everyone a look as if to say, "I can no longer tolerate the sight of you," and stalk off to his office in the old pantries, where he presumably took naps. We did not leave our seats while he was away, or speak above whispers. We soon learned that he might pop back again at any minute, saying nothing, but giving that chilling stare, far more effective than words, that seemed to be directed, like the eyes in a photograph, at each separate individual.

We called him Simon Legree. It seemed clever to have unflattering nicknames for certain teachers. Mr. Owens was Andy Gump, Miss Webster, with her blackheads and her dank hair braided into earmuffs, we called Greasy Webster. The fat French teacher was called Fatty Arbuckle.

Mr. Owens was a pale ugly young man with a high forehead and a wide bony jaw, so thin that when he sat down he folded up like a collapsible chair. Some disease of the skin had scarred and pitted his face. His unattractive appearance, his expression of extreme frustration, as if he had exhausted himself plotting a means of escape from some tormentor, invited ridicule. Within a week we had all learned that he was no more capable of keeping order than a scarecrow. He was said to write poetry, too. Miss Webster, in such a continuous state of nerves that her voice seemed on the point of going off into a shrill scream, also invited ridicule, and got plenty of it. Nine mornings out of ten her moist eyes and swollen cheeks suggested that she had spent the night crying in the little house where she lived with her widowed mother. Untroubled by any feelings of guilt or compassion, for my desire to be liked came before everything else, I joined in the persecution of these two. I could not risk not joining in the laughter of the crowd.

Mr. Stuart, the new physics teacher, who roomed at our house, was the only one not given a nickname. He was too much admired, being young and good-looking and single. I fell in love with Mr. Stuart—Frederick, as I dared to call him in my dreams—and since I could not, for fear of being laughed at, expose my unrequited passion to any person, I was driven to keeping a diary. But I could not commit my true feelings to paper, nor refer to my idol by name. I called him 'he.' "Yesterday I opened the door for him, as he had forgotten his key. He said 'What a day!' (it was raining) and went upstairs before I could think of anything to say to keep him there." "Today I went into his room with Mrs. Walsh to help change the sheets. His towels smell of Lifebuoy soap, which he keeps in a soapdish in his room. He leaves letters lying around. They are from his mother, not from girls. He is twenty-eight years old."

I was not the only one who had a crush on Mr. Stuart. Because of him, because he lived at our house, Jess and I found ourselves, shortly after the school year began, enjoying the unusual and heady sensation of being popular with other girls, who wanted to learn every detail of his private life.

"Is he engaged?" they asked us. "Does he have a girl's picture on his dresser?" He had three pictures, one of his parents and one each of his two sisters. "Does he get *letters* from girls, then? You must see what mail he gets. . . . Goodness, I don't see how you can *sleep* with him in the same house. Doesn't it give you a funny feeling knowing he's in the next room? Well, all right, then, on the next floor. . . . What is he like? I mean, what does he do? Does he ever sit in his room reading? Does he like sports?" He played tennis with Mr. Brooks, who kindly took him under his wing, introduced him to town society and even handed over a couple of girls that he, Mr. Brooks, had grown tired of.

Being popular was such a new thing for Jess and me that we hardly knew how to deal with it. We did not trust it to last. The least jolt might disturb it, we thought. Mr. Peters delivered such a jolt when he played one of his practical jokes on us. He let on to a few of his more disreputable acquaintances that our house was a speak-easy, and for about a week a procession of strange men made their way to our door to ask in a furtive whisper if they could buy a case of our "special."

Miranda soon caught on—Hattie told her, in fact—and said, "How dare he play one of his childish tricks on me! I could sue him for defamation of character. I *will* sue him. A common little butcher that I wouldn't lower myself to spit on, daring to ridicule me!" She went to see a lawyer the next day.

After a talk with him she was forced to conclude that the country was in worse shape than she had supposed. The lawyer told her that, even supposing Mr. Peters had told every person in the country that we were in the bootlegging business, Miranda still wouldn't have a case against him, since she had suffered no actual damage as a result.

"If that's what you call justice in this country!" she grumbled to Hattie. She had no one but Hattie to confide in, for Jack Williams had gone on another trip to New York, and was not expected back for some weeks.

Miranda did confide in Mr. Parker, when he came home for the week end. He was indignant enough for everyone. "That little pig!" he said. "It's just like him to pick on an innocent woman. He'd have thought twice about playing a trick like that on you if there'd been a man around to protect you. We'll see how brave he is when it comes to dealing with me. I'm going to give Mr. Smarty Peters a piece of my mind."

"No, you mustn't do that."

"I won't have anyone mistreating you."

"I've made up my mind to ignore the whole thing. That's the only way to treat people like that. He's beneath my contempt."

"Well, you let me know if he starts any more funny stuff. I'll deal with him."

But no more customers came. Mr. Peters had got what fun he could out of us and had gone on to someone else.

Of course we stopped buying meat at his shop, and Miranda was careful to be looking the other way when she saw him on the street. Then one night, about a week after we had stopped dealing with him, he came around, barefaced as if nothing had happened, to deliver a package of meat we had not ordered.

" 'Ere we are, your ladyship," he said in his most jovial Cockney voice. " 'Ere's today's special. Pork chops, half price to our regular customers, for one day only." He pushed his way into the kitchen to lay a brown-paper parcel on the counter, then took an order pad and a pencil from his pocket. "Tomorrow's special: corned beef," he announced. "I'll put you down for—let's see—three pounds be okay?" He flipped the pad into his pocket and lounged toward the door. "Well, ta ta, ladies. I'm off to home and mother, as the man said."

"One moment, Mr. Peters!" Miranda snapped. "I don't recall ordering anything from your shop."

He allowed an indulgent smile to spread across his face, as if he had caught her out in some prank. "Forgot to, didn't you? Well, sir, that's the kind of service I give my customers. They forget to phone in their orders, I don't let them go hungry. I just ramble around with the day's special as per usual."

Miranda said in an icy tone, "Now will you be so kind as to take your damned special and ramble off with it?"

His jaw dropped in an exaggerated expression of dismay. "Aw, gee whiz, are you *mad* at me?"

"Mad at you! I wouldn't lower myself."

"What have I done?" He was all innocent bewilderment.

Miranda had never intended to give him the satisfaction of knowing his little joke had upset her, but this was too much. "You know very well!" she snapped. "I suppose you thought it was very funny, sending those people up here, telling them my house was a speak-easy. I suppose you thought that was very funny indeed!"

Mr. Peters sighed. "Well, that's life, I guess. Here I thought I was doing you a favor, bringing a few extra customers your way. I thought you'd appreciate it."

Miranda tensed with fury. "How dare you insult me!" She picked up the meat and took a threatening step toward him. "Get out of my house this minute!"

He pretended to be frightened, but his eyes glittered with sly mirth. "No fair hitting a man with glasses!" he cried, and ducked outside just as the parcel hit the doorpost. We could hear him laughing all the way up the alley to his own house.

Miranda stormed about the kitchen, and threw some dishes into the sink so hard that two cups broke. "Oh, the insolence!" she cried. "Daring to show his face in my house!" Every name she called Mr. Peters and every dish she broke made her feel better, but Jess got up and closed the doors leading to the dining room and the hall. Even so, we could not be sure that Miranda's voice would not penetrate to the second floor where all the roomers, including Mr. Stuart, were listening.

Jess said suddenly, "For heaven's sake, calm down. There's no need to let the whole town in on your quarrels."

The sharpness of her voice made Miranda stare. "Now, don't you start," she said.

"Well, you shouldn't have thrown that meat at him. It wasn't a ladylike thing to do."

"Don't you criticize me!" Miranda's head reared back.

"I do any criticizing that's to be done around here," she said.

As soon as the dishes were cleared away she set up the sewing machine, for she was putting these dull evenings while Jack Williams was away to good use, running up some new dresses and underwear for herself.

"More new clothes?" Hattie said when she came in later. "Aren't you getting to be the fashion plate! Now where, in Southport, do you expect to wear a dress like that? It looks more like something you'd wear to a wedding. . . . And what is *this* gorgeous creation?" She held up some peach-colored satin with lace attached. "A nightgown?"

"Put that down. I haven't finished basting it yet."

"A nightgown like that would come in handy if the house caught fire at three o'clock in the morning. You could rush out into the street in it, looking like the Queen of Sheba. Otherwise, I can't see where you'll get the good of it—a woman sleeping alone."

"I like nice things," Miranda said.

"That's obvious," Hattie observed. "I daresay if the truth were known you *have* plans for wearing these fancy garments—plans that you're keeping to yourself. However, if you prefer to keep your best friend in the dark, not to mention your own children, far be it from me to criticize. You know best, no doubt. What's the latest from your boy friend?" she asked idly, draping a length of red chiffon over one shoulder and turning before the mirror.

Miranda pressed one foot down harder on the treadle and did not answer.

Hattie waited for the whirring to subside. "He does keep running off to New York, doesn't he? Hardly a month goes by but he pops over there on some excuse or other.

What's the attraction, I wonder? He must think a lot of those friends he visits. Who are they? Do you know them?"

"He is in New York on business," Miranda said.

"Really. Well, I only wondered. As I've mentioned before, he does keep his friends to himself. When they come to Southport to visit him, I mean. You could hardly say they put themselves out to hobnob with the natives, could you? You didn't by any chance happen to meet the two who were here last month—the old thing with the Queen Mary hats and her daughter or niece or whatever?"

Miranda had seen these two women, though she had not met them. The daughter was a tall woman in her late twenties, with pale straight hair and a prim little nun's face. Miss Dorothea Reynolds and her mother.

"They are his grandmother's friends."

"So you mentioned before. Well, as I say, it does seem funny. . . . Are they the ones he's visiting now? Oh, you did say he was on a business trip, didn't you? I suppose you've had letters."

"None of your business, nosey," Miranda said.

One result of Mr. Peters's prank was that Jess refused to pay another visit to Elliot's, the store near the waterfront where we bought the malt to make home brew. "It's not a nice place for girls to go," she told Miranda. "It's always full of men sitting around snickering and making silly remarks."

"You needn't pay any attention to them."

"But why keep on doing things when it makes people laugh at us?"

"Oh, stop being so silly. As if it matters what people say."

"It matters to me," Jess said. "I won't go there again, so there's no use asking."

"All right, if you're going to be so selfish. . . . Rose will go, won't you, love?"

"Rose is not to go, either," Jess said sharply. "I won't allow it." This was her first attempt at outright rebellion, and it made her eyes wet and defiant. "You don't have to drink beer. It makes people think you're fast."

"Fast? I wish you'd stop being ridiculous."

"Well, other women don't drink."

Miranda gave her a long hard stare. "Now who's been putting ideas into your head? Who's been stuffing you with that nonsense?"

"It's not nonsense. You might as well know: Rose and I are not going to make any more beer. If you must drink you can buy it from Mr. Dove. But I wish you'd remember that in this town drinking beer is not considered lady-like."

"Don't you tell me how to behave."

What Jess had meant to be a stern look, designed to warn Miranda that she had decided upon certain rules of conduct and intended to see that they were followed, turned out to be not much more than a stubborn glare. "It's time somebody did," she said.

It was a poor attempt at reform, but I had an idea Jess would do better the next time.

When Jack Williams returned from New York, the news of his engagement preceded him by one day. His grandmother let the cat out of the bag during her weekly marcel at the beauty parlor. The girls, Selena and Gertie and the two juniors, said nothing to Miranda, who, in her new position of manageress, now spent her days behind a pink desk in the reception room, answering the telephone and greeting customers.

Old Mrs. Williams took a keen interest in the business.

She dropped in several times a week to inspect the premises and offer suggestions. For the sake of her future—and because if she expected to retain her position she could not do otherwise—Miranda tolerated these meddlesome visits, though she disliked Mrs. Williams intensely. The memory of past insults simmered inside her like a banked furnace.

"You mustn't let me interfere," the old lady said. "I'm sure you're running things beautifully." She changed the name from Betty's Beauty Parlor to The Powder Puff Beauty Salon, and advised the girls to call themselves beauticians.

When, that Friday afternoon, she said to Selena, "My grandson is engaged to be married, you know," the shop was full of customers, and the news spread quickly around town. Hattie dropped in to see us that evening. Her air of tactful solicitude, as if she were entering a sickroom, puzzled us.

"What's wrong?" Miranda asked. "I thought you were going to see Roy's father tonight."

"I changed my mind. I thought I should come here instead."

"Well, make yourself at home. There's no beer. The girls have suddenly decided that drinking beer is not ladylike." Miranda gave a cross laugh.

"Beer is fattening, anyway." Hattie stuck her feet on the kitchen table and stared gloomily at her plump calves. Then, remembering why she had come, she said in a bright voice, "Do you know what I thought? I thought, tomorrow night, wouldn't it be fun if we all went to the county fair? You've never seen it, Miranda. Everybody in town will be there. They have fashion shows and a ferris wheel, even a dance marathon. You needn't look at the exhibits unless you want to."

"You know Jack is coming home tomorrow," Miranda said, and frowned at Hattie's askance look, which she did not understand.

"But will you be seeing him?"

"I expect to. Why?"

"Nothing. I only wondered. . . ." Hattie swung her feet off the table and reached for a cigarette. "He hasn't written to you? About anything special, I mean?"

"If it's any of your business, Paul Pry, I got a note the day before yesterday, saying he'd be home tomorrow."

"He didn't say anything else?"

"You're getting damned inquisitive, I must say."

"You needn't bite my head off," Hattie said. Having come prepared to offer sympathy, she probably felt that she had reason to be offended. "Perhaps he wants to surprise you," she said.

"What do you mean?"

"Oh, damn, I didn't mean to say that!" Hattie's face went all out of shape. "I could kick myself. But look—" She fished for a handkerchief, in case what she was about to say brought tears. "It's all over town that Jack has got himself engaged to that stuck-up thing from New York, that Dorothea Reynolds."

Miranda went white, but quickly got hold of herself. "What nonsense! Where did you hear that?"

"Roy heard it down town. As soon as he told me, I telephoned a few people. They had heard it, too. So finally I called up the *Gazette* office and asked Fud Sweeney was it true or not, and he said *they* got it from old Mrs. Williams. So that's all I know about it."

"That old woman. I might have known." Miranda laughed in an unnatural way. "Can you imagine Jack marrying an old-maid thing like Dorothea Reynolds? It's too ridiculous. He's going to marry me."

Hattie's eyes popped. "You mean it's all settled? You mean he's engaged to *you?*"

"Not formally. You must remember that poor Alfie's been gone less than a year."

"But it *is* settled?"

"It will be soon," Miranda said. Her confidence had returned. She stood up and looked at herself in the mirror beside the window, flattening the little curls around her temples, pouting her lips, looking pleased with what she saw.

Jess and I looked at one another, seeing our bleak future.

The following night, Saturday, Mr. Parker took Jess and me to the county fair. We left Miranda at home, waiting for Jack Williams.

When we returned home some time after eleven, she was still there, sitting beside the dying coals of the living-room fire. She was alone in the house. Later, when I had gathered some details of what passed between her and Jack Williams, it seemed to me like an act of Providence that all the roomers had decided to go somewhere else that night. I could not have borne it if any of them were listening.

Miranda swiveled around and glared at us. "Where on earth have you been?" she demanded in an angry voice. "Leaving me here all alone!" Her eyes filled with tears.

"Oh, look here!" Mr. Parker hovered anxiously. "Is something wrong? We thought you were with Mr. Williams."

"He's been gone for hours. I sent him packing."

"Good for you!" Jess said.

"Oh!" Miranda buried her face in Jess's shoulder and burst into tears. They were tears of rage, not heartbreak, but Mr. Parker did not know that. He pulled out his handkerchief and said, "Oh, now, look here, you mustn't!" It was exactly the way he had spoken to Clara the time she decided to run away to Hollywood.

"Don't be an old silly, now," Jess coaxed. We both knew it was no use trying to make Miranda stop crying before she was ready to, but we fussed over her and petted her, while Mr. Parker stood fussing by himself, saying, "Oh, dear, dear, isn't there something we can do?"

"He's going to marry that damned old maid," Miranda wailed.

"The two-faced thing!" Jess hugged her and patted her back. "You don't care."

"Oh, the liar! Letting me think all along that he was rich, when he hasn't got a penny to his name!" Miranda was beginning a story she would improve before morning. "That old woman has it all."

"I always thought he was sneaky."

"Shall I make a nice cup of tea?" Mr. Parker asked, on tiptoe with concern.

"Even his car belongs to her!"

When Miranda cried, she did not get soppy and red-nosed, the way most women do. She held her face up and let the tears stream down over her cheeks until all her make-up had been washed away. When, finally, Mr. Parker was able to pat her upturned face with his handkerchief, her lashes were all stuck together and the skin under her eyes was faintly blue.

"Now don't cry any more," he said in that placating voice people accustomed to dealing with invalids acquire. He dabbed away clumsily—for he was trying to avoid any appearance of overfamiliarity—but gently. When Miranda raised her still-brimming eyes to his, his face whitened with such an intensity of feeling that I was embarrassed, and looked away.

He tucked his handkerchief into his pocket and said to Jess and me, "Why don't we take your mother for a nice drive?"

"It's late," we reminded him.

"I know, but your mother is in no condition for sleeping. What she needs is a bit of fresh air. It's a lovely night, too. The harvest moon is out."

We piled into his car and he drove out of town, along a road by the sea, through fishing villages where no light showed in any window. Miranda sat in front. Beside her, Mr. Parker kept a sort of conversation going, dredging up observations about this and that, and scraps of information about the places along the way. "This village is called such-and-such. Look at the funny little houses. Everyone must be in bed. No, there's a man with a lantern, coming up from the wharf. What do you suppose he's doing out so late?"

Jess and I, in the back seat, soon fell asleep. I vaguely remember a moonlit seascape with rocks, and the sucking sound of the tide on shingle as we stopped at some little cove, turned around, and headed home. We were only half awake when we stumbled up the stairs to our bed.

Jess was awake enough to say, "Well, thank the lord for that. Now as soon as Mr. Parker's wife dies, Miranda can marry him."

I think I am safe in assuming that Miranda lay awake planning how she could rearrange the truth and present it to the world without losing face. What had really happened, as I pieced it together later, went something like this:

Shortly after Jack Williams arrived that night, Miranda told him in a joking way that she had heard he was planning to marry someone else. Instead of denying it instantly, as she had expected him to do, he seemed annoyed because the secret had leaked out. He finally admitted that, yes, he was engaged to Miss Dorothea Reynolds, but he hadn't intended to announce the engagement until the following spring, since the wedding was not scheduled to take place until June.

Having got the worst over at the beginning, he then went on to explain and placate and lay the blame for his behavior at someone else's door. It was his grandmother's fault. The old girl was so unreasonable. She had been after him and after him to marry and settle down. *She* had arranged the marriage. . . . Well, yes, of *course* he loved Miranda—they'd had some good times together, hadn't they?—but the old girl had such queer ideas.

She expected him to raise a family, for one thing, and he didn't think Miranda would want to start that all over again. He may even have said "at your age," but I think not. He was trying too hard to appear guiltless and put-upon, a victim of other people's selfishness.

At some point in the evening Miranda threatened to sue him for breach of promise. Then he had to tell her that not one cent of the Williams's money belonged to him. He hadn't a bean. And his grandmother had threatened to cut him out of her will if he didn't marry the girl of her choice. So didn't Miranda see what a spot he was in? How he was being sacrificed? He'd give anything in the world to marry Miranda, had told his grandmother so, in fact, but the old girl simply wouldn't hear of it.

After this insult, he made the mistake of trying to kiss and make up—on a temporary basis. What was doubly wounding, he allowed Miranda to see that he thought she would jump at the chance. His wedding would not take place for another eight months, and why could they not enjoy one another's company until then?

Miranda flew into a temper and reminded him that she was not some little shopgirl that he could use and then cast aside.

All these accusations and explanations and attempts at reconciliation took a good deal longer than I have indicated. I am only giving the highlights, and mostly guessing at that. I am not absolutely certain about the breach-of-promise threat, for instance, though I suspect, from something Miranda let slip later on, that she did make it. At any rate, she finally patched up her wounded dignity enough to send him packing, and warned him not to show his face around our house again.

By morning, Sunday, she had changed the story of the jilting of Miranda Arnold into the jilting of poor Jack Williams. When Hattie came in, which she did on her way home from church, bursting with curiosity, Miranda had her new story all ready. It did not matter to her that Hattie already knew half the true facts.

Jess and I were greatly relieved to think that we had seen the last of Jack Williams, but no daughter likes to see her mother jilted in favor of another, especially when the reason appears to be that she had failed to measure up to the standards required in a wife. So we felt nothing but admiration for Miranda's inventiveness when she said, "Poor Jack, I hope he doesn't take it too hard." She was sitting up in bed eating a noon breakfast, with cold cream on her face. She spread honey on a piece of toast and popped it into her mouth before she added, "I had to tell him I couldn't marry him."

When Hattie, not unreasonably, asked why, she said, "Did you know that he's practically penniless, living on his grandmother's charity? Of course I had to tell him it would be useless to go on seeing him."

Hattie, loyal friend that she was, pretended to swallow

this. She said in a prompting voice, as if supplying some detail Miranda had forgotten, "But he'll get his grandmother's money when she dies."

"Some of it, perhaps. There are other relatives. And she may live forever."

"And what about that girl in New York?"

Miranda laughed. "He even threatened to marry her, if I turned him down."

"Poor dcvil, he must be in a bad way," Hattie said.

Chapter Eleven

If Miranda was nursing a broken heart, she made a good job of concealing it. No one caught her looking sad. In the beauty shop, the best place in the world for spreading propaganda, she did not make the mistake of not mentioning Jack Williams's name. She mentioned it to everyone who came in, including his grandmother. Poor Jack, she called him, in the half-tender, half-laughing voice women use when speaking of castoffs.

"Poor Jack, what he needs is a wife. There must be some nice girl who would marry him." As there had been no further word of his engagement—no announcement in the *Gazette*—this convinced a lot of people he really was a rejected suitor, and planted the suspicion that he had been rejected because of some inadequacy.

On the street, looking as unlike a native as possible— she had all those new clothes—Miranda did not avoid meeting him, either, but waved and smiled and sang out hello as if he were some old thing she was being kind to because nobody else would bother. It disconcerted him, you could see. He didn't know what to make of it. He made the mistake of attempting to stop and talk with her, to find out, and was left looking a little foolish when she patted his arm as if he were an unreasonable child, and told him she was busy.

It was a convincing performance. It fooled everyone. Jess and I were proud of the way she carried it off.

With Jack Williams out of the picture, our future began to look brighter. We no longer faced the worry of losing Miranda. And, thanks to Mr. Stuart, we were popular with other girls at school. We might in time even cease to be regarded as outsiders, we thought.

Being popular went to my head. It made me greedy, and I used every means I could think of to ingratiate myself further. I found, for instance, that I could pass as a wit by inventing disparaging quips about the teachers. When these evoked laughter, I was encouraged to discover additional ways of earning approval. Lessons improperly learned, homework half done or not done at all, classes skipped, were all applauded as disloyalty to the school and to education in general. I never skipped one of Mr. Stuart's classes, though, and was on my best behavior there.

That autumn the girls in my class went through a phase that all teen-agers seem to go through sooner or later: we thought it was terribly clever to filch small articles from the counters of the five-and-ten. Four or five of us would lag up and down the aisles in the late afternoon, after school, fingering the glass beads and gilt compacts and bottles of nail polish, trying on rings, with such a studied air of innocence that I wonder how we failed to arouse suspicion.

Perhaps before leaving one of us would actually make a nickel purchase, to draw attention from the others. Outside, we would walk half a block before casually displaying our loot. Clara, one of the best of us at this game, might hold one hand under her chin in an affected manner until we caught sight of the ring she was wearing.

"Clara, you devil!" we would squeal admiringly. "How did you do it? That clerk never took her eyes off you." Clara would shrug modestly and say, "It's just a knack, I guess," and the rest of us would go into fits of laughter.

I could never get up enough courage to take anything. I was so ashamed of this, and so afraid of inviting ostracism, that I went down to Woolworth's by myself one Saturday afternoon and purchased a number of inexpensive articles such as cigarette holders, gilt tie clips, and the like—anything more usable would look suspicious, I thought—and thereafter when I went scrounging, as we called it, with the girls, I pretended to have stolen one of these items. The compliments heaped upon me, though undeserved, were consoling.

Jess was more discriminating in her search for friends than I was. Perhaps she did not feel as strong a need to be like everyone else. She did not appear to feel that she was being slighted if she had to walk home from school by herself. At the Campfire Girls meetings, she made no obvious effort to be a member of some clique; sometimes she isolated herself deliberately, to talk with Miss Anderson. She even took to attending the Sunday-evening services at the nearby Methodist church by herself.

It soon dawned on us that Jack Williams was not prepared to fade out of the picture just because Miranda had sent him packing. It may be that she knew he would not give up so easily. At any rate, he set out to enchant her all over again, though he gave no indication that he meant to break off his engagement to someone else. He sent roses, which Miranda kept but did not thank him for.

When he telephoned, she was cool and evasive, saying she was sorry she could not see him, she was too busy. Leaving the telephone after one of these conversations, she would have an icy glitter in her eyes. Make a fool of her, would he? She'd show him that she had as much pride as the next one. Jess and I did not miss an opportunity to remind her that he *had* made a fool of her, or tried to.

At the same time we were conducting a subtle campaign to show her what a suitable husband Mr. Parker would make. That he already had a wife was an obstacle our minds simply jumped over like an old gate that could be pushed to one side at any time. It chills me, nowadays, when I look back and realize with what cold-blooded certainty we anticipated Mrs. Parker's death, as if we thought that by removing herself from the scene she was doing no more than her duty.

We began so many sentences with "Mr. Parker says" and "Mr. Parker thinks" that Miranda laughed at us and said, "You do seem to have a crush on him."

"It's not a crush," we assured her. "We just think he's nice. He's got a nice fatherly manner."

"Yes, I suppose he has. You don't usually show such affection for people. What specifically do you like about him?"

Jess said, "He's something like Dad."

On the occasional Sunday afternoon when he drove us out to the cemetery to lay flowers on Alfie's grave, we asked him to go home by way of another street so that we could pass his own house, a gabled white cottage with green shutters, which was rented out to other people. It was near the edge of town, where stretches of country separated the houses. Snugged down under its trees, surrounded by worn lawns and latticed arbors, it gave an impression of comfort and friendliness. Jess and I gazed wistfully at it as we passed, and said to Miranda, "Wouldn't you love to live there?"

Our fondness for Mr. Parker was genuine. Jess scolded him, a sure sign of affection. "Look at those socks! You ought to be ashamed." In a little while he brought his whole collection of socks down to be examined and mended where needed. In return, he gave us presents of books and games. We looked forward to his arrival each week end. He was the only person, aside from Miranda, that we could confide in.

We even told him about the man who had put his hand on Jess's leg in the movies. "What would you have done if you were me and a man did that?" she asked him.

"I'd have slapped his face good and hard," Mr. Parker said indignantly. "You do that, too, if it happens again. What *did* you do?"

We had left the theatre and run all the way home, and had not mentioned the incident to anyone except Miranda. Aside from Jess's embarrassment, the furtive creeping of the man's hand in the dark, like some night animal, was not a thing she cared to dwell upon. Miranda said, "The dirty thing! Next time you carry a hatpin and gave him a good jab."

On Saturdays Mr. Parker helped around the house. He fixed the furnace and took out ashes, repaired leaky faucets, puttied loose windows, tightened doorknobs; in fact made himself generally indispensable. While Mrs. Walsh and I were upstairs changing beds and counting sheets, he would be in the cellar helping Jess with the part of the weekly wash that we did at home. Later he would take the bundle of dirty sheets down to the Chinese laundry and pick up the clean ones. On the way home, anticipating an invitation to lunch with us, he would buy some gristly pork pies or a pound of wieners. Jess would scold him for being extravagant. At two o'clock he would go to the sanatorium to visit his wife.

On Saturday nights James and Clara might come over to try out the new games. Mr. Parker would join in, trying hard to make everyone have a good time at what he thought of as his party, since he provided the refreshments —the baskets of apples, stacks of Sweet Marie bars, boxes of fig newtons; a treat for James, after all those doughnuts. It was the food that drew James. Clara came in the hope of seeing Mr. Stuart, who was almost always leaving with

Mr. Brooks for some social affair when she arrived.

We tried to induce Miranda to join these parties, but she never did. Instead, she would go down town shopping, or to the Palace with Hattie, returning home around ten o'clock. "Aren't you having a lovely time!" she would say, standing in the doorway smiling at us. "It's very kind of you to amuse these children, Mr. Parker."

When Clara and James had gone she would put the kettle on and say, "Would you care for a cup of tea, Mr. Parker?"

"Yes, I'd enjoy that, Mrs. Arnold."

"Run along now, girls, get your beauty sleep." Miranda would shoo us off to bed. Jess and I would exchange covert glances, hiding our satisfaction at seeing them chatting cozily over their teacups.

"I'll be along in ten minutes," Miranda would call after us, but sometimes we were asleep when she came up.

That youth resents guidance and discipline is one of the great myths of the twentieth century. Whoever subscribes to this belief cannot have gone through that unsettled, seeking period of adolescence himself.

For some time it had been obvious to me that Jess was doing better than I was in the search for some kind of a model on which to pattern her life. I was not consciously aware I was searching for a model, for I had not completely acknowledged that Miranda could not teach me what I wanted to know; but when Jess let fall observations regarding rules of conduct or good taste, I tucked them away in my mind to be mulled over later on.

When she said to Miranda, "Those beads are too flashy; you ought to wear something simple with that dress," I saw at once that she was right, though I might not have reached this conclusion on my own.

"Flashy?" Miranda's head reared back. "Whatever do you mean? I know how to dress, thank you."

And when Miranda made disparaging remarks about some local custom or manner of speech, Jess said severely, "It's all very well to have lived in London, to have seen the world, but we aren't living in London now, we're living in a Canadian town."

"I *know* where I'm living," Miranda said, "and I wish to God I was somewhere else."

"Well, you ought to try to get on more with the people. Adaptation to the community is one of the prime requisites of proper living," Jess said, obviously quoting from some book.

Miranda rolled her eyes and groaned. "What next? Sometimes I wonder about you, Jess. I really do."

One Indian-summer day I slipped away from Clara and her friends after school and walked out to the cemetery, which stood on a rise behind the town. This cemetery was as old as the town itself. Near the gates, behind the ivy-smothered chapel, great trees brooded over the headstones and kept off the sun, encouraging moss. October leaves drifting on the paths added to the smell of age.

Our plot was in the newer section, where the trees had less authority. Sunlight filtered through them to warm the neat remembered graves. Alfie's headstone was cut from dark-gray native granite. There was nothing on the polished face but his name and the dates of his birth and death.

Jess was sitting on her schoolbag beside the grave with her back to the path. She had uprooted the frostbitten geraniums we had planted in the summer, and clipped the grass around the stone where the caretaker always missed. Grass clippings, scissors and dead geraniums were in a little pile beside her, and propped against them was her *English Poets*—a school book; I had one in my bag, too—open at a poem by Rupert Brooke, the "If I should Die" one. Hearing my footsteps, she dropped forward on one knee and pretended to be busy with the scissors.

"Oh, it's you," she said, going back on her heels again. "What are you doing here?"

"Nothing. I brought these." On the way up I had reached through the pickets into someone's garden and taken three red chrysanthemums.

"There's nothing to put them in. Someone's taken the vase." Jess closed her book and thrust it into her school-bag.

I said, "I didn't know you came here—on weekdays, I mean."

"Just to tidy up sometimes. If you want to help, those clippings go in the trash box, over behind the trees."

When I returned, she had placed the three chrysanthemums against the headstone and with a twig was brushing away some dried bird droppings. "Yes, I come here sometimes," she said in a more confiding tone. "I sit here and read." She spread her faded serge skirt out behind her to save the pleats. "I'm glad, anyway, that this place is way out here, not in town."

She looked off through the trees. "It's real country beyond that fence, with wild blueberries and cattle." She spit on her handkerchief and tried to rub away the white stain from the bird droppings with it. "There ought to be something more on this stone; something to show that Dad belonged to us. Years from now, how will anyone know he wasn't alone?"

"There's room for our names under his."

"Yours and mine, anyway. Miranda's name won't go here, if she marries Mr. Parker."

"But we might not be here. We might be somewhere else when we die."

"I'll be here." Jess spoke briskly to cover a slight tremor in her voice. "I'm not going to leave. In the first place, he shouldn't be here. He didn't like this town. But now that he is here, somebody's got to stay and see that he's remembered." She rose to her feet and stood waiting as a figure came into view at the far end of the path. "If nobody remembered afterward, what would be the use of anybody's living?"

Miss Anderson came along the path carrying our vase and some pale asters. "I'm late," she said, handing the vase to Jess. "I filled this, since I was going by the pump anyway. And someone else has put flowers on Mother's grave. Could I leave these here? Oh, you've got those lovely 'mums."

So they had been meeting here all along, I thought. This was where Jess had been getting those ideas about how we should and should not behave. It must have been going on for a long time, too, since early spring.

Miss Anderson wore a brown tweed suit, leather brogues, and the kind of brimmed felt hat later made fashionable by Garbo. I recalled Jess's saying to Miranda, some weeks before, "Why don't you ever wear tweeds?" and Miranda's looking at her suspiciously, wondering where she had ever got such an idea.

"I visit Mother's grave every Friday," Miss Anderson told me as she arranged her mauve asters with my stolen red 'mums.

I took this to mean that I could join the weekly meetings if I cared to. I was not sure that I did care to. I made some excuse and wandered off by myself. I hid behind the privet hedge near the chapel and watched them strolling companionably toward the gate, Jess in her schoolgirl reefer and pleated skirt, her old childish beaver hat pushed up off her forehead, her armful of books clutched against her stomach, talking away, more than she ever talked at home.

I was always seeing, in other girls, the kind of daughters Jess and I were not, the pert vivacious kind that Miranda felt she deserved and still hoped, I think, that we would by some miracle turn into overnight. I had never looked at it the other way around, never visualized us deserving a different kind of mother. (The nearest I had come to that was years ago with Mrs. Saunders.)

But that afternoon as I sat spying among the mossy gravestones, watching Jess and Miss Anderson sauntering along out there in the sunshine and drifting leaves, though I was angry with Jess for what I told myself she was doing—going over to the enemy camp—I did envy her. I wished that I had someone like Miss Anderson to talk with. I tried to picture Miranda in a brown tweed suit and flat brogues, walking along a sunny path with me, dis-cussing . . . what? Here my invention failed. I could think of questions— How and what shall I be? Where can I find a pattern?—but no answers.

In bed that night I said, "What were you and Anderson gabbing about?"

Jess told me that they had been discussing careers. "It's time I decided what I want to be," she said. "I wouldn't mind being a nurse."

"Another bouquet from the rejected suitor?" Hattie asked one night in late November, viewing the red roses on the hall table. "He doesn't give up easily, does he?"

"He's wasting his money, as far as I'm concerned," Miranda said.

"He's got it bad." Hattie gave her an admiring glance. "Not many women your age have a rich young man pant-ing after them the way he is after you."

"My age?"

"Well, you're not sweet sixteen any more, not by a long shot," Hattie said with her usual honesty. "Do you know, it wouldn't surprise me at all if he got rid of that girl he's engaged to, now he's learning he can't have his cake and eat it, too."

"I know nothing of any engagement," Miranda said, sticking to her version of the break-up.

"Would you take him back if he did?"

"Did what? I refused Mr. Williams's proposal of marriage for financial reasons, as you very well know. If he wants to keep on sending me roses, telephoning me at all hours of the day and night, that's his privilege. He's not the first man who's made a fool of himself over me."

"Well, I give him another month, two at the outside, before he breaks down and asks Miss Dorothea Reynolds to send him back his ring, so he can place it on the finger of his own true love, namely you." Hattie added, "I had no idea you were such a *femme fatale*."

Miranda smiled. She had known all along.

One night in December I was awakened, late, by Miranda's slipping past our doorway in the dark. She was in her nightgown. I listened as she crept down the stairs, assuming she was going down to take a bath. There was no tub in our third-floor washroom, so we were forced to bathe at odd hours, when no one else was likely to want the bathroom on the second floor.

After a time it occurred to me that I could not hear the gushing sound the plumbing made when the water was turned on downstairs. I thought of various other things Miranda might be doing. Perhaps she had been unable to sleep, and had gone down to the kitchen to make herself a cup of tea.

She might be feeling lonesome. It was around this time, last year, that Alfie had died; the darkest part of the year. There had been days of rain, with cold drafts creeping through the house, and up there under the roof the wind sulked and moaned and tapped branches against the shingles like a petulant ghost. It was enough to make anyone feel sad. Miranda might be crying down in the kitchen, alone. I eased out of bed and tiptoed down the stairs in the dark.

When I reached the first landing I heard someone say "Hush!" behind Mr. Parker's closed door. His room was my old one, opening off the narrow back-stairs landing. The door between this and the main hall, which shut his room off from the others on the second floor, was closed.

I stood on the bottom steps of the narrower attic stairs and heard Miranda say, "There's no one here."

"I thought I heard someone."

"It's only the wind. This old house is full of creaks."

A listening silence, then the bedsprings creaked and Mr. Parker said, "I'd better have a look."

The heels of his slippers slapped across the carpet as he came to the door in his pajamas and stuck his head out. I pressed back into the shadows, as far as I could from the gray light that came into the hall from the narrow window. What saved me from being caught there like a Peeping Tom was Brownie's padding up the stairs from the kitchen.

Mr. Parker said in a relieved voice over his shoulder, "It's only the dog." He scooped Brownie up and carried him downstairs. I scurried up to my room.

I crept in beside Jess, trying not to waken her. It was not disbelief or horror that made me breathe warily. I knew it was improper for a man and a woman who were not married to sleep together, but it did not become a crime until they were found out. What worried me was that someone else might stumble onto what was going on in Mr. Parker's room.

I lay in one position until my arms ached, then shifted cautiously, as if my slightest movement could rouse the sleeping roomers on the second floor, make them sit up in bed listening, and finally send them out into the hall to ask one another, "Is something going on?"

After a while I became aware that Jess was not breathing like a person asleep. "Are you awake?" I whispered.

"Yes. I heard you snooping around. I hope they didn't catch you."

"Do you *know* where Miranda is?"

"She was there last night, too, and lord knows how many other nights. Last night was when I caught on."

We talked in whispers, with the sheets pulled over our heads like a tent. Jess complained, "She might have waited until they were married."

"He's as much to blame as she is."

"No he's not. He's the kind that lets a woman wrap him around her little finger. I suppose he'd go out and steal for her, if she asked him."

I did not dispute this. Young as I was, I recognized Mr. Parker as the sort of man who is happiest under a woman's thumb.

"What if someone else finds out?"

"Oh, God!" Jess groaned and pressed the sheet to her forehead. "Listen!" she hissed. "Is that someone in the hall now?"

We strained our ears. A door on the floor below opened and someone fumbled along the hall to the bathroom. For a time we heard only the spitting sound of the radiator at the head of the stairs and, outside, rain gurgling through the downspout. Then the footsteps went back along the hall.

"That was only Mrs. Walsh. She wouldn't tell, even if she knew."

"I wouldn't trust her, even. I wouldn't trust anybody. If one person knew, it would be no time at all before the whole town was talking about it. Imagine what Clara's mother would say!" Jess rolled over and buried her face in the pillow as if she hid her eyes from some horrifying sight.

"I don't think Miranda would care."

"Well, I would."

After a time Jess turned her head sideways on the pillow and said philosophically, "There's one thing we don't have to worry about now: Jack Williams. I was beginning to think he might break his engagement to that girl, as Hattie said, and we'd have him back on our hands again." She added, "Thank the lord it's Mr. Parker, not *him*."

If it had been anyone but Mr. Parker I would have been more upset but less surprised. Miranda had never laughed with him in corners, or given him those secret sidelong glances. The shock of realizing that I would not have been surprised to find her sleeping with someone like Sidney in London, or Dan Murphy in the valley, or Jack Williams, came back again and again to make me lie awake and wonder.

I slept now and then. Thoughts of Miranda and various men tumbled about in my dreams. Sidney was the most vivid. He was the first one I could remember. Then another idea began to creep, insidiously, around the outer edges of consciousness. What if someone like Sidney were my real father, not Alfie? What if someone else were Jess's father? Toward the gray end of a troubled night is the time for such ideas to take form, and flourish. Drifting from confused sleep to wakefulness and back again, I began to substitute this revelation for the real one, and to search for evidence to substantiate it.

I remembered Florrie, in her cluttered sitting room in Madam's house, standing Jess and me up against a little fan-shaped fireplace, saying, "Now who do they take after, dearie? The father?" (The father, not Alfie.) Jess took after Miranda, she could see that. She could not decide about me. "This one's not like you. Where did she get that coloring?"

Miranda said, "Alfie's fair."

"Is he, now?" Florrie appeared to marvel.

As Jess grew older, she became less like Miranda. Some features were the same, but were worn in a different way. I had always taken it for granted that I resembled Alfie, because we were both fair-haired. But was this really enough to go on? Was there any other resemblance?

I fell asleep and dreamed of trying to find myself in a clouded mirror. Nothing was reflected back; it was not a mirror, after all, but a dark opening. Then I realized that I could not remember what Alfie had looked like. The harder I tried to recall his features, the more faceless he became. In a senseless dream panic I went through the house turning out drawers, scrabbling through albums for snapshots of him. Someone had been at every picture with a soft pencil, had obliterated every face. . . .

I woke in time to see Miranda slipping quietly as a ghost up to her own bed. It was getting light outside.

Chapter Twelve

For some time after that Jess and I lived in a state of apprehension, uneasy with our friends, on the lookout for any change in their manner toward us. At school, on my way to the cloakroom during the gossip period between classes, I dreaded what I might overhear. If the laughter stopped suddenly when I opened the door, if the girls looked away, I would know what they had been talking about. I dared not be the first to leave a group, in case they had something to say after I had gone.

Our affection for Mr. Parker did not suffer much, for our discovery of the affair between him and Miranda only strengthened our conviction that he intended to do what we wanted him to. He meant to marry Miranda, as soon as he was free, which would not be long, we hoped. She would give up her job and be at home all day, we would move into his house—the cozy white house with the green shutters—and it would be almost the same as it had been when Alfie was alive. In bed at night Jess and I cheered one another with references to this ideal future, ignoring present anxieties.

"We could have a garden," I said, remembering the spring evenings at the farm when Alfie had helped us to prepare the tiny plots where we grew vegetables. This memory was associated with the calling of robins, because one warm night just at dusk I had heard one singing far away and had asked if it were a nightingale. Alfie laughed, then grew wistful, and went indoors to tell Miranda that I had mistaken a Canadian robin for a nightingale.

Jess, who had learned that there is comfort in prayer, persuaded me to accompany her to the Sunday-evening services at the Methodist church, and join her in asking God to protect us from scandal.

"What shall I say?" I asked her. I had voiced such private petitions as "Lord, please let it not rain," but these were not much more than mechanical addresses to some vague fate, and had little to do with religion.

"I say, 'Oh, God, let not the neighbors find out about Miranda and Mr. Parker, for Thy name's sake, amen.'"

"I hope you don't say it out loud."

"Of course not. Don't be so smarty." She was half afraid I might laugh at her, but was determined to enlist my support. "I say it over and over in my mind, with my eyes shut, while they're singing hymns, or during the sermon."

I followed her example, and found that it was comforting to shift one's worries onto the shoulders of a complaisant God. When we left the church we both felt better, reasonably confident that we would be spared any unpleasantness for another week.

That my school work was suffering I was well aware. I was too busy trying to ingratiate myself in other ways to spend much time on lessons. High marks did not win applause from my classmates, but exasperating the teachers —other than Mr. Stuart—by inattention and laziness did. The teachers began to look at me with that expression of distaste reserved for stupid or wayward pupils. Finally a note of complaint was sent up from the principal's office, and Miranda took it upon herself to discuss my lack of progress, not with Mr. Stanley, who had sent the note, but with Mr. Stuart.

She called me into the living room, where the discussion had taken place. I had no warning that they were talking about me; in fact, when I entered the room, they seemed to be having a cozy chat about one of those spiny seashells that are used as ornaments in homes near the sea. Miranda was holding it up to her ear, listening. He, looking handsome and jaunty in a white knitted pullover, bent toward her. The way they smiled into one another's eyes suggested intimacy, and my heart lurched with jealousy.

Miranda saw me and her expression changed. She put down the shell. "Mr. Stuart tells me you've been neglecting your studies. What have you got to say for yourself?"

I had nothing to say. I stood like an idiot, blushing.

"How do you ever expect to amount to anything, if you're going to waste your time playing the smart-aleck? Neglecting your studies, being rude to the teachers—I ought to smack your bottom!"

My humiliation was so great that I wanted to die. In Mr. Stuart's classroom I had been a model pupil, abject in my eagerness to have him think well of me. Before I ran to my room I gave him one hurt look, and saw that he was embarrassed too. He had not expected Miranda to scold me in front of him.

I threw myself on my bed and wept. I hated Miranda. She had made me appear ridiculous, childish, in front of the one person whose opinion I valued. I told myself that she had ruined my life.

I had not finished crying when Clara came up, carrying Brownie. "Miranda told me you were up here sulking," she said. "What's wrong? Oh, Brownie, you sweet thing!" She held him up to her face. "God damn my mother—just because she doesn't like dogs! Are you under the weather? I am. Can you tell?" She turned her face for inspection. Someone had told her that men could tell. "Have I got dark circles under my eyes?"

"No."

"Well, you have. What are you crying about? Has something happened? I've got cigarettes if you want to smoke. Go ahead, try one. They're good for the nerves." She opened the window to let out the smoke and said, "I don't see the point of our being such friends if you won't tell me what's wrong."

"There's nothing wrong."

"Oh, well, if you don't care to confide in me. . . ." Clara wandered around the room, finally sitting on the bed to look through a photograph album. It was the one with the snapshots of Alfie in it. A photograph of Alfie and Miranda, taken on their wedding day, was stuck under the back flap.

"Who are these people?" she asked. "Oh, your parents! My God, don't they look funny. Did Miranda really wear her hair like that, with those cootie garages?"

The gap between generations was never greater than in those days. The world had emerged from primitive darkness around 1920, we thought. The yellowed photograph, taken in 1912, was a shock to Clara. It reminded her that Miranda was a grown woman in the age of antiquity before the war.

"Those funny old-fashioned clothes!" Clara said, turning over the pages of the album. Some of the pictures in it dated back to the London days. There was one of Alfie and Uncle Bertie in Kew Gardens, against some stone steps with griffons.

"Is this London?" Clara asked. "Is that the house you lived in?"

"That's the front steps. You can't see much of the house." I pointed to the next picture, which had the Saunders' house in the background. "That's the house we lived in before we moved here." Lies came easily, for I had nothing more to lose.

"Is this your father? You don't look much like him, do you?"

I had been crying because Miranda had turned against me, because I was ashamed of myself; and from the sheer sadness of being fourteen and in love with a man who thought so little of me that he would discuss me with my mother as if I were a fractious child. At Clara's words I began to cry about something else.

"Now what have I said?" Clara was losing patience with me. "I wish you'd tell me what's wrong. It can't be a man because you haven't been out with one—unless you've been keeping something from me." She gave me a suspicious look, then said, "What I came to tell you was a really awful scandal my mother got hold of today, about someone you know, too. Lord, you're jumpy! You look as if you thought there was a ghost behind you—but I'm not going to tell you if you're going to sit there crying just because I said you didn't look like your father. My goodness, you wouldn't *want* to, would you? I mean, he was very nice, and not bad-looking for a man, but a *girl* wouldn't want to look like him. What if you were in my shoes? What if you had to live with a couple of ignorant peasants who weren't even your parents?"

"Alfie wasn't my father," I said.

Children never delve into the reasons for behaving as they do. Often there is no reason except a desire to shock. Perhaps I hoped, by occupying Clara's mind with an invented scandal, to make her forget what she had been about to tell me, which I was sure concerned Miranda and Mr. Parker. (Later on I learned that it was about two other people.)

It certainly took her mind off it for the time being. There was a stunned silence, during which she absorbed what I had said, and I felt the dizzy relief people must feel when, having hung on the edge of a cliff for some time, they close their eyes and jump.

"My God, Rose!" Clara's voice squeaked with excitement. She widened her eyes in entranced excitement, all agog to hear more. "Who *was*, then?"

"There was a man in Mrs.— in our house in London, a man called Sidney. . . ."

"Well, go *on*. Tell me about him. When did you first know?"

Too late, I considered backing down, but I saw that a retraction was the last thing in the world Clara would accept. This was better than her story of being kidnapped in a Boston park. Now that it was out, I was beginning to believe it myself, too. It gave me something to cry about without acknowledging the real reason. It is only in adolescence that we know how to cherish unhappiness and dramatize it fully. Later on we lose the knack; common sense spoils the pure enjoyment of misery.

"You won't tell anyone?"

"Of course not!"

"Promise you won't tell a soul."

"Don't you trust me, for heaven's sake? What did he look like? Was he handsome? Did your father—I mean Alfie—ever find out?" Clara kept on asking questions. She was frantic to hear the whole story. To postpone supplying details, and to avoid dwelling on how I would face the consequences if she did tell anyone else, I threw myself face downward on the bed and wept aloud. I could not shut out the picture of myself, in the dreaded future, an outcast in all decent homes, an enormity no mother would allow her child to associate with. "I can't bear to

think about it," I moaned. "Oh, Clara, don't make me
talk about it."

She tried her best to comfort me. "No wonder you're
upset, you poor thing. Look, stuff this pillow under your
head and have a good cry. Then you can tell me all about
it."

I had nothing more to tell. The vague conjecture I had
arrived at during one sleepless night now stood, through
my own doing, as a statement of fact, but nothing led up
to it or away from it. After I had been crying for some
time, I made a stab at retracting it.

I sat up and said, "What I told you about Alfie not
being my father—it wasn't true."

Clara would have none of that. She gave me a forgiving
smile and said, "You don't trust me!"

"I don't know why I said it."

"You needn't worry. I won't tell a soul."

"It was just something I thought up because I was worried about something else."

"Aren't we friends?" Clara looked injured. "Well, then,
you might as well tell me the rest. I promised to keep it
secret, didn't I? I thought that's what friends were *for!*"
She added, "Perhaps you don't want to *be* friends."

The worst thing about lies is that they are often more
attractive than the truth. Clara was sulking when she left.
"All right, then, *don't* tell me," she said. "As if I give a
damn!"

As Mr. Stuart went home for the Christmas holidays, I
was spared, for two weeks, the pain of meeting him face
to face. By the time he returned my embarrassment had
begun to lessen, and I dared to hope that by turning over
a new leaf I might still win a place in his affections.

Something else happened during the Christmas holidays. Mrs. Parker died. She died with a minimum of fuss, as if, having suddenly realized what a burden she was, she wanted to slip away as quietly as possible and be forgotten. As she had grown up in another town, and was taken there for burial, there was not even a funeral to go to. Mr. Parker simply went away for a week, and when he returned he was a widower.

Around this time, Hattie went to Boston to visit her sister. "Well, I'm off to Beantown," she told us when she came to say good-bye.

"What I'd give to be in your shoes!" Miranda said.

"I'm looking forward to the bright lights, I can tell you," Hattie said. "The shops and everything. Betty's moved out to Lynn, did I tell you? She's bought herself a little beauty parlor there. Doing quite well, too. She always had a good business head. I'm trying to talk Roy into giving up his pokey job at the jail and moving to Boston. He could find work there, I'm sure. You ought to come, too," she added. "Betty might give you a job in her shop. Betty's Salon de Beauté, she calls it. Sounds very high class, don't you think? French."

"Do you really think she'd give me a job?" Miranda asked.

"It certainly wouldn't hurt to make inquiries. Betty always said you were the best operator she ever had."

Miranda turned to Jess and me. "Would you like to live in Boston, girls?"

Jess said "No!" emphatically for both of us.

"Why not?"

"Would *you*?" Jess asked her in a startled voice.

"I'd like nothing better. I'm sick of this godforsaken little town."

"Well, I won't go."

"Now you're just being childish," Miranda said. Then, noting Jess's expression, she gave her a second look. "I don't know where you get these silly ideas. I suppose that Anderson woman has been at you, planting all sorts of notions behind my back. I wish to God I knew what that woman is up to, with all those innocent adoring Campfire Girls." She turned to Hattie. "Do you know Jess's great ambition? To be a nurse." Her laughter dissolved in irritation.

Jess threw an accusing glance at me, knowing where Miranda had got this information.

"When the girls were small I had such dreams for them," Miranda went on. "I dreamed of them becoming great beauties, or famous actresses—not movie stars, I mean real actresses like Sybil Thorndike; or dancers like Pavlova. You never saw Pavlova dance, did you?"

Hattie looked down her nose and patted her hair, a mincing gesture meant to convey sarcasm. "Not unless she danced at the old Opera House before they tore it down. A touring company used to come there every so often with *East Lynne* and *Smilin' Through*. . . . I think the girls are pretty. And clever, too," she added.

"But who would want to be a nurse? Emptying bedpans and giving enemas! I don't know where they get these ideas. Yes, I do. They get them from that Miss Anderson."

Jess's face had gone set and heavy. She stared at the table. Neither of us suspected that Miranda might be jealous.

Hattie said quickly, to change the subject, "What would you like me to bring you back from Boston, Miranda? A hat? There's a little hat shop next door to Betty's place where I can get things wholesale, so Betty wrote me. The latest styles. I'll bring back something for the girls, too. What would you like, Jess? How about a nice red-leather handbag—or one of those velvet tam-o'-shanters that are all the rage now? Which would you like?"

Jess said in a controlled voice, "I'd love a tam."

"Good. I'll buy two. What's your favorite color? A nice red?"

"Yes, red would be lovely."

"And blue for you, Rose?"

"Oh, God, to go into a real shop!" Miranda said. "I'd leave this damned little town in a minute. . . . And, Jess, if you start sulking again, I'll . . . I won't have it, do you hear?"

In bed, later, Jess said, "Do you think she'd really drag us off to Boston to live?"

"She doesn't like it here, I know that."

"What about Mr. Parker? We couldn't go off and leave him. Miranda's practically married to him. I thought we could plan for a September wedding."

"He could come to Boston, too, I suppose."

"To live, do you mean? How could he do that? His job is here. Anyway, the whole *point* of her marrying him is —" Jess checked herself. After a minute she said defiantly, "She needn't think she can make me go to Boston, even if everyone else does. I won't go, that's all. And another thing: what have you been telling Clara?"

"I haven't told her anything."

"What was she going on about the other night, talking about some secret you two had?"

"That wasn't anything."

"Well, you be careful. You know what would happen if her mother ever started snooping around. Then we would have to leave here."

"I don't care where we live, anyway."

"You're as bad as Miranda." Jess drew away from me and a cold silence fell between us.

I remembered the afternoon I had gone to the cemetery and found her sitting beside Alfie's grave, and the way she had said, "Somebody's got to stay here and see that he's remembered." I began to wonder whether the real reason she was so anxious for Miranda to marry Mr. Parker was to make sure we would stay in Southport, and never leave Alfie's grave to strangers.

Was it *only* his memory she wanted to keep alive, or did she have some idea that his ghost was there in the cemetery—lonely, homesick for some place with happier associations, crying for us to stay forever and keep him company? This thought bothered me more because Jess was not usually given to irrational fancies. In the past year, during which she had taken charge of the house so efficiently, she seemed to have become much more adult, to have begun, at least, to acquire enough judgment and common sense to guide me—Miranda too, when she would listen—along some sort of approved path of conduct.

Not that I always listened to her advice, or followed her example. Her preoccupation with the idea that the only way to keep Alfie's memory alive was to visit his grave and put flowers on it made me think she was slipping back into childhood again, where she could never set standards for me to follow.

Try as I would, I could not derive much comfort from visiting the cemetery. I went there alone one afternoon, skipping a school class to do so, and being coldly reprimanded afterward, to test myself. In winter people forget about tending graves. Not a person was in sight. Melting rabbit tracks crisscrossed one another in the first thin snow, but mine were the only human tracks. I sat on my schoolbag and tried to imagine how Jess would feel if she were in my place. I held myself still and waiting, but Alfie's ghost was not there.

Chapter Thirteen

I suppose all young people feel that they are unique, that their problems are too exceptional ever to have been encountered by anyone else. My troubles, at fourteen, arose from uncertainty as to what sort of person I should strive to be. (This had nothing to do with lofty ideals. All I wanted was to be the same as everyone else, and to be liked.)

I was learning, too, that mistakes do not rectify themselves. I could not correct the ones I had made, and I did not know how to avoid making more in the future. In spite of my resolution to turn over a new leaf for Mr. Stuart's sake, I had not succeeded in making myself popular with the teachers at school. They regarded my reformed behavior with cold disbelief. At times the one thing I wanted was to discard myself and be someone completely new.

I had read all those books that used to be written—and perhaps still are—for the enlightenment of growing girls, about some undesirable young person who was reformed overnight by a kind act, or was made to see, while weathering some crisis, how to become a deserving citizen. I kept hoping that some such revelation would come to me, but nothing happened.

Clara, with her conspiratorial airs and veiled phrases, was a great worry to me. I had to make certain that she was never alone with Miranda, for one night, ignoring my frowns and covert headshakings, she had bombarded her with seemingly casual questions.

"When you lived in London, did you know a man named Sidney?" she asked.

"Sidney? You mean Sidney Wilkinson? Wherever did you hear of him?"

"I think one of the girls mentioned him," Clara said in an offhand way. "Who was he?"

"Are you coming, Clara?" I asked sharply. We were due at a meeting of the Campfire Girls in half an hour. Jess had already left.

Miranda turned to me with an idle reminiscent smile. "Fancy you remembering him! That was years ago."

"Who was he?" Clara asked.

"Sidney was the chauffeur at . . . at my aunt's house." Miranda always paused in the middle of any statement involving her life in London, perhaps to make sure it tallied with previous statements.

"Not your own house?"

"I lived with my aunt, you know."

"Sidney Wilkinson." Clara repeated the name. "What was he like? Was he good-looking?"

"I'm going alone, then," I said from the doorway.

"You needn't be so grumpy," Clara complained, catching up with me at the end of the walk. "You never tell me anything."

"I told you I was lying that time. Don't you believe me?"

"Imagine him being the chauffeur!" Clara said. "That's not very nice for you, is it? I mean, it would be nicer if he'd been an actor, or a writer—somebody famous, anyway."

She had given up asking me questions, and now contented herself with what scrapings she could glean from other sources. These she built into a story to suit herself. Our friendship was cooling. Clara was tired, she implied, of mistrust and evasions on my part.

Her admiration for Miranda had increased, for she now thought of her as a woman with a past, a woman who had lived—in fact, the kind of woman Clara herself hoped to be some day. It did not surprise her to know that Jack Williams still sent Miranda flowers.

Miranda did not encourage Jack, though when he called her on the telephone her voice was less cold. Jess and I kept a wary lookout in his direction, but we were fairly confident that Miranda was through with him, and meant to marry Mr. Parker.

One other thing bothered us somewhat. Hattie had returned from Boston with a message for Miranda from Mrs. Fuller. There was not, in the slack winter season, an opening for Miranda in Betty's Salon de Beauté. "But Betty said to tell you that business is sure to pick up in the spring, and when it does, she'd like nothing better than to have you on her staff," Hattie said. It pleased her to think she was doing someone a good turn.

"Betty's going to write you about it later. She figures around April or May she'll be well enough established to offer you a job. So there you are. Now, if I can only talk some sense into Roy—get him to pull up stakes and head for Beantown, too—everything will be hunky-dory. You're going to love Boston, Miranda; all the lights, and the people; my God, I never saw the like of the crowds on the streets. It makes you think, I can tell you. There's no doubt about it, prosperity is here to stay."

We wondered what was going on in Miranda's mind as she heard this. She talked excitedly to Hattie about moving to Boston, but what did she really want to do? She seemed to be looking in two directions at once.

"Spring is a long way off," Jess said to me when we were alone. "A lot could happen before then." By this she meant that by spring Mr. Parker and Miranda would be making plans for their wedding.

In hoping to promote this union, we thought we were concerned only with Miranda's future, but I have wondered since whether we were really thinking of her or of ourselves. It was wholly obvious to Jess, less obvious to me, that Miranda needed some stabilizing influence. Subconsciously, we may have been trying to shift the responsibility of supplying this influence onto Mr. Parker. With Miranda settled, safe, we could concentrate on the difficult task of managing our own lives.

And yet, pushed to the back of our minds like the memory of some indiscretion that is best forgotten, was the knowledge that we were simply being Pollyannas when we told ourselves any real problems would be solved by marrying Miranda off to Mr. Parker. He could never change her. He would not even try. *He* would do the changing, because he was that kind. He would spend the rest of his life trying to please her.

We never let this knowledge come right through to the surface of our minds, for to admit that Mr. Parker was spiritless would be the same as saying that Alfie had been spiritless, too. This made us go on like someone in a boat who knows there are hidden rocks ahead, but hopes to miss them.

"Nothing pleases you these days," Clara grumbled as we left the school grounds one day in February. "You go around with a chip on your shoulder. Look what you said to Andy Gump. If you hadn't learned that poem, why didn't you skip his class, or say you were sick, instead of standing up like that saying you forgot? It gets him into such a hell of a temper with the rest of us. Lillian said you were simply showing off."

For weeks I had watched Lillian Blake, the postmaster's daughter, usurping my place as Clara's best friend.

Lillian herself, a sturdy tennis-playing girl with a heavy backside, came galloping along in her flapping galoshes to join us. "Too bad about your *English Poets* homework," she said to me with false kindness. "I thought everyone knew that old Rupert Brooke thing off by heart."

"I did know it. I just didn't want to recite it."

"Well, you're entitled to your own ideas, I suppose." Lillian gave a shrug, excusing this whim. "Shall we go shopping?" she asked Clara.

"If Rose wants to." Clara had not deserted me entirely.

Boys streamed past us on bicycles as we stood on the corner deciding. James hopped off his for a moment to say in an undertone, "Shall I bring my books over to your house tonight? I might help you with that thing you missed today. The way to learn those old poems is to go over them with someone else."

Lillian watched him pedal off, his thin knees angled out. "Is he your boy friend?"

"He just lives next door."

"He strikes me as a big sissy. I could never feel anything for a boy who turns blue in cold weather. . . . Are we going to stand here all day?"

We walked down to the business district and stared at all the shop windows. Lillian suggested going into White's Market, the largest grocery store in town. We browsed along the counters and shelves for some time, hung over the open boxes of fancy cookies and the great round of cheese with a wedge cut out of it, and wondered if there might be a tarantula in the banana cluster suspended from the ceiling. Then Lillian bought a five-cent package of chewing gum, and we left. Across the street in the five-and-ten we lounged against a radiator to get warm.

"Feel my leg," Lillian invited, and went into a fit of giggles when we discovered that she had a pound of butter tucked under the elastic of her bloomers.

"Lillian, you *devil!*" Clara shrieked, then covered her admiring laughter with her hand. This was the most daring and comical thing any of us had ever done. A whole pound of butter, stolen under the very noses of the clerks in White's. It became funnier still when the heat from the radiator melted the butter and made it run down Lillian's leg.

She sunned herself in Clara's approval. "I bet Rose wouldn't dare swipe anything as big as this."

"Would you, Rose?" Clara asked.

"I might."

"Well, then, I dare you to swipe one of those." Lillian indicated a glass case holding a great mound of assorted chocolates. Some one-pound bags had been filled and placed on the counter. "You wouldn't have the nerve to snitch one of those," she said.

"Yes I would."

"Prove it, then."

"Go ahead, Rose." Clara gave me a push. "We'll keep the clerk busy."

We loitered along the aisle, craning at the glass jars of humbugs and peanut crunch. The girl behind the counter gave us a bored look, then let her gaze wander into the street again. She yawned with her fingers over her mouth.

"How much are these boxes of peppermint wafers, please?" Clara asked in her carrying voice. Reluctantly, the clerk went to that end of the counter. During the second her back was toward me I slipped a bag of chocolates into the pocket of my coat. As soon as this was done I felt someone behind me. With affected nonchalance, but unable to control a great glowering blush, I turned around and faced Mr. Stuart. He flicked me one glance of extreme aversion, then stalked on down the aisle as if he could not bear to breathe the same air.

In the morning I doubled over in the bathroom making retching noises, and almost succeeded in throwing up. I had lain awake half the night inventing ailments which would prevent me from attending school for months to come. A pain in the side might turn into appendicitis, pains in the head might be the forerunner of a nervous collapse, aching joints and fever might lead to complete paralysis. I would rather be an invalid for the rest of my days than have to face Mr. Stuart again.

"My poor baby!" Miranda tucked me back into bed. "Now, hurry and get well, dear. We can't have anything happening to you. I'll send Mrs. Walsh up with some nice broth."

I lay in bed all morning, reading, isolating myself in a world of fiction, as if by taking no physical part in the day, by keeping out of sight, I might erase all thoughts of me in the minds of others. At noon I heard Mr. Stuart in his room below mine. He tapped out a few lines on his typewriter, then went whistling along the hall to the bathroom. I imagined him standing before the mirror gazing at his handsome reflection as he brushed his teeth. I wondered how I could go on living.

Jess came up with another bowl of soup for my lunch. Feigning sleep, I watched her tiptoeing around, brushing her hair, changing into a clean middy, preparing to go out and mingle with other people—where I could never go again, I thought. When she had gone downstairs I wondered if I might absorb some of her infallibility by reading her diary. One more misdeed would not count against me, not in a house where the truth was the last thing anyone wanted known, I thought, as I rummaged in the box under the window seat.

I found a number of books: *The Story of an African Farm, Sunshine Sketches of a Little Town, Our Village.* I knew before I turned back the covers whose name would be written on the flyleaf. "To our leader, Miss Anderson. Merry Christmas from the junior group." "To Harriet, happy birthday from Papa." The diary was not where I thought Jess kept it.

When I was sure Jess had left for school, I got up and dressed, selected two or three exercise books containing my best stories, and carried them downstairs.

"You're never going out!" Mrs. Walsh exclaimed when she saw me with my hat and coat on. "You'll catch your death, going from a sickbed into this damp." She made me wear an extra sweater.

I took the trolley to Miss Anderson's house, arriving there around two o'clock. I rang the doorbell and after quite a long wait, the maid answered it. She looked rather taken aback, I thought, as I stepped into the hall and announced that I had come to see Miss Anderson. She hesitated as if she could not decide where to put me, then led me to a small sitting room at the back of the house. I was left alone to wait and wait.

I was unaware that Miss Anderson, like all the ladies of Southport's better families—those who could afford maids—followed a certain daily routine. Her mornings were devoted to household matters: telephoning orders to the butcher and the grocer, supervising the one maid of all work, mending the linen, writing checks. After the noon meal she took a bath and changed into an afternoon dress, while the maid put on a fresh apron and cap.

Around half past two, and no sooner, they were ready to be seen, though friends would know better than to call before half past three at the earliest and then only on Thursdays, which was Miss Anderson's day At Home. On other days she would change her book at the library, or shop, or attend a meeting of the Ladies' Aid, or, at four o'clock, call on whichever of her friends was At Home that day.

The long wait made me realize that I had not picked the proper time to pay a call. My confidence oozed away. Miss Anderson might not even remember that she had once said she would like to read my stories. I wondered why I had not been asked to wait in the big front parlor. Perhaps that was reserved for more important callers.

The room I was in had a shabby comfortable air, as if it had seen a good deal of use. The chairs wore flowered cretonne slipcovers, and the faded carpet had roses of a different variety. Pale amateurish watercolors of local scenes hung on the walls. At one end of the room was a small fireplace, freshly laid, ready to be lit, and on the mantelpiece above it a gilt clock ticked in a hurried way, as if it apologized for making the only sound in the room. Books were stacked here and there, and some half-finished tapestry work had been dropped carelessly across the arm of a chair.

I considered tiptoeing out, but Miss Anderson might think it queer if I did that. Besides, the maid had taken my coat. So I sat on, clutching my exercise books, and wished I had not come. The stories were only an excuse, a conversation piece to break the ice. After she had praised them, and encouraged me to keep on writing, Miss Anderson would offer to teach me all I needed to know to manage my life. She would say, "You must be this way or that way, you must do such and such; you must have this or that goal. I will guide you along the path you must go."

By the time she came downstairs, smelling of lavender soap, I was miserably regretting the impulse that had sent me to her. When I saw that she was wearing a hat, and carried a coat over her arm as if she were going out, I knew it had been a great mistake. I thrust the stories out of sight behind my back.

She greeted me warmly. "Rose, what a nice surprise!" But I saw her cast a quick glance at the clock. She was calculating how much time she could spare.

I began to stammer apologies. I had just dropped in. . . . I happened to be passing. . . .

For ten minutes she tried her best to carry on a conversation; then I invented a pressing engagement of my own. As I rose to go she caught sight of the exercise books, and said in her most encouraging voice, "Have you brought some of your stories for me to see?"

"Oh, no!" I spoke as if she had accused me of something. "This is just some school work."

As I walked home in the damp February chill, I hoped I would never see her again.

When Jess came home from school I was back in bed again. She brought me up a sandwich, which I refused to eat. In the dreary dusk of late afternoon, with winter branches clashing and shivering outside the window, I wanted nothing but to be alone with my misery.

"Where were you today?" Jess asked, kicking off her shoes and settling at the foot of the bed with her arms wrapped around her knees. "Mrs. Walsh said you went out."

"I wasn't anywhere."

She rested her chin on her knees and looked at me. "You're not really sick, are you? Something else is bothering you. Are you in trouble at school?"

"I only want to be left alone."

"Or have you quarreled with your friends?"

"I haven't *got* any friends."

"What about Clara?"

"Clara hates me."

"Have you been fighting with her?"

"Fighting with her? I wouldn't lower myself."

"Well, what about James? He likes you."

"That damned sissy. I'm ashamed to be seen with him."

"Don't cry. Can't you tell me what's wrong—why you say you haven't got any friends?"

"Nothing's wrong. Only . . . sometimes I wonder why life gets more and more complicated, the older we get. If it's like this now, what will it be like when we're old—when we're thirty?"

"Thirty?" Jess said, unable to visualize herself at this great age. "Like *what*, now?" she asked.

"We don't get any happier."

Jess considered this. "Isn't that what we're supposed to be learning now?" she said. "To face the future?"

"I'd just as soon not face it."

"Don't talk nonsense," Jess said, getting ready for a lecture. She thought for a minute, possibly trying to recall more quotations from whatever book she had been reading, then changed her mind and said, "You'll never guess who I walked home from school with."

"Who?"

"Mr. Stuart. He asked after you, too."

"He did not!"

"Yes he did. He said he missed you—I mean, he noticed you weren't in his class today. And guess what else he said about you. He said you were one of his favorite pupils."

"That's a damned lie! He never said any such thing."

"Cross my heart."

"I don't believe one word of it. You're just a plain bloody liar. . . . What else did he say?"

"That was the only thing he said about you, except that he was sorry you were sick. He talked all the way home, though." Jess hugged her knees, and her eyes grew dreamy. "He talked about his college days. The college he went to was in a small town, about the size of this one, and he said the students used to drive people crazy with their pranks. Especially the first-year students, because they like to show off more.

"There was a little tuck shop where they used to go after classes to buy cakes and doughnuts to eat in their rooms at night, and it got to be sort of a fad to steal things from that shop. Mr. Stuart said once he stole a pie, a whole apple pie. He put it inside his coat, and then someone bumped against him and squashed it, right there in the shop. He said he was never so embarrassed in his life." Jess put her hands to her face and rocked with laughter. "Can you imagine that? Can you imagine Mr. Stuart doing such a thing?"

I looked sharply at her to see if she was being subtle, but she was not. She wore an indulgent smile, thinking of Mr. Stuart and his apple pie. It struck me that she was in love with him, too. She was still glowing from her walk home with him.

I realized that he must have told her that story—knowing she would repeat it—for my benefit, to let me know that he did not think too badly of me. My heart began to lift. Anxiety seemed to fall away in layers, and I found that I could eat the sandwich Jess had brought up, after all. She turned on the light and the room was filled with comfort. Downstairs, we heard the click of Mr. Stuart's typewriter. "He's writing a letter to his mother," Jess said, as if this were a rare and excellent thing for a man to do.

When one is young and first in love, dreams are enough. If a dream came true, the shock would be too much; there would be no way of dealing with it and nothing more to dream about. I never did more than anticipate a declaration of love from Mr. Stuart, and so was spared the ordeal of coping with realization. I never saw him again after that winter, but for years afterward he remained in my mind as a figure of romance.

"I ought to be downstairs helping Mrs. Walsh." Jess looked at the alarm clock on the dresser. "But I want to show you something first." She felt behind "Madame Le-Brun and Daughter," which had been moved up from her old room on the second floor, and found a letter. "Read this," she said, handing it to me.

The letter was from Mrs. Fuller to Miranda, saying that one of her girls had left unexpectedly and that Miranda could have the job if she wanted it. "Let me know as soon as you *can*," Mrs. Fuller had written in a heavy sprawling hand with frequent underlinings. "I *hope* you will decide to come. Properly trained operators are *scarce* here." There followed some details about salary and hours, then, "I know you will like Boston, and feel more at home here than in a small town, as you are accustomed to city living. There are some lovely *flats* within walking distance of the shop. Please advise if you wish me to inquire about them. I understand they are quite *reasonable*, and very modern."

"When did this come?" I asked.

"Yesterday."

"Has Miranda seen it?"

"Of course not, stupid."

"Aren't you going to show it to her?"

"No, I'm not." Jess reached over and took the letter from my hand. She added in a threatening voice, "I hope you're not getting any ideas."

"What if Mrs. Fuller writes again?"

"I'll handle it. I'll answer it myself, and say—well, I'll say that Miranda's decided she doesn't want to leave Southport." Jess folded the letter and tucked it in her pocket. She wore what Miranda called her mulish look, a look of dedicated determination.

The discovery that she had been driven to stealing other people's letters—what amounted to an act of desperation, seeing that under ordinary circumstances she would not even dream of *reading* anyone else's mail—filled me with uneasiness, for I knew there was more behind it than her desire to see Miranda and Mr. Parker married. There was her obsession with the idea that none of us must leave this gray little town where Alfie was buried.

I was not particularly anxious to leave Southport myself. Aside from wanting to be near Mr. Stuart, I had made one or two friends—for in spite of what I had said to Jess, I still considered James and Clara my friends—and the prospect of starting all over again, in a new country full of strangers, was somewhat intimidating. On the other hand, there was a certain excitement in the thought of far-off places, a feeling that perhaps we had not found what we had set out from England to seek; that since we had come this far we ought to see what was beyond the horizon.

"Do as you please, I don't care," I said, turning away. "You seem to be in charge. You seem to have decided that you're the head of this house."

"Well, somebody's got to be. Miranda doesn't always know what's right."

"And you do, I suppose?"

"I think I'm learning," Jess said seriously. "I'm trying to learn, and that's something Miranda won't do. She thinks that because she does a thing, it must be right."

"I suppose it's right to go stealing other people's letters?"

Jess looked as hurt as if I had slapped her.

"Why didn't you burn the damned old letter, instead of hiding it behind that picture? If you've already decided to keep it from Miranda, why bother showing it to me? Now I'm as guilty as you are."

"Oh, God, I don't know. I just wanted to tell someone. It seemed underhanded enough, just hiding it. . . ." Jess leaned toward me and said in an anxious coaxing voice, "You're not going to be an old cross-patch, are you?" She sounded like a little girl who is not sure she has done the right thing.

At an age when conventionality means everything, one of the most embarrassing things for a young girl is to acknowledge that her mother inspires in others a lack of respect. I had always known that Miranda's refusal to conform to local standards made some people suspicious, and that others were angered when she looked down her nose at native customs. In retaliation they made fun of her, imitating her British accent and haughty manners. I wished she would conform more, but had learned to accept the fact that she would not. Actually, I swung between wishing she would be the same as everyone else, and being proud of her because she was not.

But when Mr. Peters made suggestive remarks, I could

not help seeing that he regarded her as the sort of woman men say such things to. One night about a week after Jess told me about the letter, he dropped in as usual to deliver the next day's meat. Lingering with one hand on the door-knob, also as usual, he told a joke that made Miranda's head rear back.

"I'll thank you to remember where you are, Mr. Peters," she said.

"Oh, come off it, Duchess. Don't give Uncle Fred the old bunko." He grinned slyly at her. "Innocent as a little white lamb, aren't we, kiddo?"

Miranda slammed the door in his face and stalked up-stairs, leaving Jess and me in the kitchen to wonder.

"He wouldn't dare talk like that to anyone else," Jess said angrily. Her face was still red.

"Men think they can say anything to her."

"Oh, God, I hope nothing's leaked out." Jess put her hands to her face. "The way he said that—it sounded as if he had heard something about her. Oh, I wish spring would come, so that Miranda and Mr. Parker could an-nounce their engagement and all this worry would be over. . . . And that Jack Williams phoned again last night. Miranda got to the telephone first, or I would have told him she wasn't at home. They talked for ten min-utes, and when I asked her what they had been talking about, she said it was none of my business. . . . What is she doing upstairs now?"

"I'll go up and see."

Miranda was doing her face. One of her best dresses was laid out on the bed. "Are you going out?" I asked her.

"Yes, I am."

"With Hattie?"

She gave me a sharp look and said nothing.

I reported to Jess, "She's going out. She wouldn't say where, but she's got her red dress laid out."

Miranda had not come downstairs when we looked out and saw Jack Williams's car pull up in front of the house. "*Now* look who's coming," Jess said. "So that's what Miranda's up to!" We watched Jack swing jauntily out of his blue sedan and start up the walk, carrying a bunch of red roses. "You run upstairs and keep Miranda busy until I get rid of him," Jess said. "I'll tell him she's not at home."

Miranda was just about ready to come down, and I had to think fast to keep her in her room. When she asked me to fetch her patent-leather pumps from the closet, I stuffed them into the pocket of an old coat and said, "They're not here."

"They must be. I put them there myself," Miranda said. The floor of her closet was littered with fallen coat hangers as well as shoes. She came and raked through the jumble herself. "Look under the bed, then. They're here somewhere." We looked under the bed. Miranda was getting more impatient by the minute. "I'll have to wear something else, then. Not those runover things, idiot! For heaven's sake," she said when Jess came in, "is everybody going to congregate here? A person would think this was a public waiting room."

"Have you lost something?" Jess asked.

"I can't find my damned shoes." Miranda opened a drawer, looked inside, and slammed it shut.

"I didn't know you kept them in drawers." Jess sat calmly on the bed and said, "Mr. Williams just telephoned that he won't be able to see you tonight. His fiancée has arrived unexpectedly from New York."

Miranda straightened as if she had been shot. "*Who* telephoned?"

"Mr. Williams." Jess looked her straight in the eye. "Just a few minutes ago. He asked me to tell you that his fiancée has arrived, so he won't be able to see you tonight." She added with a note of reproof, "You didn't tell us you were expecting him. Was he coming here on business?"

"Oh!" Miranda's eyes blazed. She looked at the pair of shoes I had handed her, and flung them to the floor. "His fiancée?" she cried suddenly, as if the word had just registered. "Oh, the liar! He told me he had broken his engagement."

Jess shrugged. "He's liable to tell you anything."

"Are you sure he said fiancée?"

"Certain." Jess nodded. "It looks to me as if he's trying to make a fool of you," she added.

"I'd like to see him do it!"

"Did he really tell you he had broken his engagement to that girl?" Jess looked as if she could hardly believe this. It struck me that she had inherited more of Miranda's inventiveness than I had supposed.

Miranda was working up into a rage. Jess helped her by saying, "I hope he didn't think you'd be fool enough to swallow that."

"After he swore up and down he'd never see that girl again!" Miranda ripped off her dress and threw it in a heap on the bed. "After the way he's been mooning around, making promises! Oh, I never heard of anything so deceitful!"

We watched her going through the familiar routine. When she had calmed down a little, Jess blotted up her tears and said, "Now, don't cry any more. You don't want to waste tears on him. Let's forget about him. Shall I brush your hair?"

One thing Miranda loved was to have someone brush her hair and massage her back and do her nails. We fussed over her for an hour, as if she were a doll we were playing with, making her smile, coaxing her into a good humor. We even gave her a mudpack and painted her toenails while the greenish mask was drying.

In the middle of it Jess went downstairs. She returned, carrying a mug of beer.

Miranda drank it in gulps. "I didn't know there was any left."

"I ran across and bought some from Mr. Dove," Jess said. "There's more downstairs if you want it."

Miranda raised her eyebrows. "I thought you said drinking beer wasn't ladylike."

"Well, I wanted to cheer you up."

"That was sweet of you." Miranda nuzzled her cheek.

She had completely recovered from her bad temper, but Jess waited another half hour before she said: "Would it be too soon for you to announce your engagement to Mr. Parker?"

Miranda looked at her in utter astonishment. "What on earth are you talking about?"

"His wife's been dead for two months now."

"What's that got to do with me?"

"Well, you are going to marry him."

"Marry Mr. Parker?" Miranda burst out laughing. "Whatever gave you that idea?"

Jess stared at her. "We thought you had it all planned . . . we thought it was all settled . . . that you and Mr. Parker. . . ."

"I'd as soon marry a wooden Indian. Mr. *Parker*, for heaven's sake!"

Jess stood up. Her face reddened and her eyes grew damp. "Then why have you been sleeping with him?" she asked.

Miranda did not react quickly. There was a long pause

during which her shoulders tensed and her eyes gathered sparks. When she spoke, her voice kept on rising steadily as the enormity of Jess's question sank in.

"Now, look here, Jess," she said, "if you're going to be vulgar, you just go to your room until you learn how to behave. If there's one thing I will not tolerate it's people asking vulgar questions. Casting aspersions at people in that common way! I'm sure I don't know where you pick it up. I've tried to bring you up like a lady. It's all those common people you associate with. People like that Miss Anderson. If I had known we'd be forced to associate with people like that, I would never have come to this country."

When Jess said nothing, but looked at her with that reproachful wide-eyed stare, Miranda went on, using one of her favorite threats. "I ought to smack your bottom! After the way I've worked and slaved to give you a proper upbringing, to be insulted in that vulgar way by my own daughter!"

"Oh, stop it!" Jess spoke so sharply that Miranda jumped. "There's no use pretending with us. All we want to know is, are you going to marry Mr. Parker or not?"

"I'm sure I don't know where you get such ideas." Miranda's eyes faltered momentarily but she tilted her chin and looked defiantly back at Jess. "I have no intention of marrying Mr. Parker, so will you kindly mind your own business from now on? The trouble with you is," she said, picking up steam again, "you're too big for your breeches. Meddling in other people's private affairs—you ought to be ashamed! Now, you go to your room and stay there until you learn some manners."

"You've been sleeping with him for months now," Jess said, not moving. "What have you been doing that for if you don't intend to marry him?" She added, when Miranda drew herself up and prepared for a denial, "There's no use looking so innocent. We've known about it since before Christmas."

"I had no idea you had taken to snooping into other people's private affairs. Creeping and spying—I must say I expected to find a little privacy in my own home."

"He wants to marry *you*, doesn't he?" Jess persisted.

Miranda gave up. She tried another defiant tilt of her chin at Jess, and got such a dark look in return that she threw out her hands in a gesture of resignation. "Yes, he does," she admitted. "I don't know what I'm going to do with him. He looks so damned po-faced."

"Why *not* marry him?"

"Are you out of your mind?"

"Well, you can't go on like this. I think half the town must know about you and him by now."

Miranda's pained look was for the nosey townspeople. "Is there no privacy in this damned town? My God, when I think of the way people spy on one another—"

"You should have known better."

"Peeping Toms, going around sniffing at one another's private lives—"

"What sort of an example are you setting for us?" Jess demanded.

"Country nobodies. Who cares what they say?"

"I'm not sure that it has leaked out yet, but for heaven's *sake*, Miranda, don't you ever stop to think of your reputation? Of *our* reputation? No wonder Mr. Peters thinks he can talk to you the way he does."

"People have such dirty minds," Miranda complained. Then, seeing that she was getting nowhere with Jess, she changed her tactics. "Oh, ducky, don't scold me!" She lifted her face and some tears started from the corners of her eyes. "Where's a hankie, love?" She fumbled in the pocket of Jess's middy for a handkerchief which she held against her chin, where there were no tears yet. "He was so lonely," she said. "I wanted to cheer him up. What are we here for, if not to help others?"

"Don't make excuses," Jess said coldly. "If you can't behave yourself, you had better find someone to look after you. Rose and I won't be here forever."

At this, Miranda burst into real tears. Jess softened a little and said, "I meant, someone like Mr. Parker. You know he'd do anything for you. Don't you like him?"

"But I couldn't *live* with him."

"Why not?"

"I couldn't *marry* him. He's so dull. Oh, lovie, don't be cross." Miranda laid her wet cheek against Jess's. "I can't help the way I am," she said.

"Well, *I* give up." Jess lay on her back with her hands behind her head. We had undressed in silence, and lay side by side without speaking for a long time after we had turned out the light. Outside, a damp wind crept around the chimneys and brushed at the windows.

"She might change her mind and marry him."

"No she won't. She's got her eye on bigger game. *He'll* be back," Jess said, meaning Jack Williams. "He'll be prancing up the walk again with his bloody red roses. Don't fool yourself."

"Miranda won't see him."

"Don't fool yourself about that, either."

I was on the verge of tears. "Doesn't anything ever turn out the way you want it to?"

I expected Jess to scold me for being babyish, but she did not. After a silence she sat up in bed and rested her chin on her drawn-up knees. "What really frightens me is that someone *will* find out about her and Mr. Parker—or that someone has already. Mrs. Dove gave me the funniest look tonight, when I went there to buy the beer.

"I tried to get away without seeing her, but she came out just as I was leaving. She looked at me—oh, I can't describe it—as if she had something up her sleeve. It made me go cold all over. Do you remember the letter she wrote that time, to the woman who had the flat up the street— the one who was running around with the married man —telling her to get out of town? All the neighbors signed it, remember?"

"Miranda wouldn't sign it."

"All the other women on the street did. Well, I was coming home behind the garages, and I looked back—it's spooky out there at night, so dark—and I got the funniest feeling, as if I could look right through the walls of their house and see Mrs. Dove sitting there with that look on her face, writing the same sort of letter to Miranda. . . . That's why I asked Miranda about the engagement. I got in a panic."

As soon as Jess put the picture in my mind I saw Mrs. Dove, too, sitting upright at the dining-room table where she wrote letters, with that threatening sign above her. She would write quickly, for she had written the same kind of letters before, and knew exactly what to say. Her pen would stab through the paper when she came to words like "respectable" and "tolerate." And when she had signed her name she would knock at every door on the street, with the letter in her hand.

Then I imagined us, Jess and Miranda and me, ostracized, pursued by scandal, hurrying off down the street with our belongings, while everyone watched from windows and mothers called their children indoors.

I sat up and said, "What are we going to do?"

Jess bounced to a new position on the hard mattress. "You heard what Miranda said: she can't help the way she is."

"But I thought people were supposed to try. You keep saying that."

"Miranda will never change." Jess thought about this, and added, "*We're* the fools, for expecting her to."

"We only wanted her to be like other mothers."

"Nobody's perfect. What if we had a mother like Clara's?"

"But I never wanted her to change *that* much."

"Well, you can't have it both ways. The thing is, next time we won't expect so much."

"Next time?"

"It's too bad she's spoiled herself for this town. I liked it here. However. . . ." Jess lay back with a sigh, like someone who is relieved to drop out of a contest. "It won't kill us to live in Boston."

"You mean you're going to give her that letter from Mrs. Fuller?"

"Well, if Miranda's going to be the way she is, we can't stay here. This isn't the sort of place she should be. She ought to be in a crowd, where she won't be watched. Tomorrow I'll seal up that letter and pretend it just came."

What this decision cost Jess I can only guess. She was not the kind who went around airing her feelings. Duty meant a great deal to her, and I suppose she suddenly realized that her duty lay in seeing Miranda through whatever she got into next; that we ought to live in whatever place was best for Miranda. Perhaps Jess even got some altruistic satisfaction out of sacrificing her own desires in the service of others; but it must have been hard on her, just the same.

In the morning, when Miranda had read the letter and handed it around, Jess said, "Now, Miranda, I think you ought to accept Mrs. Fuller's offer."

As Miranda was still being a penitent little girl from the night before, she said meekly, "Oh, ducky, do you really think so?"

"Well, if you're tired of living here, as you keep saying, this is your chance to get away."

"Then it's all right with you if I write to Mrs. Fuller and tell her we're coming?"

"I'd do it right away, if I were you. She might change her mind. This letter's over a week old, too. It must have been delayed. Why not send a telegram?"

"Whatever you say, Grandmother dear. You know best." Miranda gave Jess a second look. "You are a funny girl. I thought you'd raise a fuss about leaving here. I thought you'd be upset about leaving your friends."

"I'll send the telegram myself," Jess said. "You might forget."

Children take root anywhere, and they do it quickly because they feel the need to become settled and familiar, to establish a pattern, to do the same things and see the same faces day after day. Each time we moved I felt as if I actually had been uprooted and transplanted. I was always homesick for the place before.

Miranda wasted no time on backward looks. She was too busy planning another fresh start, preparing for the move to Boston; though Jess did most of the actual planning. We sold off such household furnishings as had belonged to us, gave the roomers their notice, and arranged interminable interviews with the immigration authorities. This latter took up a good deal of time, since we were not Canadian citizens.

Miranda was put out when she discovered that Canadian immigrants were more welcome in the United States than those from England; that if it had not been for the fact she had a job waiting for her in Boston we might not have been given permission to enter the country. It seemed to her that this showed a great lack of intelligence on the part of the Americans. "I simply cannot understand the reasoning of such people," she said. "Who *would* they let in, if not us?"

As she did have a job waiting for her in America, the preparations for entering the country were rushed through, and in two weeks we were ready to start.

During this time I watched Miranda and wondered about her, not realizing that I was for the first time trying to understand her instead of wishing she understood me. I saw that, though she sometimes pretended to take offense, she was really pleased when Jess said, "Now, Miranda," in that new authoritative voice, and told her what to do. "Now, Miranda, I want you to straighten out these accounts. There's a bill from the telephone company that hasn't been paid. We don't want to go off owing people money."

"You help me then, dear." Miranda looked more helpless than she was.

I wondered, too, whether Miranda felt any sadness at leaving the few friends she had made. Mr. Parker, for instance—could she go off and leave him without a backward glance?

At first I thought she did not notice how he stood around with a stricken expression, as if the world had fallen in on him. Then it dawned on me that she did notice it, and that it was the way she expected him to look. She expected him to be sad for a long time after she was gone. Months, perhaps years later, when she was in low spirits, it would shore up her self-confidence to look back and think of him still faithfully pining away.

It was not until twenty years later that I learned how the affair between Miranda and Mr. Parker had begun. Hattie told me. She was a gray-haired widow by this time, still ready for a good laugh, but saddened somewhat by the way time had flown by. Miranda was also, for the time being, widowed, having recently lost her third husband. Two sods, one grass, as Hattie put it.

We were all visiting Jess at the time, at her summer home near Portland. Miranda was out somewhere with her fiancé, a building contractor who was cleaning up a fortune on the post-war boom, and Jess had taken the children to the village on some errand. Hattie and I sat on the beach and talked about the old days in Southport.

She told me that news of the affair between Miranda and Mr. Parker *had* leaked out, and was the talk of the town for some weeks after we left. "If you ask me," Hattie said, "half the ones who did the most talking were simply jealous. I never blamed her. Such a little thing. And after all, when everything's said and done, what was it but pure kindness on her part? Your mother had a heart of gold, Rose. She couldn't bear to see people unhappy.

"She told me about going up to Mr. Parker's room one night with some fresh towels. He'd just got back from seeing his wife, and he was feeling pretty low. You know how sad he always looked, as if he hadn't a friend in the world. He started to tell her about his wife, and when he had to stop and put his hands over his eyes she said to him, 'Oh, you poor thing!' and threw her arms around him. You know how she was; impulsive.

"She said to me, 'Hattie, I swear I don't know how it happened, but the next thing I knew I was in bed with him. Oh, it did cheer him up.' I've no doubt it did." Hattie gave one of her famous laughs. "So then she told me that having cheered him up once, it did seem mean not to try again, when it was doing him so much good. Pure kindness. . . ." Hattie gazed for some time at the sea.

"Miranda got more out of life than I ever did. She made people happy, whatever faults she had. She made you and Jess happy, once you got over trying to reform her and took her as she was. . . . Oh, I always thought how nice it would be if people would gossip about *me* for a change. It must give a woman a lift. But, there; I never gave them anything to talk about. . . . It's *living* that's kept Miranda young.

"You used to say she didn't think. Well, what if she didn't? Maybe the rest of us think too much. We go on trying and trying to be what others tell us we ought to be, till one fine day we wake up and realize that it's almost over—life—and what have we done with it? *That's* what you've got to watch out for," Hattie said darkly.

"Look at me. I never caught on till it was too late." She sighed and glanced down at her body that was growing old. "And look at Miranda. Past fifty-five, a grandmother six times already, and still as full of beans as ever. She knows there's less to be alarmed about in life than people think. It's all in the way you look at things. There's more to laugh at than not, too, only you've got to look for it. You've learned as much by this time, I hope."

I had, by that time, but I had not learned it when I was fourteen.

The day we went out to visit Alfie's grave for the last time, Miranda wept all through the afternoon. The snow was melting in the lengthening days, a damp wind blew, and the trees looked more bereft than ever. Jess stood with her face screwed up against the wind, not even glancing at the flowers we laid against the headstone, but I knew that she had been out by herself the day before.

As soon as we returned home Miranda took out the sepia portrait of Alfie in uniform and wept over it. It had been taken during the war. He stood against a backdrop of painted clouds, looking at something over the photographer's head. "Oh, I can't bear to think of him not being here now," Miranda said, gazing at the portrait and blotting up the tears that fell on it. "When we're getting a fresh start. . . ."

"Don't cry, there's a good girl," Jess said.

Miranda wiped her eyes with the back of her hand. "Alfie was always saying that. You sound like him."

"Don't *you* be taken in by that fresh-start business," Jess said to me when we were alone. "Nothing's going to change."

"We'll be in a new place."

"But Miranda will be the same. She says we'll put everything behind us, but we never do. We go on being the same wherever we are. You watch: we won't be in Boston a week before she meets someone else, one of those roving-eyed sheiks that she always seems to fall for. We'll go through the same thing all over again. Only this time," Jess said, "we'll know better than to expect miracles."

Almost at the last minute we learned that we would have to leave Brownie behind. I could not bear the thought of handing him over to strangers.

"Let me keep him," Clara begged. She picked him up and hugged him against her chest. "I'll take good care of him."

"Your mother doesn't like dogs. She wouldn't have him in the house."

"Yes, she will. I'll make her. I'll threaten to run away.

Oh, please let me keep him. I'll be good to him. I'll brush him every day." Brownie put out his tongue and licked her chin. Clara looked at us with swimming eyes. "He loves me," she said.

Whatever pressures she brought to bear, her mother did finally give in and agreed that Brownie could stay with them. Clara brought him to my room when she came to say good-bye. "Don't be surprised if I turn up in Boston one of these days," she said. "Next year, or the year after. I won't be able to stand it here much longer than that. We'll come together, Brownie and me." She looked away from me and said, "I wanted to tell you—I'm going to put flowers on your father's grave."

"You are?"

"Yes, I'll go on Sundays. It will be a nice walk for Brownie." She added in a self-consciously casual voice, "You look a lot like your father, did you know? I mean, anyone could tell that you were his daughter."

I knew what she meant, and gave her a grateful look, which she pretended not to see.

Two days later we stood at the rail of the Boston boat looking down at the people on the wharf. It was a much smaller, much less demonstrative crowd than the one we had left at Liverpool. There were no songs, no tears— except Miranda's—and no laughter. But this time there were four people we knew, four people who had come to see us off: Hattie, Mr. Parker, Clara, and James.

After five years in Canada we had made that many friends. They stood in a little knot, looking chilled and unhappy, staring somberly up at us. When the boat began to move away they seemed relieved that the time had come to wave and call out good-byes.

When Jess's face lit up suddenly I looked where she was

looking and saw Miss Anderson hurrying down the side street from the shopping district. She broke into a dignified run, then stood with one hand lifted in a gesture of farewell.

Miranda leaned on the rail, calling, "Good-bye! Good-bye!" She was the only one crying.

The boat moved away. Our friends grew smaller, then they turned to follow the rest of the crowd up the side street to the more cheerful part of town; to the shops, and their homes.

We watched the warehouses and the fishing boats slide past, then went forward as the boat churned out of the harbor into the open sea. The horizon lay ahead of us, and beyond that we could not see.